THE CUSTOMS CONSPIRACY

A Corporate Fraud Thriller

by

Jackie L. Smith

THE CUSTOMS CONSPIRACY

Published and Printed by Jackie L. Smith

Cover design by Jessica Stacey

ISBN: 979-8-9959280-9-6 (paperback)

Printed in the United States of America

Dedication

For my brothers and sisters in arms, who understand pressure.

For those who choose integrity over comfort.

And for everyone who thought it was too late— it never is.

Contents

Chapter 1: The Pattern

Friday afternoon settled into the office with the particular weight of approaching weekend. Jack had learned, over the years, that offices had their own weather.. Not the kind that came from the sky, but the kind that settled into cubicles and conference rooms - moods that shifted with deadlines, egos, and whispered conversations that traveled faster than emails. On the twelfth floor of a glass-and-steel building overlooking the river, Jack spent most of his days navigating that invisible climate with deliberate calm.

He worked as a Risk Compliance Analyst for a regional logistics firm, a job that rewarded precision and punished carelessness. He liked that about it. Numbers behaved. Processes made sense. If something failed, there was a reason, and reasons could be fixed. He wore the same quiet uniform most days - pressed shirt, dark slacks, sleeves rolled just enough to suggest effort without invitation. He spoke plainly, listened carefully, and kept his personal life sealed behind a professional distance that had become part of his reputation.

People noticed.

They always did.

Jack wasn't flashy, but he was steady. Tall without looming, attractive without courting it. He moved through the office with purpose, a man who did not linger in doorways or lean too long against desks. When he smiled, it was brief and genuine. When he set boundaries, they were unmistakable.

That reputation hadn't come easily.

Early on, a coworker had mistaken Jack's politeness for permission - small touches that lingered, comments that edged toward invitation. Jack addressed it directly, professionally, and once. When it continued, he filed a formal complaint without drama. The message traveled fast. By the time the matter was resolved, people understood something important about Jack: flirtation did not interest him, and persistence would not be tolerated.

It made him respected. It also made him alone.

But Jack wasn't truly alone. He'd learned that lesson the hard way - first in marriage, then in divorce, and finally in the careful reconstruction of what family meant. Three children called him Dad, though they didn't live with him anymore. Sarah, sixteen. Michael, fourteen. And Emma, eleven. Their mother, Jennifer, had moved on years ago, remarried to a decent man named David who treated the kids well. Jack couldn't ask for more than that.

They'd divorced when Emma was three - amicably, which seemed impossible to most people. But Jack and Jennifer had figured something out that others struggled with: you could fail at marriage without failing at parenthood. They'd built separate lives that intersected every other weekend, every Wednesday dinner, every school event and holiday negotiated with calendars and text messages.

This Saturday was his. Sarah had a soccer game. Michael wanted help with a history project about Vietnam. Emma just wanted to show him the new book she'd been reading, something about dragons and kingdoms that she described with breathless enthusiasm.

Vietnam.

The word still carried weight, even after all these years. Jack had been twenty-two when he'd shipped out with the Navy, young and convinced of his own invincibility. He'd served on river patrol boats - PBRs they were called - navigating the Mekong Delta's maze of waterways. The war had been winding down by then, but it hadn't felt like it. Ambushes still happened. Firefights erupted without warning. And one morning in December 1972, a rocket-propelled grenade had torn through the boat's hull and sent shrapnel tearing through Jack's left side.

He'd survived. Three of his crew hadn't.

The doctors had pulled most of the metal out, but not all of it. Pieces remained, too small or too dangerous to extract, embedded in muscle and scar tissue. On cold mornings or before rain, Jack felt them - a deep ache that started in his ribs and radiated through his shoulder. A permanent reminder that survival came with a price.

Michael's history project would cover the war's end, the fall of Saigon, the bitter homecoming veterans received. Jack had promised to help, though he wasn't sure how much of his own experience he'd share. Some things were better left in the past. Others needed to be remembered so they wouldn't be repeated.

By the time he shut down his computer that evening, the office had thinned. The city below glowed in orderly lines, a grid of intention and habit. Jack gathered his things, nodding to the security guard on his way out, and let the elevator carry him down in silence. He liked the quiet moments between roles - the pause between who he was at work, who he was as a father, and who he was when no one was watching.

Ruby entered his life during one of those pauses.

They met months earlier, by accident rather than design. A mutual acquaintance, a birthday gathering, a conversation that stretched longer than expected. Ruby had been sitting on the arm of a chair, glass untouched, listening more than speaking. When Jack joined the circle, their eyes met briefly - an acknowledgment, nothing more. Later, they found themselves alone near the kitchen, talking about unremarkable things: books that stayed with you, cities that felt like home, the comfort of routines.

What struck Jack wasn't her beauty, though she had that in an understated way - dark hair worn loose, a small scar near her temple she didn't try to hide, a face shaped by both laughter and restraint. It was her attention. When Ruby listened, she listened fully, as if the world narrowed to the space between words. She asked questions that mattered. She didn't rush to fill silences.

Their relationship unfolded without urgency, which made it feel inevitable. Dinners became regular. Conversations deepened. They learned each other's habits - the way Jack organized his thoughts aloud when stressed, the way Ruby traced patterns on the table when nervous. There was affection early, then something warmer, heavier, more anchoring.

She'd known about the divorce from the start. Jack had been direct about it - he had children, an ex-wife he respected, obligations that came before anything new. Ruby had nodded, asked good questions, and told him that a man who honored his responsibilities was worth waiting for.

That night, Jack arrived at Ruby's apartment just after sunset. The space reflected her - clean but lived-in, books stacked horizontally and vertically, a throw blanket folded with care. She greeted him with a kiss that was neither rushed nor hesitant, her hands resting easily at his waist.

They moved together with familiarity born of trust. There was no need for performance, no proving. Their intimacy was slow, deliberate - shared breaths, whispered laughter, the kind of closeness that made time irrelevant. Jack felt grounded in those moments, present in a way that nothing else demanded. When they finally rested, Ruby's head against his chest, the world felt briefly uncomplicated.

Later, as they lay tangled in sheets, Ruby traced a line along his arm.

"You're thinking," she said softly.

"Always," Jack replied.

"About work?"

"About balance," he said. "About how people build lives without noticing the weight they're carrying."

She smiled faintly. "You carry a lot."

He didn't deny it.

Jack's mother, Helen, occupied a steady place in his thoughts, though not his daily routine. He visited when needed, checked in regularly, made sure she had help where she required it. Since his father's death, Jack had quietly arranged support - home maintenance, errands, someone to assist with the things that had become difficult. Helen accepted his care with grace, though she never stopped reminding him that she was still capable.

That night, Jack didn't go to her house. He didn't need to. She was settled. Safe. His children were with Jennifer this week, tucked into their own routines in a house across town. That knowledge allowed him to stay where he was, to invest in the life unfolding beside him.

Ruby shifted, propping herself on one elbow. "You should introduce me to your mother sometime."

Jack looked at her, surprised by the directness. "You want to meet Helen?"

"Eventually," Ruby said. "When you're ready. No pressure."

He thought about that - Ruby at his mother's table, the two women in his life sizing each other up with the careful politeness that preceded either acceptance or distance. Helen would ask questions. Ruby would answer them honestly. It could work.

"Soon," Jack said. "I think you'd like her."

"And your kids?" Ruby asked carefully. "When do I meet them?"

That was a bigger question. Jack had been careful to keep his dating life separate from his children. They'd met a few of Jennifer's boyfriends before David, and he'd seen how confusing it was for them when relationships ended. He wouldn't put them through that unless he was certain.

"When I'm sure," Jack said. "When this is something that lasts."

Ruby nodded, not hurt, just understanding. "That's fair."

Ruby studied his face. "You don't talk much about your family."

Jack exhaled slowly. "There's not much left to talk about."

He told her then - about siblings who hadn't lived long enough to grow old, about the silence that followed their absence, about a father who had made mistakes before becoming the man Jack remembered. Prison had been part of that story, though it wasn't the whole of it. Redemption rarely fit neatly into timelines.

Ruby listened without interruption. When he finished, she reached for his hand.

"You're not broken," she said.

"I know," Jack replied. "But I'm careful."

She squeezed his fingers. "So am I."

They fell asleep that way, the city outside indifferent to the quiet commitments forming within those walls. Jack dreamed lightly, without the usual edge of vigilance. In the morning, he would return to the office, to spreadsheets and meetings and expectations. On Saturday, he'd pick up his children, watch Sarah dominate the soccer field, help Michael understand a war Jack had fought in, and listen to Emma's stories about dragons.

But for now, in the stillness of Ruby's apartment, he allowed himself the rare luxury of feeling exactly where he belonged.

Chapter 2: The Call

The phone call came on Monday morning, during a stretch of ordinary hours that felt deceptively stable. Jack was at his desk, navigating spreadsheets and coordinating shipments, when his cell buzzed with an unfamiliar number. He let it go to voicemail. The second call, ten minutes later, came with a name he recognized: St. Catherine's Hospital.

He stepped into an empty conference room before listening.

The voice was professional, calm, practiced at delivering news without drama. Helen had been admitted earlier that morning. A neighbor found her disoriented, struggling to speak clearly. Stroke, they suspected. Tests were underway. She was stable for now. Could he come?

Jack stood very still, the hum of the fluorescent lights suddenly too loud. His mind raced through logistics automatically - how long it would take to drive there, what he'd need to cancel, who he should notify. Underneath that, quieter but insistent, was the weight of knowing things had shifted irrevocably.

He called Ruby first.

"I'm on my way to the hospital," he said, voice steady but clipped. "My mom."

"I'll meet you there," Ruby said immediately.

"You don't have to-"

"Jack." Her voice was firm. "I'll meet you there."

He didn't argue.

The second call went to Jennifer. She answered on the first ring, her voice bright with the chaos of getting three kids ready for school.

"Jack? Everything okay?"

"My mother had a stroke. I'm heading to St. Catherine's now."

The background noise stopped. "Oh God. Is she-"

"Stable. They think she'll be okay, but I don't know details yet."

"Should I tell the kids now, or do you want to wait until you know more?"

"Tell them. I don't want them hearing it from someone else at school or getting blindsided. Let them know she's stable and I'll call them tonight with more details."

"Of course. Jack, if you need anything - if Helen needs anything - you call me, okay?"

"I will. Thanks, Jen."

The drive felt both endless and too short, the city blurring past while his thoughts churned. Helen had been fine three days ago. Tired, maybe, but fine. He replayed their last conversation, searching for signs he might have missed. Had she seemed weaker? Had her words slurred slightly? He couldn't be sure. Guilt settled in his chest, familiar and unwelcome.

The sensation reminded him of triage - that cold assessment of priorities he'd learned in the Navy. Who could be saved. Who couldn't. What mattered most when everything mattered. He'd carried wounded men through firefights, made impossible calculations about who got evacuated first. The shrapnel still buried in his ribs ached with the memory.

But this was his mother. There was no triage here. Only getting to her as fast as possible.

By the time he reached the hospital, Ruby was already in the waiting area. She stood when she saw him, and the relief on her face steadied him more than any reassurance could have. She didn't ask questions. She just fell into step beside him as they navigated the sterile hallways toward Helen's room.

Helen looked smaller in the hospital bed, diminished by tubes and monitors. Her eyes were closed, her breathing steady but labored. A nurse was adjusting an IV, making notes on a clipboard.

"You're the son?" the nurse asked.

Jack nodded.

"She's resting now. The doctor will be in shortly to go over everything." The nurse's tone was kind but efficient. She'd done this many times before.

Jack pulled a chair close to the bed and sat. Ruby stayed near the door, giving him space but present. He reached for Helen's hand

- cool, papery, still recognizably hers. Her fingers twitched slightly, and her eyes fluttered open.

"Jack," she said, the word thick and uneven.

"I'm here," he said.

She tried to smile, but only half her face responded. The asymmetry was jarring, a visible mark of what had been taken. Jack kept his expression neutral, unwilling to let her see his fear.

"You... worry too much," Helen managed.

"Occupational hazard," Jack replied softly.

The doctor arrived shortly after - a woman in her forties with efficient movements and a direct gaze. She explained what they'd found: an ischemic stroke, moderate severity, affecting motor control and speech on her left side. Early intervention had helped, but recovery would take time. Rehabilitation. Possibly permanent limitations. They'd know more in the coming days.

Jack listened, absorbing every detail, already calculating what would need to change. Helen couldn't live alone anymore. That much was clear. The house would need modifications, or she'd need to move somewhere with more support. He'd have to coordinate care, manage logistics, ensure she wasn't left vulnerable again.

Ruby stepped forward then, standing beside him. "What does the timeline look like?"

The doctor glanced between them, clearly reading Ruby as part of the equation. "A few days here for monitoring. Then likely a rehab facility for a few weeks. After that, it depends on her progress."

Jack nodded, filing it all away. When the doctor left, he sat with Helen in silence, his mind already three steps ahead while his heart stayed stubbornly present. Ruby touched his shoulder gently.

"I'll get us some coffee," she said.

When she returned, Jack was still sitting beside Helen, who had drifted back to sleep. Ruby handed him a cup and sat in the chair beside him. They didn't speak for a long time. The beeping of monitors filled the space, rhythmic and unrelenting.

"You're already planning," Ruby said eventually.

"Someone has to," Jack replied.

"You don't have to do it all alone."

He looked at her, something in his chest loosening slightly. "I know."

Over the next few days, Jack's life narrowed to a new rhythm: mornings at the office handling what couldn't be delayed, afternoons and evenings at the hospital. Ruby came when she could, fitting her schedule around his without making it a point of discussion. She brought food he barely touched, sat with Helen when Jack needed to make calls, and never once acted as though her presence required justification.

On the second evening, Jack finally called his children. He waited until after dinner, knowing they'd be settled, knowing Jennifer would have prepared them.

Sarah answered, her voice careful. She was sixteen and old enough to understand that grown-ups sometimes lied to protect you.

"Dad? How's Grandma?"

"She's stable," Jack said. "The stroke affected her left side - her arm and her speech - but the doctors think she'll recover most of it with therapy."

"Can we see her?"

"Not yet. She needs rest right now. But soon, I promise." He paused. "How are you doing?"

"I'm okay. Michael's been quiet. Emma keeps asking if Grandma's going to die."

Jack closed his eyes. Emma was eleven - old enough to understand death, young enough to be terrified of it. "Can you put her on?"

A rustle, then Emma's small voice. "Daddy?"

"Hey, sweetheart."

"Is Grandma going to die?"

Jack had learned not to lie to his children. They could smell dishonesty the way dogs could smell fear. "Everyone dies eventually, Em. But Grandma's not dying now. She had something happen to her brain - it's called a stroke - and it made part of her body stop working right. But the doctors are helping her, and she's getting stronger every day."

"Will she be okay?"

"I think so. It'll take time, but yes, I think she'll be okay."

"I want to see her."

"You will. Very soon. I promise." He heard her sniffle. "Em, you know I wouldn't lie to you about this, right?"

"I know."

"I love you."

"Love you too."

Michael came on next, his fourteen-year-old voice deeper than Jack remembered from just last week.

"Dad, do you need help? I could come stay with Grandma when she gets home."

The offer caught Jack off guard. Michael was at that age where he bounced between childhood and adulthood, sometimes awkward, sometimes surprisingly mature. "That's really thoughtful, buddy. But you've got school, and Grandma's going to need professional help for a while. What I need from you is to keep being a good big brother to Emma. She's scared."

"I know. I told her Grandma was tough."

Jack smiled despite himself. "She is. You all are." He paused. "We still on for that Vietnam project this weekend?"

"If you have time. I know you're busy with Grandma."

"I'll make time. I promised, didn't I?"

"Yeah. Thanks, Dad."

After he hung up, Jack sat in the hospital corridor, the phone heavy in his hand. The building hummed around him with its ceaseless machinery of care and crisis. He thought about his children - Sarah trying to be strong, Michael trying to help, Emma trying not to be afraid. They were good kids. He and Jennifer had done something right, even if they'd failed at staying married.

Helen's condition stabilized, though progress was slow. Speech therapy began almost immediately - frustrating, exhausting work that left her drained. Her left arm remained weak, her movements uncertain. The doctors were cautiously optimistic, but Jack had learned early that optimism was often a polite way of managing expectations.

One evening, as Jack sat reviewing care facility options on his laptop, Helen reached for his hand.

"You can't... fix everything," she said, the words halting but clear.

"I can try," Jack replied.

She shook her head slightly. "You need... to live, too."

"I am living."

"With her?" Helen's gaze shifted toward the hallway where Ruby had stepped out to take a call.

Jack hesitated. "Yes."

Helen's expression softened. "Good."

That night, after Ruby drove him back to his apartment - a rare concession to exhaustion - Jack stood in the shower and let the water run until it turned cold. The weight of everything pressed down: Helen's fragility, the life he'd have to reorganize, the future that suddenly felt more uncertain. His children needed stability. His mother needed care. Ruby needed to know she wasn't investing in someone who'd disappear under pressure.

But beneath it all was something steadier - the knowledge that he wasn't navigating it alone.

When he finally climbed into bed, Ruby was already there, reading. She set the book aside and turned toward him.

"How are you holding up?" she asked.

"I don't know yet," Jack admitted.

She reached for his hand, threading her fingers through his. "You will."

Jack believed her. Not because he had answers, but because she didn't need him to.

The rehabilitation facility was better than Jack expected - clean, well-staffed, structured in a way that suggested competence. Helen was transferred there a week after the stroke, and within days, she'd begun the slow, grueling work of relearning basic tasks. Jack visited daily, adjusting his schedule ruthlessly to make it possible.

On Saturday, he brought the kids.

They were quiet in the car, even Sarah, who usually filled silences with observations and questions. Jack had warned them what to expect - that Grandma might look different, sound different, that she was working hard to get better. But nothing prepared children for seeing someone they loved diminished.

Emma held his hand tightly as they walked down the corridor. "Will she remember us?"

"Of course she will," Jack said. "A stroke doesn't take away memories. It just makes some things harder."

Helen was in the common room, working with a physical therapist on grip exercises. She looked up when they entered, and her face transformed - the worry lines smoothing, the careful control releasing into genuine joy.

"My babies," she said, the words slow but clear.

Emma ran to her, careful not to jostle, burying her face against Helen's good shoulder. Sarah followed more slowly, trying not to cry. Michael hung back, his jaw tight, until Helen waved him over with her working hand.

They crowded around her chair, and Jack stood back, letting them have this moment. The therapist caught his eye and nodded approval - family was the best medicine, her expression said.

After the visit, as they walked back to the car, Sarah said quietly, "She's going to be okay."

It wasn't a question. Jack recognized the tone - his daughter convincing herself, building the narrative she needed to believe.

"Yes," Jack said. "She is."

As the weeks progressed, Helen's progress became both encouraging and sobering. She regained some strength in her left arm, enough to manage basic tasks with assistance. Her speech improved significantly, though fatigue still slurred her words by evening. But it was clear she wouldn't return to full independence. Not soon, maybe not ever.

Jack began the process of arranging long-term care. He researched assisted living facilities, interviewed caregivers, consulted with social workers. Every decision felt heavy, laden with implications he couldn't fully escape. Helen had always been self-sufficient, proud. Now she needed help with things she'd once done without thought.

One evening, as Jack sat with her going over options, Helen interrupted him.

"I don't want to be a burden," she said quietly.

Jack looked up sharply. "You're not."

"Jack-"

"You're not," he repeated, more firmly. "You've spent your life taking care of me. Let me do this."

Helen's eyes welled, but she didn't cry. She just reached for his hand and held it.

Later that night, Jack sat in Ruby's apartment, the exhaustion finally catching up with him. Ruby brought him tea, settled beside him on the couch, and waited.

"I don't know if I'm making the right choices," Jack said eventually.

"You're making the best ones you can with what you know," Ruby replied.

"What if that's not enough?"

"Then you'll adjust." She leaned into him, her warmth grounding. "That's what you do, Jack. You adapt."

He wanted to believe her. Most days, he did. But some nights, lying awake in the dark, he felt the weight of it all pressing too close - the responsibility, the uncertainty, the slow erosion of control. He'd built his life on structure, on knowing what came next. Now, everything felt contingent.

The shrapnel in his ribs ached, a reminder of other times when control had been an illusion. In Vietnam, you couldn't plan around an RPG. You couldn't predict which turn of the river held an ambush. You adapted or you died.

But Ruby stayed. Through the late nights and the tense silences and the moments when Jack's patience frayed despite his best efforts. She didn't fix anything. She just stayed.

And somehow, that was enough.

Chapter 3: Pressure Rising

Monday announced itself without ceremony. Jack arrived at the office early, the building still half-asleep, lights humming softly above rows of empty desks. He liked this hour - the illusion of control it gave him, the sense that if he came early enough, stayed sharp enough, nothing could get ahead of him.

He set his jacket over the chair, powered up his workstation, and pulled up the audit request that had unsettled him all weekend. It sat there on his screen like a polite threat, written in the careful language of corporate procedure. Everything about it looked correct. That, more than anything, made him uneasy.

Jack read it again, line by line, tracing the routing history, the approvals, the timestamps. Whoever initiated it understood the system. They knew which doors to knock on and which ones to leave untouched. This wasn't fishing. It was targeted.

By midmorning, the office had filled with the low murmur of conversation and the clatter of keyboards. Jack attended his standing meeting, contributed when needed, listened more than he spoke. He noticed things most people missed - who avoided eye contact, who lingered after discussions, who suddenly seemed too interested in matters outside their scope.

At ten-thirty, his manager, Frank Delaney, stopped by his desk.

"You got a minute?" Frank asked.

Jack stood. "Of course."

Frank's office was glass-walled and immaculate, every surface curated to suggest transparency. He gestured for Jack to sit.

"I'm hearing your name more than usual," Frank said, not unkindly. "That's not a problem in itself. But it means eyes are on your work."

"They usually are," Jack replied evenly.

Frank nodded. "True. This audit request-"

"-is premature," Jack finished. "And misdirected."

Frank smiled faintly. "I thought you might say that."

They talked through the request carefully, neither saying more than necessary. Frank trusted Jack's instincts, but trust in an organization like theirs always had limits. Jack left the office knowing two things: Frank wasn't behind this, and Frank wouldn't shield him if things turned adversarial.

At lunch, Jack ate alone at his desk, a habit he'd never broken. He used the time to pull historical data, mapping patterns across departments, flagging anomalies. Slowly, a picture began to emerge - not proof, not yet, but enough to suggest coordination.

Someone was nervous.

The realization didn't thrill him. It focused him.

His phone buzzed. A text from Jennifer: Michael's teacher called. He got into a fight at school. Can you pick him up? I'm stuck in a meeting.

Jack stared at the message. Michael didn't fight. He was the peacemaker, the one who defused situations, the kid who'd rather walk away than throw a punch.

He texted back: On my way.

Jack grabbed his jacket and headed for the elevator, already composing the explanation he'd give Frank. Family emergency. His son. The words felt strange - not because they weren't true, but because work and family rarely collided so directly.

The middle school was fifteen minutes away in light traffic. Jack made it in twelve, his mind running through possibilities. Michael was fourteen, old enough to have reasons for things, old enough to make choices that would follow him. Whatever had happened, Jack needed to understand it before reacting.

The vice principal's office smelled like stale coffee and teenage anxiety. Michael sat in a chair outside, his face swollen on one side, his knuckles scraped raw. The other boy - bigger, older-looking - sat across from him, ice pack pressed to his nose.

Michael's eyes met Jack's, a mix of defiance and shame that Jack recognized from his own youth.

Vice Principal Harris emerged from her office, a woman in her fifties who'd clearly dealt with this scenario a thousand times.

"Mr. Mercer. Thank you for coming so quickly."

"What happened?"

"According to witnesses, Kyle here made some comments about Michael's grandmother. Michael responded physically. Three punches before a teacher intervened." Her tone was carefully neutral. "We have a zero-tolerance policy for fighting."

Jack looked at the other boy. "What did you say about his grandmother?"

Kyle shifted uncomfortably. "I just said... I heard she had a stroke and was probably gonna die soon. I didn't mean-"

"You meant it," Jack said quietly. "And my son reacted to a deliberate provocation."

Harris's expression tightened. "Mr. Mercer, I understand emotions are running high in your family right now, but violence is not-"

"I'm not condoning violence," Jack interrupted. "I'm acknowledging that my son was provoked. Deliberately. This boy-" he gestured at Kyle "-knew exactly what he was doing. He wanted a reaction."

"Both boys will serve one-day suspension," Harris said firmly. "That's policy."

Jack nodded. "Fair enough. But I want it noted in the record that my son was defending his family's honor after a targeted, cruel comment. That context matters."

"It will be noted," Harris said. "Michael, you can go with your father."

They walked to the car in silence. Michael kept his head down, shoulders hunched. Jack waited until they were both inside, doors closed, before speaking.

"You want to tell me what really happened?"

Michael's jaw worked. "He's been saying stuff all week. About Grandma. About how old people are useless. About how she should just die and stop wasting everyone's time." His voice cracked. "I tried to ignore it. I did. But today he said... he said maybe someone should help her along. Put her out of her misery."

Jack's hands tightened on the steering wheel. He understood violence - had dealt it, received it, survived it. He'd learned in the Navy that some situations required force, that restraint wasn't always strength. But he'd also learned that violence had consequences, that every fight left scars whether you won or lost.

"You hit him three times," Jack said.

"Yes, sir."

"Did you win?"

Michael looked up, surprised. "I... yeah. He went down."

"Good." Jack started the car. "Here's what you need to understand. Fighting has a cost. You got suspended. That's the price. But some things are worth the cost. Defending your grandmother's honor? That's one of them."

"You're not mad?"

"I'm proud you stood up for what matters. I wish you'd tried other options first - telling a teacher, walking away. But I understand why you didn't." Jack glanced at his son. "Next time - and there will be a next time, life guarantees that - you walk away first. You tell a teacher. You give the system a chance to handle it. Only when all else fails do you use your fists. Understand?"

"Yes, sir."

"And Michael?" Jack waited until his son looked at him. "If you're going to fight, fight to end it. Three punches, he goes down, you stop. That's discipline. That's control. You protected yourself and your family without going too far. That's the right balance."

Michael nodded slowly, something settling in his expression - understanding, maybe, or relief that his father wasn't disappointed in him.

They drove to a diner Jack remembered from when the kids were younger. Over burgers and fries, they talked about Helen's recovery, about Sarah's upcoming soccer tournament, about Emma's dragon book. Normal things. Safe things. The fight became context, not the entire story.

"Dad?" Michael said as they were finishing.

"Yeah?"

"Were you ever in a fight? Like, a real one?"

Jack thought about the Mekong Delta. About firefights that erupted without warning. About the morning the RPG hit and everything turned to chaos and blood and screaming. About fights that weren't about honor or pride but survival.

"Yes," he said. "More than one."

"Did you win?"

"I survived. That's the only victory that matters in a real fight."

Michael absorbed that. "Is that why you have that scar? On your side?"

Jack had never hidden his scars from his children, but he'd never explained them in detail either. They'd seen them during summers at the pool, asked casual questions, accepted vague answers.

"Vietnam," Jack said. "Shrapnel from a rocket. I was your age plus eight years."

"Did it hurt?"

"Yes."

"Does it still?"

"Sometimes. When it's cold, or before rain. The metal that's still inside reminds me it's there." Jack paused. "But that's the thing about surviving fights, Michael. You carry them with you. The trick is not letting them define you."

They sat in comfortable silence for a moment, father and son, connected by shared experience and unspoken understanding.

Jack dropped Michael back at Jennifer's house. She met them at the door, took one look at Michael's face, and sighed.

"School called," she said. "Suspension tomorrow."

"I know."

"You okay with how we handled it?" Jack asked.

Jennifer looked at Michael, then back at Jack. "He defended his grandmother. I can't be mad about that. But Michael-" she turned to their son "-this doesn't become a pattern. Understood?"

"Yes, ma'am."

"Good. Go ice that face."

After Michael went inside, Jennifer stepped onto the porch, closing the door behind her.

"How's Helen doing?"

"Making progress. Slow but steady."

"And you? You look tired."

"I am tired. But managing." Jack hesitated. "Jen, if something happens - if I need help with the kids while I'm dealing with Helen's care - can I count on you to be flexible?"

"Of course. We're a team, Jack. We always have been, even after the divorce." She studied him. "You're seeing someone, aren't you?"

Jack blinked. Jennifer had always been able to read him.

"Yes."

"Good. You deserve that." She smiled. "When do we get to meet her?"

"Eventually. When I'm sure."

"The kids will like anyone who makes you happy, Jack. Don't overthink it."

That evening, Jack went straight to Ruby's apartment. She answered the door, took one look at his face, and pulled him inside without a word. They sat on the couch, and he told her about Michael, about the fight, about the conversation in the diner.

"You handled that well," Ruby said.

"Did I? I basically told him fighting was okay."

"No. You told him there were consequences to fighting, and sometimes those consequences were worth it. That's different." She leaned against him. "Your son was defending someone he loves. You validated that while teaching restraint. That's good parenting."

Jack exhaled slowly. "Jennifer asked about you."

"What did you tell her?"

"That I'm seeing someone. That it's serious."

Ruby was quiet for a moment. "Is it? Serious?"

Jack turned to face her. "Yes. At least, it is for me."

"For me too," Ruby said softly.

They sat together in the quiet apartment, the day's chaos settling into something calmer. Outside, the city moved through its rhythms - traffic, sirens, the endless pulse of urban life. Inside, Jack felt the pieces of his world arranging themselves into a pattern he hadn't planned but recognized as right.

His mother was recovering. His son had learned something important about standing up for family. His ex-wife remained a supportive partner in raising their children. And Ruby - Ruby was becoming the kind of constant he'd stopped believing existed.

But beneath it all, the work pressure remained. The audit request. The careful maneuvering. Someone at the company was nervous about something, and they'd decided Jack was the threat.

That would need to be dealt with. Soon.

But tonight, Jack let himself rest. Let himself be just a father, a son, a partner. Tomorrow would bring its own demands.

Tonight, he was exactly where he needed to be.

Chapter 4: No Safe Options

The restaurant Ruby had chosen was quieter than their usual spots - a corner bistro with exposed brick and low lighting that suggested conversation over spectacle. Jack arrived first, claimed a table near the back, and ordered water while he waited. His mind was still half at the office, replaying the audit request, tracing the approval chain, looking for the pattern beneath the surface.

Ruby appeared in the doorway, scanning the room with the methodical attention Jack had come to recognize. She spotted him, smiled, and navigated through the tables with easy grace. She'd come straight from work, still dressed in a charcoal suit that managed to look both professional and effortless.

"Sorry I'm late," she said, leaning down to kiss him briefly. "Client call ran long."

"You're fine. I just got here myself."

They ordered - Ruby choosing the salmon, Jack opting for steak - and settled into the familiar rhythm of their evenings. She asked about Helen first, the way she always did, and Jack gave her the update: physical therapy progressing, speech improving, frustration mounting as Helen realized the extent of her limitations.

"She asked about you again," Jack said.

Ruby raised an eyebrow. "What did she ask?"

"When she's going to meet you properly. Not just glimpses in hospital corridors."

"And what did you tell her?"

"That I'm working up to it." Jack paused. "She said I overthink things."

"She's not wrong."

Jack smiled despite himself. "No, she's not."

Their food arrived, and they ate in comfortable silence for a few minutes. Jack noticed the way Ruby cut her salmon into precise portions, the methodical approach that spoke to something fundamental in her character. He'd learned early that Ruby's mind worked in patterns and systems, that she saw order where others saw chaos.

"How's work?" Ruby asked eventually. "You've seemed distracted the last few days."

Jack considered his answer carefully. He'd told Ruby about the audit request in passing, framed it as a routine annoyance. But it wasn't routine, and the more he looked at it, the less routine it became.

"Something's off," he admitted.

Ruby set down her fork, attention sharpening. "Off how?"

"There's an audit request circulating. On the surface, it looks legitimate - proper routing, correct approvals, reasonable justification. But the timing's wrong. The scope's wrong. And the person who initiated it doesn't usually handle this kind of review."

"What's the scope?"

"My department specifically. Shipment reconciliation, documentation verification, customs clearance records for the past eighteen months." Jack leaned back slightly. "It's targeted. Someone's looking for something."

Ruby was quiet for a moment, her expression thoughtful. "Or someone's looking to see if you've found something."

The observation landed with precision. Jack had been circling that possibility without naming it directly.

"Yeah," he said. "That occurred to me too."

"What have you found?"

"Nothing concrete. Just... inconsistencies. Small ones, but consistent. Certain routes always seem to have documentation gaps. Nothing that raises immediate red flags, but enough to make me wonder if someone's being deliberately sloppy or deliberately careful."

Ruby reached for her wine, took a small sip, her mind clearly working. "You said eighteen months. That's specific. Why that timeframe?"

"That's what the audit request specified."

"Right, but why? Audit scopes are usually annual, quarterly, or comprehensive. Eighteen months suggests they're either avoiding something older or targeting something recent." She paused. "Do your inconsistencies fall within that window?"

Jack thought about it. The patterns he'd noticed had started appearing roughly two years ago, maybe a little less. Eighteen months would capture most of them.

"Yes," he said slowly. "They would."

Ruby set her glass down carefully. "Jack, I don't want to overstep, but this sounds like someone trying to either find out what you know or position themselves to discredit whatever you might report."

"You're not overstepping."

She studied his face. "What do you want to do about it?"

That was the question, wasn't it? Jack had spent his career respecting institutional processes, following proper channels, trusting that systems worked when good people operated them honestly. But he'd also learned - in Vietnam, in divorce, in the thousand small crises of daily life - that systems only worked when the people running them wanted them to work.

"I want to understand what I'm looking at before I make any moves," Jack said. "Right now, I have suspicions. I need evidence."

"Can you pull data without raising flags?"

"Some. My access is broad enough that routine queries won't trigger anything. But if I start digging into specific accounts or routes, people will notice."

Ruby was quiet for a moment, clearly thinking. When she spoke again, her tone was careful, almost tentative.

"I could look at it," she said. "If you wanted a second set of eyes."

Jack studied her. "What kind of second set of eyes?"

Ruby smiled faintly. "The kind that used to do this for a living."

She'd mentioned her background before - corporate accounting, eventually moving into audit work - but always in passing, without detail. Jack had sensed there was more to the story but hadn't pressed.

"Tell me," he said.

Ruby set her fork down, gathering her thoughts. "I worked for Hammond & Associates for six years. Big Four firm, forensic accounting division. We did fraud investigation, litigation support, regulatory compliance work. I was good at it."

"Was?"

"I left three years ago." She paused. "I found something I wasn't supposed to find."

Jack waited.

"One of our major clients - a manufacturing conglomerate - was cooking their books. Not small stuff. Systematic revenue recognition fraud, hundreds of millions over multiple years. I found it during what was supposed to be a routine audit." Ruby's expression hardened slightly. "I reported it through proper channels. To my supervisor, to the engagement partner, to the ethics committee."

"And?"

"The partner killed the investigation. The client was too valuable, the relationship too important. They buried my findings, reassigned me to different work, and made it very clear that my career prospects depended on forgetting what I'd seen." Ruby's voice was steady but cold. "I didn't forget. I took everything I'd found to the SEC."

Jack felt something shift in his understanding of the woman sitting across from him. "What happened?"

"The SEC investigated. Quietly, for eighteen months. Eventually, they brought charges. The company settled for a massive fine, several executives were removed, the firm paid penalties for failing to report." Ruby met his eyes. "I was fired three days after the settlement was announced. Officially for 'poor judgment and violation of client confidentiality.' Unofficially for being a whistleblower they couldn't retaliate against directly."

"Jesus."

"I was blacklisted in corporate accounting. No Big Four firm would touch me. Most mid-sized firms wouldn't either. The message was clear: I'd betrayed the industry's unwritten rules." She picked up her wine glass again but didn't drink. "So I went independent. Small business clients, individuals, nonprofits. People who needed competent accounting but couldn't afford the big firms. It pays the bills. It's honest work. And nobody tells me what I'm allowed to find."

Jack absorbed this, seeing Ruby differently now - not just as the woman he'd grown to care for, but as someone who'd faced a version of what he might be facing. Someone who'd chosen principle over security and paid the price.

"Do you regret it?" he asked.

"No." The answer was immediate, certain. "I regret trusting the system to do the right thing. I regret thinking that following proper channels would be enough. But I don't regret exposing what I found. Those executives were stealing from shareholders, lying to investors, destroying pension funds. Someone had to stop them."

"Even if it cost you your career?"

"My career in corporate accounting," Ruby corrected. "I still have a career. It's just different than I planned." She smiled slightly. "Sometimes the price of keeping your integrity is changing your definition of success."

They sat in silence for a moment, the restaurant's ambient noise washing around them. Jack understood now why Ruby had offered to look at his data. This wasn't academic for her. It was personal.

"If I show you what I have," Jack said carefully, "you need to understand what you're getting into. If there's something real here, if people are willing to run an audit to cover it up or expose me, then they're nervous. Nervous people make dangerous decisions."

"I know."

"Ruby, I'm serious. You've already paid once for doing the right thing. I won't ask you to pay again."

She reached across the table, took his hand. "You're not asking. I'm offering. And Jack? If there's fraud happening at your company, ignoring it doesn't make you safe. It makes you complicit."

He knew she was right. He'd known it since the audit request appeared on his screen. The question was never whether to investigate. It was whether to investigate alone or with help.

"Okay," he said. "I'll pull together what I have. But we do this carefully. No traces, no patterns that suggest we're coordinating. You're just a girlfriend who happens to know accounting, looking at her boyfriend's work complaints."

"Agreed." Ruby squeezed his hand. "When's your next custody weekend?"

"This Saturday. Why?"

"Because you should spend it with your kids, not buried in spreadsheets. Show me what you have during the week. I'll do preliminary analysis on my own time. We'll compare notes after the weekend."

Jack nodded. The plan was sound. Cautious. Smart.

They finished dinner, the conversation shifting to lighter topics - a book Ruby was reading, plans for Helen's next step in rehabilitation, whether Jack should finally replace his aging car.

Normal things. Safe things. The kind of conversation that reminded Jack why he valued this relationship.

Later, back at Ruby's apartment, they moved together with the easy intimacy of people who'd learned each other's rhythms. There was comfort in the familiar now, in knowing what made her laugh, what made her sigh, where she liked to be touched. They made love slowly, without urgency, and afterward lay tangled together in the dark.

"Jack?" Ruby's voice was soft, drowsy.

"Yeah?"

"When you introduce me to your kids, I want to meet them as the person I actually am. Not as some cleaned-up version who doesn't have opinions or a past."

Jack thought about that. Sarah was sixteen, old enough to appreciate complexity. Michael was fourteen, still figuring out what integrity looked like. Emma was eleven, young enough to see things simply but old enough to sense dishonesty.

"They'd respect that," he said. "Hell, they'd probably like you more for it."

"Good." Ruby shifted, settling more comfortably against him. "Because if we're doing this - really doing this - I don't want to start by pretending to be someone I'm not."

"We're doing this," Jack confirmed. "Really doing this."

She was asleep within minutes, her breathing deep and even. Jack lay awake longer, his mind returning to the audit request, to the inconsistencies in shipping records, to the careful way someone had structured their investigation to look routine while being anything but.

Ruby's story had given him perspective. She'd followed the rules, trusted the system, and been punished for it. The lesson wasn't that doing the right thing was wrong. It was that doing the right thing required understanding the actual fight you were in, not the fight you wished you were in.

If there was fraud at his company - and Jack's instincts said there was - then the people behind it had resources, institutional protection, and motivation to cover their tracks. An audit request wasn't just bureaucratic maneuvering. It was reconnaissance. They were testing his defenses, looking for vulnerabilities, preparing their next move.

Jack's hand moved unconsciously to his left side, feeling through his shirt the ridged scar tissue where shrapnel had torn through muscle and lodged against bone. The doctors had pulled out what they could. The rest stayed embedded, too close to vital organs to risk extraction. On nights like this, when stress and old injuries conspired, he could feel every fragment.

Vietnam had taught him about fighting smart versus fighting hard. About knowing when to advance and when to fall back. About the difference between courage and stupidity.

This situation required the same tactical thinking. He couldn't charge ahead without reconnaissance. Couldn't ignore the threat and hope it disappeared. Couldn't trust that institutional processes would protect him when those same processes might be compromised.

But he also couldn't do nothing.

Jack closed his eyes, feeling Ruby's warmth beside him, thinking about his children sleeping safely across town, about his mother struggling through rehabilitation, about all the people whose lives intersected with his and depended on him making smart choices.

Whatever was happening at work, whatever the audit request represented, he would handle it. Carefully. Methodically. With help from someone who understood the actual cost of fighting institutional corruption.

He fell asleep finally, his last thought before darkness claimed him: Some fights choose you. The only question is whether you're ready when they arrive.

Saturday morning arrived bright and cold, the kind of November day that promised winter without quite delivering it. Jack picked up the kids from Jennifer's house at nine, the usual handoff smooth and practiced. Sarah climbed into the front seat, Michael and Emma piled into the back, and within minutes, the car filled with the chaotic energy of three children competing for attention.

"Dad, can we stop for donuts?" Emma asked immediately.

"We just had breakfast," Sarah said.

"Yeah, but that was at Mom's house. Dad's mornings start with donuts."

"Not every morning," Jack corrected mildly.

"Most mornings," Michael said. "The good ones anyway."

Jack glanced in the rearview mirror, caught Michael's grin, and relented. "Fine. Donuts. But then we're going straight to Sarah's game."

The soccer field was forty minutes away, which meant they had time. Jack pulled into their usual spot - a family-owned bakery that had been operating since before Jack was born. The kids spilled out of the car, already arguing about which donuts to get, and Jack followed them inside with the resigned patience of a parent who'd learned to pick his battles.

By the time they reached the soccer field, Sarah was in game mode - quiet, focused, stretching with the deliberate precision of an athlete who took her performance seriously. She'd been playing since she was six, had developed into a strong midfielder with field vision that impressed her coaches. College scouts had started attending games this season. Sarah pretended not to notice, but Jack knew better.

He settled into the bleachers with Michael and Emma, watching Sarah warm up with her team. Jennifer and David arrived a few minutes later, claiming spots nearby. They'd long ago worked out the etiquette of shared events - close enough to present a united front, far enough to give each other space.

"How's Helen doing?" Jennifer asked, leaning over.

"Better. Doctors think she'll be ready for outpatient therapy in another week."

"That's great. The kids have been asking about visiting again."

"Tomorrow, if she's up for it. I'll call the facility this afternoon."

David nodded a greeting to Jack, then turned his attention to the field as the game began. He was a good man, David - steady, kind to the kids, respectful of boundaries. Jack had been prepared to dislike him on principle when Jennifer first introduced them. Instead, he'd found someone he could trust with his children's daily wellbeing. That mattered more than ego.

The game unfolded with the controlled chaos of competitive high school soccer. Sarah moved through it with confidence, calling plays, directing traffic, making the kind of decisions that separated good players from great ones. In the thirty-second minute, she collected a pass at midfield, saw the opportunity, and threaded a perfect ball through three defenders to their striker, who finished cleanly.

Emma jumped up cheering. Michael offered his usual understated "Nice," which coming from a fourteen-year-old boy counted as high praise. Jack allowed himself a moment of pure paternal pride.

They won 3-1, Sarah assisting on two goals and scoring the third herself. Afterward, flushed and happy, she jogged over to where the family had gathered.

"Good game," Jack said simply.

"You saw the through-ball in the first half?"

"I saw it. Perfect weight."

Sarah grinned. "Coach said the same thing."

Jennifer hugged her daughter. "You were amazing. We're all going out for lunch - you want to join us, Jack?"

It was an olive branch, an invitation to extended co-parenting. Most weekends, they kept their time separate. But sometimes, for moments like this, they bent the rules.

"Can't today," Jack said. "I promised Michael we'd work on his Vietnam project this afternoon."

"Rain check then." Jennifer squeezed his arm briefly. "Emma, you want to come to lunch with us, or go with your dad and Michael?"

Emma considered, clearly torn between french fries and her father. "Can I do both?"

"Not unless you've developed teleportation," David said dryly.

"I'll go with Dad," Emma decided. "But can we get french fries anyway?"

"We'll figure something out," Jack promised.

They parted ways in the parking lot, Sarah heading off with Jennifer and David, Michael and Emma climbing back into Jack's car. The afternoon stretched ahead, full of the comfortable routines that defined custody weekends.

Back at Jack's apartment, he set Michael up at the dining table with research materials while Emma claimed the couch with her dragon book. Jack made sandwiches, distributed them along with chips and Emma's requested french fries - frozen ones from his freezer, heated in the oven, close enough to count.

Michael had spread out papers, library books, and his laptop, clearly taking the Vietnam project seriously. Jack settled across from him, coffee in hand.

"So what's the assignment exactly?" Jack asked.

"We're supposed to pick a specific aspect of the Vietnam War and explore it in depth. I chose the end - the Fall of Saigon and the immediate aftermath." Michael looked up. "I thought... maybe you could tell me what it was like. Coming home, I mean."

Jack had known this question would come eventually. His children knew he'd served, knew he'd been wounded, knew he didn't talk about it much. But they'd never pressed for details, and he'd never volunteered them.

"What do you know already?" Jack asked.

Michael referenced his notes. "That the war ended in April 1975 when North Vietnamese forces took Saigon. That thousands of South Vietnamese who'd worked with Americans tried to evacuate. That American veterans came home to protests and hostility." He paused. "That a lot of them felt abandoned."

"That's all accurate." Jack took a sip of coffee, choosing his words carefully. "I was discharged in '73, two years before the fall. I'd been wounded in late '72, spent months in recovery, and by the time I was mobile again, my enlistment was up. So I missed the final collapse. But I knew people who were there for it."

"What was it like when you came home?"

Jack thought about the airport in San Francisco, the long-haired protesters, the signs calling him a baby killer. He thought about changing out of his uniform in an airport bathroom because wearing it felt dangerous. He thought about his own father - still alive then, still trying to rebuild his life after prison - looking at Jack with something like recognition and sadness.

"Complicated," Jack said finally. "I'd served my country, done what was asked of me, gotten hurt doing it. I expected... not gratitude exactly, but acknowledgment. Instead, a lot of people saw the uniform and saw everything they hated about the war. They didn't see individual soldiers. They saw the policy, the deaths, the waste."

"That's not fair."

"No, it wasn't. But anger rarely is." Jack paused. "The thing you have to understand about Vietnam is that it divided the country in ways that haven't fully healed. People had strong opinions - about whether we should be there, about how the war was conducted, about what it meant for America's role in the world. And soldiers became symbols in that argument, whether we wanted to be or not."

Michael was taking notes, his expression serious. "Did it make you angry? Being treated like that after what you'd been through?"

"Yes. For a long time, I was angry." Jack set down his coffee cup. "But anger doesn't change anything. It just eats you from the inside. So eventually, I had to figure out what to do with it."

"What did you do?"

"I focused on the things I could control. Got a job. Built a life. Started a family." Jack gestured around the apartment. "The war was part of my past, but it didn't have to define my future. That was a choice I had to make actively, every day for a while."

Emma had abandoned her book and was listening now, curled up on the couch with wide eyes.

"Daddy, were you scared? In the war?"

Jack looked at his youngest daughter, weighing honesty against age-appropriateness. "Yes, sweetheart. I was scared a lot."

"But you did it anyway?"

"I did it anyway. Sometimes being brave doesn't mean not being scared. It means being scared and doing what needs to be done regardless."

Emma seemed to accept this, returning to her book. Michael was still processing, clearly trying to reconcile the father he knew with the young man who'd fought in a jungle on the other side of the world.

"Can I ask about when you got hurt?" Michael said quietly.

Jack had known this was coming too. He pulled up his shirt slightly, showing the scars on his left side - pale, ridged lines where shrapnel had torn through and surgeons had stitched him back together.

"We were on river patrol. The Mekong Delta - lots of waterways, villages, places where enemy forces could hide. Our job was to interdict supply lines, provide security, show American presence." Jack's voice was steady, factual. "December 1972, early morning. We were running a routine patrol when we got hit with an RPG - a rocket-propelled grenade. It struck the boat's hull. The explosion sent shrapnel through my side."

"Did it hurt?"

"Yes. But not right away. First, there was just shock - your body doesn't process pain immediately during trauma. Then adrenaline kicks in, and you do what you're trained to do. I helped get the boat to shore, helped with the wounded." Jack paused.

"Three of my crewmates died. I lived. The pain came later, in the hospital."

Michael was quiet for a moment. "Do you still think about them? The ones who died?"

"Every day," Jack said honestly. "Not in a way that stops me from living. But they're always there. Part of why I survived was luck - six inches to the right and the shrapnel would've hit my heart. So I owe it to them to do something with the life I got to keep."

"Like what?"

"Like being a good father. A good son. A good man." Jack met his son's eyes. "Like doing the right thing even when it's hard. Like standing up for what matters."

Michael nodded slowly, understanding something unspoken passing between them. They worked on the project for another hour, Jack providing context and personal insight while Michael shaped it into a cohesive narrative. By the time they finished, Michael had the foundation for something thoughtful and personal.

As the afternoon faded toward evening, Emma convinced Jack to read the next chapter of her dragon book aloud. He settled on the couch with her tucked against his side, Michael claiming the other end with his phone. Jack read about kingdoms and magic and a young dragon learning to fly, and felt the specific contentment that came from being exactly where he was supposed to be.

His phone buzzed with a text from Ruby: *How's the dad weekend going?*

Jack typed back one-handed: *Good. Kids are happy. Will call you tonight.*

No rush. Enjoy your time with them. I'll be here.

He pocketed the phone and continued reading, Emma's breathing deepening as she started to drift off. This was what mattered - these moments, these children, this deliberate construction of a life worth protecting.

Whatever was happening at work could wait until Monday.

For now, he was just Dad, reading about dragons to a sleepy eleven-year-old while her brother scrolled through whatever fourteen-year-olds scrolled through. Normal. Simple. Perfect.

The shrapnel in his ribs ached faintly - rain coming, probably - but Jack ignored it. Some scars you carried. Some fights you survived. And some moments you just held onto as tightly as you could, knowing they wouldn't last forever but mattered precisely because they didn't.

He kept reading until Emma fell asleep completely, then carefully extracted himself and carried her to the guest room that had become her space during custody weekends. Michael had already retreated to his own room. The apartment fell quiet.

Jack stood in the hallway for a moment, looking at the closed doors behind which his children slept, and felt the weight of responsibility settle familiar and solid across his shoulders.

He would protect them. Whatever it took. Whatever it cost.

That was the promise he'd made the day each of them was born, and it was a promise that didn't expire just because he and their mother had divorced.

Some things were non-negotiable.

Family was one of them.

Chapter 5: The Trap

Monday arrived with the particular weight of unfinished business. Jack spent the morning in back-to-back meetings, his attention split between the discussions happening in conference rooms and the patterns forming in his mind. By lunch, he'd managed to carve out an hour alone at his desk.

He pulled up the shipping database, running queries that would look routine to anyone monitoring his activity. Regional volume reports. Documentation completion rates. Standard compliance metrics. The kind of thing a Risk Compliance Analyst reviewed constantly.

But Jack wasn't looking at the standard metrics. He was looking at the outliers.

Three routes kept appearing in his analysis: Los Angeles to Shanghai, Miami to Rotterdam, and Houston to Singapore. High-volume corridors, complex regulatory environments, multiple handoffs between carriers and customs authorities. Exactly the kind of routes where discrepancies could hide in legitimate complexity.

Jack exported the data to a spreadsheet, scrubbed of any obvious identifying markers, and saved it to a thumb drive. He'd give it to Ruby tonight; let her forensic accounting mind find the patterns he suspected were there.

His phone buzzed. A text from the rehabilitation facility: *Helen asking for you. Nothing urgent, just wants to talk.*

Jack checked his calendar. He could visit during his lunch hour if he skipped eating. He texted back: *On my way.*

The facility was twenty minutes across town, a modern building that managed to feel clinical and comfortable simultaneously. Jack signed in at the front desk, nodded to nurses he'd come to recognize, and made his way to Helen's room.

She was dressed and sitting in the chair by the window, working through exercises with a hand therapy ball. Her left hand still moved with visible effort, but the progress since the stroke was undeniable.

"You didn't have to come during work," Helen said, her speech clearer now though still slightly thick.

"I wanted to." Jack pulled up a chair beside her. "How are you feeling?"

"Like I'm eighty years old and rebuilding myself from scratch." She set down the therapy ball. "But better than last week."

They talked for a while about her progress, about the kids' visit the day before, about small domestic matters that filled the space between larger concerns. But Jack could tell Helen had something specific on her mind. She had the same expression she'd worn when he was young and she was working up to a difficult conversation.

"What's wrong?" he asked finally.

Helen studied him with the unsettling perception of a mother who'd spent sixteen years reading her son's moods before words could hide them.

"You're carrying something heavy," she said. "I can see it in how you hold yourself."

Jack considered deflecting, then didn't. Helen had earned honesty.

"Work situation. Nothing dangerous, just... complicated."

"The kind of complicated that keeps you up at night?"

"Sometimes."

Helen was quiet for a moment, her good hand tracing patterns on the arm of her chair. "Your father used to get that same look. When he was wrestling with something at the construction company."

Jack rarely heard his mother talk about his father in specific terms. The man had died eight years ago, the memories still tender in ways Helen didn't often expose.

"What would he do?" Jack asked.

"Depends on the problem." Helen's gaze drifted to the window. "Most times, he'd work it out himself. Figure the angles, find the solution, and move forward. But there was one time..." She trailed off, then seemed to decide something. "You were young. Maybe seven or eight. Your father was working as a project manager for a mid-sized construction firm. Good job, good pay, building toward something."

Jack waited.

"They were bidding on a municipal contract. Big project, would've secured the company for years. Your father was putting together the cost estimates when he found discrepancies in the materials projections. Someone had deliberately underestimated costs to make their bid more competitive."

"Fraud," Jack said.

"Yes. But the kind that's hard to prove if everyone involved denies knowing. The kind where speaking up means accusing your bosses of intentional wrongdoing." Helen's expression hardened slightly. "Your father went to his supervisor first. Was told he'd misunderstood the numbers. Went to the owner next. Was told to mind his own business and focus on his assigned work."

Jack had heard pieces of this story before, but never the full version. His father's time in prison had been explained as "making a mistake" when Jack was young, then "refusing to participate in corruption" when he was old enough to understand nuance.

"So he reported it?" Jack asked.

"He refused to sign off on the bid. Told them if they submitted fraudulent numbers, they'd do it without his name attached." Helen's voice carried old pride mixed with old pain. "They fired him. Then they reported him to the licensing board, claimed he'd been the one falsifying documents. It took two years to clear his name, and by then he'd lost his license, his savings, and any chance of working in the industry again."

"Jesus."

"That's when things got hard. Really hard. He took whatever work he could find, but we had three kids and a mortgage. Eventually..." Helen paused, the next part clearly difficult even decades later. "Eventually he got desperate. Made real mistakes, not imagined ones. Ended up in prison for eighteen months."

Jack knew this part. The fraud conviction, the jail time, the way his father had emerged quieter and more deliberate. What he hadn't known was the full context - that his father's fall had started with refusing to participate in someone else's crime.

"Why are you telling me this now?" Jack asked quietly.

Helen turned from the window, met his eyes directly. "Because you're facing something similar, aren't you? Found something wrong, wondering whether speaking up will cost you everything."

Jack didn't deny it.

"Your father used to say that doing the right thing doesn't guarantee the right outcome. Sometimes good men lose. Sometimes the corrupt win." Helen's good hand reached for his. "But he also said that you can't build a life worth living on compromised ground.

That if you let fear of consequences stop you from acting on your principles, you've already lost the only thing that really matters."

"His principles put us in poverty," Jack said carefully. "Put him in prison. Nearly destroyed our family."

"Yes, they did. And he paid for that every day for the rest of his life." Helen's grip tightened. "But Jack, he never regretted standing up to that corruption. What he regretted was what he did after - the shortcuts, the desperation, the real crimes he committed trying to survive the consequences of doing right. He told me once, near the end, that if he could do it over, he'd make the same choice about the bid. But he'd plan better for the aftermath."

Jack absorbed this, seeing his father differently now. Not as a man who'd failed, but as a man who'd fought and lost and then made new mistakes trying to recover. A cautionary tale with layers he was only now old enough to understand.

"What would he tell me to do?" Jack asked.

"He'd tell you to document everything. Build your case carefully. Don't go to war until you know you can win, or at least until you've protected the people who depend on you from the fallout." Helen paused. "And he'd tell you to find allies. He tried to fight alone. That was his mistake."

Jack thought about Ruby, about her offer to help, about her own experience fighting institutional corruption. About Paul in IT, who'd been quietly helpful. About Monica Chen, who'd hinted at her own concerns.

"I'm not alone this time," Jack said.

Helen smiled, the asymmetry from the stroke giving it a lopsided quality that was somehow more genuine. "Good. That woman of yours - Ruby? She seems smart. Capable."

"She is."

"Then trust her. But Jack?" Helen's expression turned serious. "Whatever you're facing, don't let it consume you. Don't let it take away from your kids, from building the life you want. Your father's other mistake was letting the fight become everything. Even after he got out of prison, part of him never left that battle. Don't do that to yourself."

Jack nodded, feeling the weight of his mother's wisdom and experience pressing against his own instincts. The shrapnel in his ribs ached - rain coming for sure now - and he thought about all the old wounds that never fully healed, just became part of you.

"I should get back to work," he said finally.

"Go. And Jack? When you're ready to introduce me to Ruby properly, I'd like that. She's important to you. That makes her important to me."

Jack kissed his mother's forehead, careful of the fragile places, and left her to her therapy and her memories.

The drive back to the office felt longer than it was, his mind turning over his mother's story, seeing the parallels and the differences. His father had fought without preparation, without allies, without understanding the full scope of what he was up against. Jack wouldn't make the same mistakes.

But he also wouldn't ignore what he'd found.

Back at his desk, Jack spent the afternoon in a carefully orchestrated dance of productivity and investigation. He attended meetings, responded to emails, handled routine compliance reviews. But in the margins, he pulled data, cross-referenced accounts, built the foundation of understanding.

By four o'clock, he'd identified something concrete: a shell company that appeared repeatedly in customs documentation for the three routes he'd been tracking. Pacific Meridian Holdings. Listed address in Delaware, minimal online presence, no obvious business operations. But it showed up as an intermediary on dozens of high-value shipments.

Jack ran the company name through every database he had access to. What he found was carefully constructed absence - a company that existed on paper, met minimum legal requirements, but did nothing that would attract attention. The perfect vehicle for moving money or goods without scrutiny.

His phone buzzed. Ruby: *Dinner at my place tonight? I'll cook.*

Jack: *Perfect. I have something to show you.*

Ruby: *Work thing or personal thing?*

Jack: *Work. The thing we discussed.*

Ruby: *Okay. Come whenever you're ready.*

Jack shut down his workstation at five-thirty, the thumb drive secured in his pocket. As he walked to his car, he noticed Derek Vaughn in the parking lot, leaning against a Tesla and talking on his phone. Their eyes met briefly. Vaughn nodded - professional, cordial, empty of meaning.

Jack nodded back and kept walking.

But as he drove away, he checked his rearview mirror more often than usual. The prickle of awareness from Vietnam had returned - that sense of being watched, of being in someone's crosshairs even if you couldn't see the shooter.

He took an indirect route to Ruby's apartment, watching for tails, seeing nothing obvious but trusting his instincts enough to be cautious. By the time he arrived, he was reasonably certain he hadn't been followed.

Ruby answered the door in jeans and a soft sweater, her hair down, already working on dinner. The apartment smelled like garlic and herbs.

"You're paranoid," she observed, reading something in his expression.

"Professional caution," Jack corrected.

"Mmm." She kissed him quickly. "Wine?"

"Please."

They moved into the kitchen, working in the easy synchronization they'd developed - Jack setting the table while Ruby finished cooking. Over pasta and salad, Jack walked her through what he'd found: the routes, the patterns, the shell company.

Ruby listened with the focused attention of someone who understood exactly what he was describing. When he finished, she set down her fork.

"Can I see the data?"

Jack pulled out the thumb drive. "It's scrubbed of identifying information, but the patterns are all there."

Ruby took the drive, walked to her laptop, and plugged it in. For the next thirty minutes, she worked in silence, occasionally making notes, running calculations, cross-referencing information. Jack cleaned up from dinner and gave her space.

Finally, she looked up.

"This is layering," she said. "Classic money laundering structure. Pacific Meridian Holdings is probably one of multiple shell companies in a chain. They receive payments for legitimate-looking services - customs brokerage, freight forwarding, trade facilitation - but the actual services are minimal or non-existent. The money moves through the shell, gets mixed with legitimate funds, then resurfaces somewhere else looking clean."

"How much money are we talking about?"

Ruby pulled up a spreadsheet she'd created. "Based on the documentation here and assuming standard fee structures, Pacific Meridian has processed at least twelve million dollars through your company's shipments in the past eighteen months. Probably more - this is just what I can track from incomplete data."

Jack felt something cold settle in his stomach. Twelve million dollars. That wasn't bookkeeping errors or sloppy accounting. That was systematic, intentional, organized.

"Who's behind it?" he asked.

"Can't tell from this data. But someone senior enough to approve routing decisions, authorizes payments, and ensures documentation doesn't get flagged." Ruby closed the laptop. "Jack, this is serious. We're not talking about small-scale fraud. This is either money laundering, import duty evasion, or both. Possibly tied to smuggling."

"Smuggling what?"

"Could be anything. Counterfeit goods, controlled substances, embargoed materials. The shell company structure hides the actual cargo and its origin." She paused. "Or it could be purely financial - using the logistics network to move illicit money under cover of legitimate trade."

Jack thought about Derek Vaughn, about the audit request, about the careful way someone had been testing his awareness.

"They know I'm looking," he said.

"Probably. The audit request was either preparation to discredit whatever you found, or an attempt to see how much you knew." Ruby came to sit beside him on the couch. "What do you want to do?"

That was the question. Jack had found something real. Ruby had confirmed it, quantified it, explained the mechanism. Now he had to decide what came next.

"I need more evidence," he said. "Right now, I have patterns and a shell company. That's enough to raise questions but not enough to prove anything. I need to trace Pacific Meridian further, find out who controls it, document the actual flow of money."

"That's going to take time. And it's going to increase your exposure."

"I know."

Ruby was quiet for a moment. "There's another option. We could take what we have to the FBI now. Let them investigate."

"With incomplete evidence? They might look into it, or they might file it away as speculative. And the moment the FBI starts asking questions, everyone involved will know. They'll have time to destroy records, create plausible deniability, pin it on someone expendable." Jack shook his head. "No. I need to build a complete case first. Something they can't ignore and can't easily dismantle."

"That's what I did," Ruby said quietly. "With Hammond & Associates. I built what I thought was an airtight case before going to the SEC."

"And it worked. The company was charged, executives were removed."

"After eighteen months. And I lost my career in the process." Ruby took his hand. "I'm not trying to talk you out of this. I'm trying to make sure you understand what you're risking."

Jack squeezed her fingers. "I understand. But I also understand what happens if I do nothing. The fraud continues. People profit from crime. And I become complicit by staying silent."

"Like your father," Ruby said softly.

Jack looked at her, surprised.

"You visited your mother today at lunch," Ruby continued. "Came back looking like someone had handed you a piece of difficult history. I'm guessing she told you something about your father."

"Yeah." Jack explained the story Helen had shared, about the construction bid and the choice that led to everything that followed.

Ruby listened, then nodded slowly. "So now you know this is in your blood. The inability to look away from corruption even when looking costs you everything."

"Is that a compliment or a warning?"

"Both." She shifted closer, resting her head on his shoulder. "I'll help you. Whatever you need. But Jack, we do this smart. We don't take unnecessary risks. We protect your kids, your mother, ourselves. And if it gets too dangerous, we go to the authorities with whatever we have, even if it's incomplete."

"Agreed."

They sat in silence for a while, the weight of what they were committing to settling around them like weather. Outside, the first drops of rain began to fall - the storm Jack's old wounds had predicted arriving right on schedule.

"I should tell you something else," Ruby said eventually. "When I was investigating the Hammond case, I learned something important. Big fraud doesn't happen in isolation. There are always enablers - people who look the other way, people who benefit indirectly, people who are scared to speak up. And there are always enforcers - people whose job is to protect the operation, to neutralize threats."

"You think I'm being treated as a threat?"

"I think the audit request was the first move. There will be others." Ruby lifted her head, met his eyes. "We need to assume someone is watching your activity, monitoring what you access, maybe even listening to your communications."

"At work, definitely. Outside work..." Jack considered. "Possible but harder to do without being obvious."

"So we're careful. We don't communicate about this through work email or work phones. We don't discuss it where we might be overheard. We assume everything digital leaves a trail." Ruby paused. "And we start thinking about what happens if this goes bad. Where your kids go. How your mother's care continues. What assets might be seized or frozen."

Jack felt his jaw tighten. The idea of his children being affected, of Helen's recovery being interrupted, of Ruby being pulled down with him - it activated every protective instinct he had.

"I won't let them hurt my family," he said.

"I know. But wanting to protect them and being able to protect them are different things." Ruby's tone was gentle but firm. "This is where your father made his mistake. He didn't plan for the aftermath. We're going to do better."

She was right. Jack knew she was right. But planning for failure felt like inviting it.

"Okay," he said finally. "Tomorrow, I'll update my will, review my insurance policies, make sure Jennifer has all the documentation she'd need to maintain the kids' routines if something happened to me. I'll talk to the facility about Helen's care being continued regardless of my personal circumstances."

"And I'll start building a backup plan. Places to store evidence, people we can trust with information if we need it distributed quickly, contacts who might help if official channels fail." Ruby stood, pulled Jack up with her. "But tonight, we're going to stop talking about fraud and corruption and just be two people who care about each other. Deal?"

"Deal."

They moved to the bedroom, leaving the laptop and the data and the mounting evidence behind. The rain fell steadier now, drumming against the windows, and Jack let himself focus entirely on the woman beside him - the curve of her neck, the softness of her skin, the way she responded to his touch with complete trust.

Later, lying in the dark with Ruby asleep against his shoulder, Jack's mind returned to the problem despite his best efforts. Twelve million dollars. Shell companies. Money laundering. And somewhere in his company's leadership, someone orchestrating it all while preparing to neutralize anyone who got too close.

His phone buzzed on the nightstand. A text from Jennifer: *Michael wanted me to thank you again for helping with his project. He got an A on the first draft.*

Jack smiled despite everything. *He earned it. Smart kid.*

Jennifer: *Takes after his dad. Night, Jack.*

Jack set the phone down, careful not to wake Ruby. His son had gotten an A on a Vietnam project Jack had helped with by sharing difficult truths about war and consequence and choosing to do right even when right was hard.

Now Jack was facing his own version of that choice. And unlike his father, he had allies. He had Ruby's expertise. He had time to prepare. He had learned from history's mistakes.

But he also had twelve million reasons why someone might decide he was too dangerous to leave alone.

The shrapnel in his ribs ached steadily now, keeping rhythm with the rain. Old wounds and new threats, past and present, all converging in a pattern Jack was beginning to understand.

Some fights you could avoid. Some you couldn't. And some you walked into with your eyes open, knowing the cost but unable to live with the alternative.

Jack closed his eyes and tried to sleep, knowing tomorrow would bring its own complications. The investigation would continue. The risk would increase. The careful dance of appearing normal while building a case would demand everything he had.

But tonight, he had this: a warm apartment, a sleeping woman he trusted, the sound of rain washing the city clean. Tomorrow's problems would wait.

They always did.

Chapter 6: Helen's Warning

The week unfolded with deceptive normalcy. Jack attended meetings, filed reports, maintained the facade of routine compliance work while quietly assembling pieces of a puzzle that grew more disturbing with each new discovery.

On Tuesday, he found a second shell company - Hemisphere Trade Solutions, incorporated in Nevada, linked to the same shipping routes as Pacific Meridian Holdings. The two companies appeared to work in tandem, splitting fees in ways that made individual transactions look smaller, less noteworthy.

On Wednesday, he traced payment authorizations and found Derek Vaughn's signature on a dozen documents approving routing through both shell companies. Not proof of knowledge - Vaughn signed hundreds of documents monthly - but a thread worth pulling.

On Thursday, Paul Hendricks from IT stopped by Jack's desk with what looked like a routine software update but was actually a quiet warning: "Someone requested access logs for your workstation activity last month. Thought you should know."

Jack had thanked him calmly, filed the information away, and spent the rest of the day being extra cautious about what he accessed and when.

By Friday afternoon, Jack had compiled enough evidence to feel both vindicated and anxious. The fraud was real, systematic, and involved multiple parties. But he still couldn't definitively identify everyone involved or prove criminal intent beyond reasonable doubt.

He was finishing up for the day when his phone rang. Helen's rehabilitation facility.

"Mr. Mercer? This is Diane from St. Catherine's. Your mother asked me to call. She's experiencing some discomfort - elevated blood pressure, slight difficulty breathing. We're monitoring her closely, but she wanted you to know."

Jack's stomach dropped. "Should I come now?"

"The doctor doesn't think it's an emergency, but Helen would feel better if you were here. And frankly, so would we."

"I'm on my way."

Jack grabbed his jacket and headed for the elevator, texting Ruby as he walked: *Helen having complications. Going to facility now.*

Ruby's response came immediately: *Want me to meet you there?*

Jack hesitated, then typed: *Not yet. I'll call if I need you.*

The drive felt endless, traffic conspiring against urgency. Jack forced himself to breathe steadily, to not catastrophize. Elevated blood pressure. Difficulty breathing. Could be a dozen things, most of them manageable. Helen was in a medical facility. She was being monitored. She would be fine.

But the voice in his head that had kept him alive in Vietnam - the one that calculated odds and recognized danger - whispered that stress contributed to medical complications. That Helen had been worrying about him. That his investigation might be affecting more than just his own life.

He found Helen in her room, connected to monitors, a nurse adjusting her IV. She looked small again, diminished in ways that the stroke hadn't fully accomplished.

"You didn't have to rush," Helen said, her voice weak but clear.

"Yes, I did." Jack took her hand, feeling the papery fragility of aging skin. "What happened?"

The doctor arrived before Helen could answer - a different physician than usual, younger, with the efficient manner of someone accustomed to delivering news that ranged from routine to devastating.

"Mr. Mercer? I'm Dr. Patel. Your mother experienced a hypertensive episode this afternoon. Her blood pressure spiked significantly, accompanied by shortness of breath and chest tightness."

"Is it her heart?"

"We don't think so. EKG looks stable, cardiac enzymes are normal. Most likely a stress response, possibly anxiety-related." Dr. Patel glanced at Helen, then back to Jack. "Has your mother been under unusual stress recently?"

Jack looked at Helen, who was carefully not meeting his eyes.

"She's been worried," Jack admitted. "About her recovery, about being a burden, about family matters."

"I'm not a burden," Helen said automatically.

"I know you're not. But you worry about being one, which amounts to the same thing physiologically." Jack squeezed her hand gently. "What were you doing when this started?"

Helen was quiet for a moment. "Watching the news. There was a story about corporate fraud, executives going to prison. It reminded me of... other things. I started thinking about your father, about the choices he made, about you facing similar situations." She finally met his eyes. "And I got myself worked up."

Dr. Patel nodded. "Anxiety can absolutely trigger hypertensive episodes, especially in patients recovering from stroke. The good news is we've got her blood pressure stabilizing now. I'd like to keep her overnight for observation, make sure this was an isolated incident."

"Whatever you think is necessary," Jack said.

After the doctor left, Jack pulled a chair close to Helen's bed and sat in silence for a while. The monitors beeped softly, rhythmic and reassuring. Outside the window, evening was settling over the city, lights beginning to glow in the dusk.

"I'm sorry," Helen said finally.

"For what?"

"For adding to your stress. For being another thing you have to worry about."

"Mom, you're not a thing. You're my mother. And worrying about you isn't a burden, it's what family does." Jack paused. "But I am sorry that my situation is affecting your recovery."

"It's not your fault that criminals exist."

"No. But it's my choice whether to confront them." Jack studied his mother's face, seeing the worry there, the fear she was trying to hide. "Do you want me to walk away from this? From what I've found at work?"

Helen considered the question seriously. "I want you to be safe. I want you to be there for your children. I want..." She trailed off, then started again. "But I also want you to be able to look at yourself in the mirror. Your father couldn't, after he compromised himself. That ate at him more than the prison time ever did."

"So what would you have me do?"

"Be smarter than your father was. Build your case, but build your protection too. Don't stand alone in the spotlight waiting to be knocked down." Helen's grip on his hand tightened. "And for God's sake, don't let trying to do the right thing destroy the good things in your life. Your father did that. Don't repeat his mistakes."

Jack nodded slowly. The same advice Ruby had given him, coming now from his mother. Both women he trusted telling him the same thing: fight smart, not just hard.

"I'm being careful," Jack said. "I have help. I'm documenting everything, building contingencies. This isn't a reckless crusade."

"Good." Helen relaxed slightly. "Then I'll try not to have a panic attack every time I see a news story about whistleblowers."

Jack smiled despite himself. "Deal."

They sat together until Helen drifted into sleep, her breathing steady and her blood pressure readings gradually normalizing. Jack stayed in the chair, unwilling to leave until he was certain she was stable.

His phone buzzed with a text from Ruby: *How is she?*

Jack: *Stable. Anxiety-triggered hypertension. They're keeping her overnight for observation.*

Ruby: *Because of the work situation?*

Jack: *Indirectly. She was worrying about me.*

Ruby: *Jack, if this investigation is affecting your mother's health...*

Jack: *I know. We'll talk tonight.*

He stayed another hour, watching monitors and thinking about consequences. About how fighting corruption didn't just risk his own career and safety, but rippled out to affect everyone connected to him. His mother's blood pressure. His children's security. Ruby's professional standing.

The cost of doing the right thing kept climbing.

By the time Jack left the facility, it was fully dark. He drove to Ruby's apartment on autopilot, his mind running through scenarios and contingencies. When Ruby opened the door, she took one look at his face and pulled him inside without a word.

"She's okay," Jack said immediately. "Really. They've got her stabilized."

"But you're not okay."

Jack sank onto the couch, suddenly exhausted. "My investigation put my mother in the hospital."

"Your mother's anxiety about your investigation contributed to a medical episode," Ruby corrected. "That's different."

"Is it?"

Ruby sat beside him. "Jack, if you stopped every time someone you loved got worried or scared, you'd never do anything difficult. Your kids worry when you're late picking them up. Your ex-wife worries about you being alone. Your mother worries because that's what mothers do." She took his hand. "The question isn't whether your actions cause worry. It's whether they're necessary and whether you're managing the risk responsibly."

"And am I? Managing the risk responsibly?"

"You're building a case methodically. You're protecting your family. You're not going in guns blazing." Ruby paused. "But we do need to talk about whether the timeline needs to accelerate or pause."

Jack was quiet for a moment. "What did you find?"

Ruby had been doing her own investigation, using her forensic accounting skills and old contacts to dig deeper into the shell companies. She pulled out her laptop now, opening files she'd compiled over the past few days.

"Pacific Meridian Holdings and Hemisphere Trade Solutions are both owned by a parent company called Nexus Global Ventures, incorporated in the Cayman Islands." She pulled up a corporate structure diagram. "Nexus Global has controlling interests in seven other shell companies, all used for similar purposes - facilitating payments, creating layers between money sources and destinations."

"Who owns Nexus Global?"

"That's where it gets interesting. Ownership is hidden behind nominee directors and bearer shares. But I found something else." Ruby pulled up a different document. "Three years ago, before the shell company network was established, there was a simpler structure. A single LLC called Pacific Trade Partners, incorporated in Delaware, with two listed owners: Derek Vaughn and someone named Marcus Chen."

Jack felt his pulse quicken. "Monica Chen's husband?"

"Could be. I haven't been able to confirm yet. But if so, it connects two people at your company to the original structure." Ruby scrolled through more documents. "The LLC was dissolved eighteen months ago, right around the time the more complex shell company network was established. My guess is they realized they needed better insulation."

"So Vaughn and possibly Marcus Chen started this operation, then evolved it into something more sophisticated."

"That's my working theory. But Jack, there's more." Ruby's expression turned serious. "I found evidence of payments flowing from Nexus Global to accounts in Hong Kong and mainland China. Large payments, irregular intervals, no clear business purpose."

"Money laundering?"

"Or payments for goods or services that aren't going through normal channels. Smuggling, most likely." Ruby closed the laptop. "We're not just looking at fraud anymore. This has international dimensions. Customs violations. Possibly organized crime connections."

Jack stood, paced to the window, looked out at the city lights. Twelve million dollars had seemed significant. Now it looked like the visible portion of something much larger.

"We need to go to the FBI," he said.

"I agree. But we need to do it right." Ruby joined him at the window. "Monday, I'll reach out to my former colleague at the Bureau. Agent Sarah Reeves, white-collar crime division. I trust her, and she'll take this seriously. We give her everything we have, let the professionals handle it from there."

"And in the meantime?"

"In the meantime, you be very, very careful at work. Don't access anything suspicious. Don't ask questions that might alert anyone. Just be the normal, competent Risk Compliance Analyst you've always been."

Jack nodded. The decision felt both right and terrifying. Once they contacted the FBI, there was no going back. The investigation would expand beyond his control. People would know he was the source. Retaliation became not just possible but likely.

"I need to talk to Jennifer," Jack said. "Tell her what's happening, make sure she knows to be careful with the kids."

"Good idea. And Jack?" Ruby wrapped her arms around him from behind. "This is the right move. Your father tried to fight alone and lost. You're not going to make that mistake."

They stood together at the window, watching the city exist in blissful ignorance of the small drama unfolding in Ruby's apartment. Somewhere out there, Derek Vaughn was probably having dinner, confident in his criminal enterprise. Marcus Chen was living his life, assuming his crimes were safely hidden. And dozens of others who benefited from or enabled the fraud were sleeping soundly, convinced they'd never face consequences.

Jack was going to change that.

But first, he had to protect his family.

Saturday morning, Jack picked up the kids as usual. Sarah had a college tour to attend with Jennifer and David, so it was just Michael and Emma for the weekend. They drove to Jack's apartment, stopped for breakfast at their favorite diner, and settled into the comfortable routine of custody weekends.

But Jack's mind was elsewhere, running through the conversation he needed to have with Jennifer. How to explain without frightening her. How to warn without creating panic. How to be honest about danger while maintaining the kids' sense of security.

Emma was absorbed in her dragon book, curled up on the couch with a blanket. Michael was supposed to be doing homework but was clearly distracted, glancing at his phone every few minutes with the furtive attention of a teenager trying to hide something.

"What's so interesting?" Jack asked.

Michael looked up, caught. "Just... texting with some friends."

"About?"

Michael hesitated, then seemed to decide honesty was easier than evasion. "There's this girl. Kaylee. She sits behind me in English. We've been talking more lately."

Jack felt the peculiar sensation of his son growing up in real-time. "Talking, huh?"

"Yeah. Just, you know. Talking."

"Does your mother know about Kaylee?"

"No. I mean, not specifically. I haven't really..." Michael trailed off, then looked at Jack directly. "How did you know you wanted to ask Mom out? Like, when you first met her?"

Jack sat down across from his son, recognizing the moment for what it was - not just teenage crush conversation, but Michael trying to understand relationships, trust, vulnerability.

"I didn't, at first," Jack admitted. "Your mother and I met through mutual friends at a party. She was smart, funny, kind. But I was just out of the Navy, still dealing with injuries and figuring out what came next. I wasn't looking for a relationship."

"So what changed?"

"She asked me to coffee. Direct, no games. I said yes because I liked her honesty. And then we kept talking, kept finding reasons to see each other, and eventually I realized I didn't want to imagine my life without her in it."

Michael absorbed this. "But then you got divorced. So how do you know if someone's right?"

It was a harder question than it seemed. Jack thought about his marriage to Jennifer - good years, real love, and then the slow recognition that they wanted different things, had grown into incompatible people. The divorce had been amicable because they'd both been honest enough to admit the truth.

"You don't know, not completely," Jack said. "Love isn't a math problem with a definite answer. It's a choice you make every day, and sometimes the choice changes as you change." He paused. "Your mother and I loved each other. We still do, in a different way. We just learned that loving someone doesn't always mean staying married to them."

"Is that why you're with Ruby now? Because you're different than you were with Mom?"

"Partly. I'm older, more settled in who I am. And Ruby... she sees me clearly, accepts what she sees, and chooses me anyway. That's rare."

Michael nodded slowly, processing. "Do you think you'll marry her?"

The question surprised Jack with its directness. "I don't know. Maybe. We're not rushing anything."

"But you want to? Eventually?"

Jack considered lying or deflecting, then didn't. Michael deserved honesty, especially about something that would affect his life.

"Yeah," Jack said. "Eventually, I think I do."

Michael smiled, the expression more mature than Jack expected. "Good. She seems cool. And you're happier when you're with her."

"You noticed that?"

"Dad, we're not blind. You text more, smile more, seem less... I don't know. Less like you're carrying everything alone."

Jack felt something shift in his chest - pride in his son's perception, gratitude for his acceptance, and a sharp awareness that this conversation was part of why he was fighting so hard against the corruption at work. These moments mattered. This relationship mattered. And anything that threatened to destroy the life he'd built was worth opposing.

"Thanks, buddy," Jack said quietly.

They were interrupted by Emma, who'd looked up from her book with wide eyes. "Are you talking about Ruby? Is she going to be our new mom?"

"No," Jack said quickly. "Your mom is your mom. That doesn't change. Ruby would be... someone else important. Someone who cares about you because she cares about me."

Emma considered this. "Like how David cares about us because he cares about Mom?"

"Exactly like that."

"Okay." Emma returned to her book, apparently satisfied with this explanation.

Michael grinned at Jack. "Well handled, Dad."

"Thanks. Now tell me more about Kaylee."

They talked for another twenty minutes - Michael sharing details about the girl who sat behind him in English, Jack offering gentle advice about respect and honesty and the difference between liking someone and being ready for a relationship. It was the kind of father-son conversation Jack had imagined having someday, back when Michael was small and relationships seemed far in the future.

Now the future was here, unfolding in real-time, and Jack felt the weight of wanting to be worthy of his son's trust.

That evening, after the kids were in bed, Jack called Jennifer. She answered on the second ring, her voice low - probably in her bedroom, not wanting to wake David.

"Everything okay?" she asked. "Kids all right?"

"Kids are fine. But I need to talk to you about something else. Something serious."

He heard her shift, could picture her sitting up straighter. "Okay. I'm listening."

Jack explained carefully, methodically. The fraud he'd discovered at work. The shell companies, the money laundering, the international connections. The FBI contact Ruby was arranging. And most importantly, the potential for retaliation.

"Jesus, Jack," Jennifer said when he finished. "Why didn't you tell me sooner?"

"Because I wanted to be sure it was real before I worried you. And because I needed to have a plan before I involved the kids."

"What kind of plan?"

"Ruby's contacting the FBI Monday. Once they're involved, the investigation becomes theirs. But between now and when arrests happen, there might be a period where the people involved know they're caught and get desperate." Jack paused. "I need you to be extra careful with the kids. Verify who's picking them up from school. Don't let them go anywhere unusual. Keep an eye out for anything strange."

Jennifer was quiet for a long moment. "You really think they might go after our children?"

"I think desperate people make unpredictable choices. I'm not trying to scare you - the risk is probably minimal. But I won't forgive myself if something happens because I didn't warn you."

"Okay. I'll talk to David, explain the situation. We'll be careful." Another pause. "Jack, are you safe? Do you need to stay somewhere else until this is resolved?"

"I'm okay. Ruby and I are being cautious. But Jen, there's something else. If this goes badly - if I get arrested or accused of something I didn't do - I need you to know the truth. I need you to believe that whatever they say about me, I was trying to stop a crime, not commit one."

"Of course I'll believe you. Jack, you're the most honest person I know. Even when we were getting divorced, even when it hurt, you never lied to me." Her voice softened. "The kids adore you. I trust you. Whatever happens, we'll figure it out together."

Jack felt his throat tighten. "Thanks, Jen."

"And Jack? This woman, Ruby. She's good for you. I can hear it in your voice. Don't let this situation mess that up."

"I won't."

After they hung up, Jack sat in the dark living room of his apartment, listening to the quiet sounds of his children sleeping in their rooms. Michael, growing up and asking about relationships.

Emma, still young enough to think in simple categories of family and home. Both of them trusting him to keep their world stable and safe.

He thought about his father, who'd tried to fight corruption alone and lost. About Helen, lying in a hospital bed because worry had spiked her blood pressure. About Ruby, risking her own professional reputation to help him. About Jennifer, trusting him even after their marriage had ended.

Some fights you chose. Some chose you. But all of them revealed who you really were when the cost became real.

Jack stood, checked on both kids one more time - Michael sleeping with his phone on the nightstand, Emma clutching her dragon book even in sleep - and returned to his own room.

Monday, they'd contact the FBI. Tuesday, the real fight would begin.

But tonight, he was just a father, listening to his children breathe, grateful for the life he'd built and determined to protect it from anyone who thought twelve million dollars in fraud was worth destroying what mattered.

The shrapnel in his ribs ached steadily, keeping rhythm with his heartbeat.

Old wounds. New battles. Same fundamental truth: you fought for what mattered, or you surrendered who you were.

Jack had learned that lesson in Vietnam. He'd relearned it through divorce, through rebuilding his life, through every hard choice that had brought him to this moment.

He wasn't going to forget it now.

Chapter 7: The Audit

Monday morning arrived with the crystalline clarity that came after difficult decisions. Jack woke early, went through his routine with deliberate focus, and arrived at the office before most of his colleagues. The building felt different now - not safer or more dangerous, just observed. Every camera, every badge reader, every digital system that tracked his movements felt suddenly significant.

He settled at his desk, logged in, and began his day exactly as he had every Monday for the past three years. Email review. Calendar check. Routine compliance updates. The performance of normalcy.

At nine-fifteen, Frank Delaney stopped by his desk.

"Morning, Jack. Got a minute?"

"Of course."

Frank's office felt smaller than usual, the glass walls offering transparency that was mostly illusion. They sat across from each other, Frank's expression carefully neutral.

"The audit request we discussed last week," Frank began. "It's been approved. They're moving forward with a full review of your department's processes for the past eighteen months."

Jack kept his expression steady. "When does it start?"

"Wednesday. External auditors, very thorough. They'll want access to all your files, documentation, correspondence." Frank paused. "Jack, I want you to know this isn't personal. This is standard procedure for departments handling high-value international shipments."

"I understand."

"Do you?" Frank leaned forward slightly. "Because I'm getting pressure from upstairs to make sure this audit goes smoothly. No resistance, full cooperation, complete transparency."

"That won't be a problem. I have nothing to hide."

Frank studied him for a long moment. "Good. Because between you and me, there are people in this company who think you've been too... meticulous lately. Asking questions, pulling data, looking at things that might be outside your immediate scope."

"I'm a Risk Compliance Analyst. Meticulous is the job description."

"True. But there's meticulous and there's making people nervous." Frank's tone remained even, but the warning was clear. "Just be smart about how you handle the next few weeks. Keep your head down, cooperate fully, and let the audit run its course."

Jack nodded, understanding what wasn't being said: Frank knew something was wrong, suspected Jack had found it, but wasn't willing to stake his own career on supporting whatever came next.

"Thanks for the heads up," Jack said.

"Don't thank me. Just be careful."

Back at his desk, Jack sent a carefully worded text to Ruby: *Meeting at usual place tonight? Need to discuss schedule changes.*

Ruby's response came ten minutes later: *6:30. I'll bring dinner.*

The rest of the morning passed in studied routine. Jack attended a department meeting, reviewed shipping documentation, responded to emails. He was acutely aware of Derek Vaughn's presence two floors up, of the cameras tracking his movements, of the digital trail every action created.

At eleven, Monica Chen appeared at his desk, tablet in hand, expression professionally pleasant.

"Jack, do you have those quarterly compliance reports? I'm consolidating data for the executive summary."

"Sure. Let me pull them up." Jack opened the relevant files, began transferring them to a shared drive. As he worked, Monica leaned slightly closer, her voice dropping.

"Be very careful this week. People are watching."

Jack didn't look up from his screen. "I'm always careful."

"I mean it. The audit isn't just an audit." Monica straightened, her voice returning to normal volume. "Thanks for these. I'll let you know if I need anything else."

She walked away before Jack could respond, leaving him to wonder exactly how much she knew and whose side she was on.

By lunch, Jack's carefully maintained calm was fraying at the edges. He left the building, walked three blocks to a small park, and called Ruby from a bench far from any obvious surveillance.

"They're moving faster than we expected," he said without preamble. "Full audit starting Wednesday."

"Did you contact your FBI friend?"

"Calling her this afternoon. But Jack, if the audit starts Wednesday, they might find evidence before we can get it to the Bureau."

"Or they'll destroy evidence," Jack said. "Either way, we're running out of time."

Ruby was quiet for a moment. "Okay. New plan. I'm calling Sarah Reeves right now, explaining the situation, asking for an emergency meeting. Today if possible."

"Can you do that? Just demand an immediate meeting with the FBI?"

"I can when I have evidence of ongoing money laundering with international connections and a forty-eight-hour window before potential evidence destruction." Ruby's voice was firm. "This is exactly what the Bureau wants - active cases with cooperating witnesses. Sarah will take the meeting."

"Okay. Let me know what she says."

Jack returned to the office, forced down a sandwich at his desk, and spent the afternoon in a state of controlled tension. Every email felt significant. Every phone call potentially monitored. Every interaction coded with meanings he might be missing.

At three o'clock, his desk phone rang. Internal number, unrecognized extension.

"Jack Mercer."

"Mr. Mercer, this is Linda from HR. Do you have time to stop by this afternoon? Just some routine paperwork regarding your benefits enrollment."

Jack's pulse quickened. HR calls were rarely routine, especially unscheduled ones.

"What kind of paperwork?"

"Just some discrepancies in your file we need to clear up. Shouldn't take more than fifteen minutes."

"I'll come by at four."

Jack hung up, immediately suspicious. His benefits enrollment was current, had been reviewed two months ago. Either this was genuinely routine, or it was the opening move in a more aggressive campaign.

He texted Ruby: *HR just called. "Routine paperwork." Feels wrong.*

Ruby: *Don't go alone. Ask if you can bring a representative.*

Jack considered, then called back. "Linda, this is Jack Mercer again. For the benefits discussion, am I allowed to bring a representative?"

Brief pause. "That won't be necessary for routine paperwork, Mr. Mercer."

"I understand it's not necessary. I'm asking if it's permitted."

Longer pause. "Of course you can bring someone if you prefer. Though I assure you, this is completely standard."

"Great. I'll see you at four."

Jack hung up and immediately called Ruby. "Can you be at my office at four? HR meeting, they're calling it routine, but I don't trust it."

"I'll be there. But Jack, I'm not an employee. They might not let me sit in."

"Then you'll wait in the lobby. I just want someone to know where I am and what I'm walking into."

"Understood. And Jack? Sarah Reeves can meet us tonight at seven. There's a coffee shop near the Federal Building - neutral ground. She'll listen to what we have."

Jack felt some of the tension ease. Progress. Finally, they were moving from investigation to action.

"Good. I'll see you at four."

The afternoon crawled toward four o'clock. Jack prepared for the HR meeting the way he'd once prepared for patrol in Vietnam - by assuming the worst and planning accordingly. He saved all his current work to the cloud, backed up critical files to his personal thumb drive, and composed a brief email to Frank explaining his concerns about the audit and the unusual HR summons. He saved it as a draft, didn't send it, but wanted it ready if needed.

At three forty-five, Ruby texted: *In your lobby.*

Jack grabbed his jacket and headed downstairs. Ruby was sitting in one of the modern chairs near the security desk, dressed in business casual, looking like she belonged. She stood when she saw him.

"Ready?" she asked quietly.

"As I'll ever be."

They took the elevator to the third floor, where HR occupied a suite of offices designed to feel welcoming and professional. Linda turned out to be a woman in her fifties with a kind face and an apologetic manner.

"Mr. Mercer, thank you for coming. And you are?" She looked at Ruby.

"VRuby Martinez. I'm here as Jack's guest."

"I'm afraid this is a confidential HR matter. Company policy requires—"

"I understand," Jack interrupted. "Ruby can wait in the lobby area. But I want it noted that I requested her presence and was denied."

Linda's expression flickered - surprise, maybe, or concern. "Of course. Right this way, Mr. Mercer."

Jack followed her to a small conference room. Seated at the table was someone he didn't recognize - a man in an expensive suit with the smooth manner of corporate counsel.

"Mr. Mercer, this is David Brennan from our legal department. He'll be sitting in on our discussion."

Jack's internal alarms went to full alert. "I thought this was about benefits paperwork."

"It is. Partly." Linda gestured to a chair. "Please, sit."

Jack sat, every sense heightened. "I think I'd like to have my own legal counsel present if your lawyer is here."

Brennan smiled - professional, unthreatening. "That's absolutely your right, Mr. Mercer. But this really is routine. We're just clarifying some questions that came up during a standard file review."

"What questions?"

Linda pulled out a folder, opened it carefully. "We've noticed some... irregularities in your recent work patterns. Extended database queries, unusual file accesses, data exports that don't align with your typical job functions."

Jack kept his expression neutral. "I'm a Risk Compliance Analyst. My job is to identify irregularities. That requires looking at data comprehensively."

"Of course," Brennan said smoothly. "No one is questioning your dedication. But we need to ensure that all data handling follows proper protocols. Particularly with sensitive financial information."

"Everything I've accessed has been within my authorization level."

"True. But authorization and appropriateness aren't always the same thing." Brennan pulled out a document, slid it across the table. "We'd like you to sign this acknowledgment that you've been reminded of our data handling policies and confidentiality requirements."

Jack picked up the document, read it carefully. The language was deliberately broad - acknowledging receipt of policy reminders, agreeing to follow proper protocols, confirming understanding of confidentiality obligations. On the surface, innocuous. In practice, it could be used to suggest Jack had been warned about improper conduct, setting up a later claim that any whistleblowing was retaliation for being caught.

"I need to have my attorney review this before I sign anything."

Linda looked genuinely distressed. "Mr. Mercer, this really is standard—"

"Then there's no harm in me having it reviewed. I'll take a copy, have my counsel look at it, and get back to you by end of week."

Brennan's smile didn't change, but something hardened behind his eyes. "Of course. Take all the time you need. Though I should mention, refusing to sign standard policy acknowledgments could be seen as non-cooperation with HR processes."

"I'm not refusing. I'm requesting time for legal review. That's my right as an employee."

The meeting concluded shortly after, tension barely masked by professional courtesy. Jack collected a copy of the document, declined to discuss a timeline for signing, and left the conference room feeling like he'd just survived an ambush.

Ruby was exactly where he'd left her, reading something on her phone. She looked up as he approached, read his expression, and stood without a word. They left the building together, walking a full block before either spoke.

"They tried to get me to sign something that could be used against me later," Jack said quietly.

"But you didn't sign it."

"No. I asked for time to have a lawyer review it."

Ruby squeezed his arm briefly. "Good. That was smart. Now let's go meet Sarah and make this officially the FBI's problem."

The coffee shop was deliberately anonymous - a chain location near the Federal Building, busy enough for privacy through crowd noise but public enough to feel safe. Ruby and Jack arrived ten minutes early, claimed a corner table, and waited.

Agent Sarah Reeves arrived precisely at seven. She was in her late thirties, dressed in practical business attire, with sharp eyes that catalogued everything about them in the first three seconds. She ordered coffee, joined them at the table, and got straight to business.

"Ruby tells me you have information about corporate fraud with international connections. Tell me what you have."

Jack had prepared for this. He pulled out a folder containing printed summaries - careful not to include anything that could be traced directly to company servers - and walked Agent Reeves through the shell companies, the payment patterns, the international transfers.

"How much money are we talking about?" Reeves asked.

"Minimum twelve million through the logistics company over eighteen months. Possibly more through channels we haven't identified yet."

Reeves made notes, asked pointed questions about documentation, timeline, involved parties. She was thorough and skeptical in equal measure - exactly what Jack needed.

"You mentioned international transfers to Hong Kong and China," Reeves said. "Do you have evidence of what's being paid for?"

"No. Just that the payments are irregular, large, and have no clear business purpose in the company's legitimate operations."

"Could be money laundering. Could be payment for smuggled goods. Could be a lot of things." Reeves closed her notebook. "Here's where we are. What you've described is interesting but incomplete. It's enough to justify preliminary investigation, but not enough for warrants or arrests."

"What do you need?" Ruby asked.

"Direct evidence of criminal intent. Communications showing knowledge of illegal activity. Documentation of actual smuggling or customs fraud. Financial records showing the money trail from source to destination." Reeves paused. "Right now, you have suspicious patterns. I need proof."

Jack felt frustration building. "There's an audit starting Wednesday. If they're cleaning house, evidence could disappear."

"I understand the urgency. But I can't launch a full investigation based on suspicion and inference." Reeves softened slightly. "What I can do is open a preliminary inquiry. That gives us authority to start looking, to coordinate with customs and IRS, to monitor the situation. If evidence surfaces during their audit, or if they try to destroy evidence, we'll know."

"And if they come after Jack?" Ruby asked. "Retaliation, termination, false accusations?"

"Document everything. Save all communications. If they take action against you, Mr. Mercer, that could actually help our case - retaliation against a whistleblower is a separate crime we can prove more easily."

Jack understood the logic but hated it. He was being asked to become bait, to absorb whatever attacks came while the FBI slowly built their case.

"How long does a preliminary inquiry usually take?" he asked.

"Weeks to months, depending on complexity and cooperation." Reeves must have seen his expression. "I know that's not what you want to hear. But financial crimes with international components take time to unravel. Rushing leads to missed connections and failed prosecutions."

They talked for another thirty minutes, Reeves taking detailed notes, asking for specific documentation, explaining what she could and couldn't do at this stage. By the time they left, Jack had agreed to provide additional evidence as he found it, to document any retaliation, and to be patient while the Bureau worked.

In the parking lot, after Reeves had driven away, Ruby turned to Jack.

"Are you okay?"

"I'm frustrated. I hand them evidence of serious crimes and get told to wait patiently while criminals keep operating."

"She's doing her job correctly. Building a case that will actually stick." Ruby took his hand. "I know it's not satisfying. But this is how it works. We gave them enough to start looking. Now we trust the process."

Jack wanted to argue, wanted to push harder, wanted immediate action. But he'd learned in Vietnam that wanting and having were different things. Sometimes you did what was possible, not what was preferred.

"Okay," he said finally. "We gave it to the FBI. Now we wait."

"Now we're very, very careful," Ruby corrected. "You go to work, do your job, cooperate with the audit, and don't give them any excuse to come after you. And we document absolutely everything."

They drove back to Ruby's apartment in separate cars - an abundance of caution that felt both paranoid and necessary. Inside, Ruby poured wine, ordered Thai food, and they spent the evening reviewing everything one more time, making sure they hadn't missed anything.

"Your HR meeting," Ruby said. "That document they wanted you to sign. Did you get a copy?"

Jack pulled it out, handed it over. Ruby read it carefully, her forensic accountant's mind identifying the traps embedded in seemingly innocuous language.

"This is clever," she said. "It doesn't accuse you of anything directly. But by asking you to acknowledge policy reminders about data handling, they create a paper trail suggesting you'd been doing something questionable with company data."

"Which I could then be accused of violating, giving them cause to terminate me."

"Exactly. And termination for policy violation looks very different from termination for whistleblowing." Ruby set down the document. "You were right not to sign it. But they'll probably try again."

"What should I do?"

"Nothing. You asked for time to have legal counsel review it. Take that time. If they push, cite your right to legal representation. If they insist, sign it but add a written statement that you're signing under protest and don't agree with the characterization of your work." Ruby paused. "Actually, you should probably get an employment attorney. Now, before you need one."

"I'll call someone tomorrow."

They ate dinner mostly in silence, the weight of what they'd set in motion settling around them. The FBI was involved now. The investigation was real, official, documented. There was no going back.

Later, lying in bed with Ruby asleep beside him, Jack thought about his children, about Helen recovering in her facility, about Jennifer trusting him to handle this situation responsibly. He thought about his father, fighting alone and losing. About the choices that defined character and the prices those choices demanded.

The shrapnel in his ribs ached with particular insistence tonight, as if his old wounds recognized the new battle beginning.

Jack closed his eyes and tried to sleep, knowing tomorrow would bring the audit closer, knowing Wednesday would start a new phase where maintaining the appearance of normalcy became the most important performance of his life.

Some fights happened in the open, all noise and fury.

Others happened in conference rooms and HR meetings and carefully worded documents designed to create legal liability.

Jack had survived the first kind in Vietnam.

Now he'd find out if he could survive the second kind in corporate America.

The principles were the same: know your enemy, protect your position, never give ground you couldn't afford to lose.

He'd learned those lessons in blood and fire.

He wouldn't forget them now.

Chapter 8: Evidence

Tuesday passed in a state of suspended animation. Jack went through the motions of his job with mechanical precision, hyper-aware of every interaction, every email, every moment that might be monitored or misconstrued. The audit was less than twenty-four hours away, and the office felt like a stage set where everyone was playing roles they didn't quite believe in.

At ten AM, Jack received an email from the external audit team - Cartwright & Associates, a mid-sized firm that specialized in compliance reviews. The message was professionally cordial, outlining the scope of their review, requesting access to specific files and systems, and scheduling an introductory meeting for Wednesday morning at eight.

Jack forwarded the email to his personal account - one of dozens of small acts of documentation Ruby had insisted upon - and sent a polite confirmation reply.

By lunch, the tension had settled into his shoulders like old familiar weight. He ate a sandwich at his desk, reviewing the files the auditors would see, finding nothing that concerned him. Everything he'd accessed was within his authorization. Every query he'd run had legitimate business justification. He'd been careful, methodical, clean.

But careful didn't mean safe. Not when the people you were investigating had institutional power and motivation to protect themselves.

At two PM, Paul Hendricks appeared at Jack's desk with a laptop under his arm.

"Got a few minutes? Need to run a security update on your workstation."

Jack recognized the transparency of the excuse but played along. "Sure. How long will it take?"

"Ten, fifteen minutes." Paul set down his laptop, pulled up a chair, and began typing commands that were entirely performative. After a moment, he spoke quietly, eyes on his screen. "You should know, they're installing keystroke logging software on compliance department computers tonight. Part of the 'enhanced security protocols' for the audit."

Jack kept his expression neutral. "That's unusual."

"Very. But it came down from Vaughn's office, signed off by legal." Paul's fingers kept moving across the keyboard. "Officially, it's to ensure audit integrity. Unofficially, it means everything you type, every file you open, every search you run gets logged and reviewed."

"Starting when?"

"Midnight tonight. IT is doing the install remotely." Paul glanced up briefly. "I thought you should know."

"I appreciate it."

Paul finished his fake security update, gathered his laptop, and left without further conversation. Jack sat very still for a moment, processing the implications. Keystroke logging meant anything he did on his work computer from midnight onward would be completely transparent. No more discrete inquiries. No more careful data pulls. The digital surveillance was escalating from passive observation to active monitoring.

Jack pulled out his personal phone, stepped into an empty conference room, and called Ruby.

"They're installing keystroke loggers on my computer tonight," he said without preamble.

Ruby was quiet for a beat. "Aggressive move. They're really worried about what you might find during the audit."

"Or what I might communicate to the auditors."

"Have you done anything on your work computer that could be problematic?"

Jack thought through his recent activity. "No. I've been careful to keep work queries looking routine. All the real analysis happened on my personal devices or yours."

"Good. Then let them log. Just make absolutely sure you don't access anything sensitive from now on." Ruby paused. "Jack, this is a good sign, actually."

"How is active surveillance good?"

"Because it means they're defensive. They wouldn't waste resources monitoring you if they weren't genuinely concerned. You've gotten close to something important."

Jack appreciated the logic but didn't feel reassured. "I'm meeting with an employment attorney at four-thirty. Figured I should have someone on retainer."

"Smart. Get everything documented - the HR meeting, the policy acknowledgment they wanted you to sign, the sudden audit, now the keystroke logging. Build your retaliation case before they make their move."

After they hung up, Jack returned to his desk and worked with deliberate caution. Every email was professional and straightforward. Every file access had clear business justification. Every communication was crafted to withstand scrutiny.

He was performing the role of Perfect Employee while his actual thoughts churned with strategy and contingency planning.

At four-fifteen, he left the office early - a rarity that would definitely be noted - and drove to the law offices of Katherine Mendoza, an employment attorney Ruby's former colleague had recommended.

Mendoza's office was in a converted brownstone downtown, the kind of place that suggested competence without corporate sterility. She was a woman in her late forties with graying hair and the direct manner of someone who'd seen every employment dispute variant and wasn't impressed by any of them.

"Mr. Mercer. VRuby Martinez spoke highly of you." They shook hands, settled into her office. "Tell me what's happening."

Jack laid out the timeline: discovering the fraud, the suspicious audit request, the HR meeting with the policy acknowledgment, the keystroke logging installation. He showed her copies of relevant documents, explained the shell companies, described the FBI's preliminary inquiry.

Mendoza took notes, asked sharp questions, and when Jack finished, she sat back in her chair.

"You're in a textbook retaliation setup," she said. "They know you've found something, they're positioning to either discredit you or terminate you with cause before you can blow the whistle publicly."

"Can they do that? Legally?"

"They can try. Whether it succeeds depends on documentation and timing." Mendoza pulled out a legal pad. "Here's what we do. First, I'm sending a letter to your company's legal department and HR, informing them that you've retained counsel and that all future communications regarding your employment should be directed through me. This puts them on notice that you're represented."

"Won't that make me look guilty of something?"

"It makes you look smart. And it creates a paper trail showing you took protective measures before any adverse action, which supports a retaliation claim if they fire you." Mendoza made more notes. "Second, we document everything from this point forward. Every meeting, every email, every conversation that could be construed as threatening or retaliatory. You keep a detailed log with dates, times, witnesses."

"Already doing that."

"Good. Third, we need to consider whether to file a formal whistleblower complaint now or wait until they make their move."

Jack frowned. "What's the advantage of waiting?"

"If we file now, before they've taken adverse action, we're making an accusation without proof of retaliation. If we wait until they fire or demote you, we have both the underlying fraud and the clear retaliation. Much stronger case." Mendoza paused. "But waiting is risky. If they move fast, or if evidence gets destroyed, we might lose the opportunity to prove the fraud."

"The FBI has our evidence. They're conducting a preliminary inquiry."

"That helps. But federal investigations take months or years. We need to assume you might be terminated before the FBI acts." Mendoza looked at him directly. "Mr. Mercer, what's your goal here? Protect your job? Expose the fraud? Ensure the criminals face consequences?"

Jack thought about his children, about Helen recovering from her stroke, about Ruby risking her own reputation to help him. He thought about his father, who'd tried to do right and paid dearly for it.

"All of the above," he said. "But if I have to choose, I want the fraud exposed and the people responsible held accountable. My job is secondary."

Mendoza smiled faintly. "That's the answer I hoped you'd give. Makes you a good witness and a sympathetic plaintiff if this goes to court." She pulled out a contract. "My retainer is five thousand dollars. I bill at three-fifty an hour. Whistleblower retaliation cases can run twenty to fifty thousand in legal fees if they go to trial."

Jack felt his stomach tighten. He had savings, but that kind of money would hurt. Still, the alternative - facing this alone without legal protection - was worse.

"I'll transfer the retainer today."

"Good. I'll send the representation letter to your company tomorrow morning. Don't be surprised if HR or legal contacts you directly trying to get you to talk without me present. Don't do it. All communication goes through me from now on."

They spent another thirty minutes going over strategy, discussing likely scenarios, and preparing for various contingencies. By the time Jack left Mendoza's office, he had a clearer picture of the legal battlefield ahead.

He drove to Ruby's apartment, stopping on the way to pick up Chinese food - an offering of normalcy in the midst of escalating chaos. Ruby answered the door in yoga pants and an oversized sweater, her hair pulled back, looking tired but determined.

"How'd it go with the lawyer?"

"Good. She's sending a letter tomorrow putting the company on notice that I'm represented." Jack set down the food, pulled Ruby into a brief embrace. "This is really happening."

"Yeah. It is."

They ate dinner with the television on for background noise, both of them too aware of the possibility that Ruby's apartment might be monitored. The conversation stayed deliberately superficial - work complaints, weekend plans, Helen's recovery progress. Normal couple talk that revealed nothing important.

Later, after they'd cleaned up, Ruby pulled out a pad of paper and wrote: *Should we assume they're listening?*

Jack considered, then wrote back: *Probably paranoid, but not worth the risk.*

Ruby nodded, wrote again: *FBI contact tomorrow. Reeves wants update on audit.*

Jack: *I'll call from burner phone.*

They'd bought prepaid phones earlier in the week - spy novel nonsense that felt ridiculous and necessary in equal measure. The phones lived in Ruby's car, used only for sensitive communications, disposed of regularly.

Ruby: *Your mom called me today.*

Jack looked up, surprised. Ruby had given Helen her number weeks ago but they'd never spoken directly.

Ruby wrote: *She wanted to know if you were okay. Said you sounded stressed Sunday.*

Jack: *What did you tell her?*

Ruby: *That you're handling a difficult work situation but you're not alone. She said to tell you she's proud of you.*

Jack felt something catch in his throat. His mother, recovering from a stroke, worried about him even while fighting her own battles. The weight of people depending on him - trusting him to make the right choices, to protect himself and them - pressed heavy on his shoulders.

He wrote: *I don't want her worrying. Stress affects her blood pressure.*

Ruby: *She's your mother. Worrying is non-negotiable. But I told her you have good support. That seemed to help.*

They abandoned the written conversation, settling on the couch to watch a movie neither of them paid attention to. Jack's mind kept circling tomorrow's audit, running through scenarios, calculating probabilities. Ruby's hand found his, squeezed gently, and he forced himself to focus on the present moment.

His phone buzzed. A text from Jennifer: *Kids want to know if they can see Grandma this weekend.*

Jack: *Probably. I'll check with the facility tomorrow and let you know.*

Jennifer: *Thanks. Also, Michael asked if he could invite Kaylee to his birthday dinner next month. Thoughts?*

Jack smiled despite the stress. His son growing up, navigating first crushes, asking permission to include a girl at family events. Normal, healthy, utterly removed from fraud and FBI investigations.

Jack: *If he's ready to introduce her to the family, I'm fine with it. Your call since you're hosting.*

Jennifer: *We're good with it. Fair warning - Emma is already planning to interrogate this poor girl.*

Jack: *Of course she is. She takes after you.*

Jennifer: *Damn right she does. Night, Jack. Be safe.*

The casual signoff - "be safe" - landed differently now. Jennifer knew about the work situation, knew there were risks. Her reminder wasn't casual. It was a wife who still cared about her ex-husband's wellbeing asking him to be careful.

Jack pocketed his phone and pulled Ruby closer.

"You okay?" she asked quietly.

"Thinking about what we're risking. All the normal things that could get destroyed if this goes wrong."

"Like what?"

"Michael's birthday dinner with his first girlfriend. Emma interrogating her. Sarah's college applications. Helen's recovery. Sunday dinners and custody weekends and all the small ordinary moments that make life worth living."

Ruby was quiet for a moment. "You could walk away. Right now. Stop investigating, cooperate with the audit, let the FBI handle it from their end without your active involvement."

"Could you? If you were in my position?"

"No," Ruby admitted. "I couldn't. Which is how I know you won't either."

They sat in silence, the movie playing unwatched, both of them understanding that some choices weren't really choices. They were revelations of character, tests that showed who you actually were when the cost became real.

Jack's phone buzzed again. This time, an unknown number. He answered cautiously.

"Mr. Mercer?" The voice was male, professional, unfamiliar. "This is Martin Cartwright from Cartwright & Associates. I'm leading the audit team that will be reviewing your department tomorrow."

"Mr. Cartwright. I wasn't expecting to hear from you tonight."

"I wanted to introduce myself personally and assure you that our review will be thorough but fair. We're not here to find fault, just to verify compliance with company policies and regulatory requirements."

"I appreciate that."

"I also wanted to give you a heads up - we'll be conducting individual interviews with all compliance department staff. Yours is scheduled for Thursday afternoon. Two PM, if that works for your schedule."

"That's fine."

"Excellent. And Mr. Mercer, I should mention that we've been informed you recently retained legal counsel. That's absolutely your right, but I want to assure you that our audit is independent of any internal company politics. We answer to the audit committee, not to management."

Jack heard what wasn't being said: Cartwright knew about the legal representation, which meant someone at the company had briefed him. The question was whether Cartwright was genuinely independent or already compromised.

"I appreciate your transparency, Mr. Cartwright. I look forward to meeting you tomorrow."

After hanging up, Jack looked at Ruby. "The lead auditor just called. Very reassuring, very professional. Too reassuring."

"You think he's been told to find something on you?"

"I think he's been told there are concerns about my data handling practices and to pay special attention to whether I've been accessing information outside my scope."

Ruby stood, paced to the window. "So they prime the auditor to look for evidence you've been doing something inappropriate, you get flagged for the very investigation that uncovered their fraud, and suddenly the real criminals are victims of an overzealous employee violating company policy."

"That's my read."

"We need to tell Agent Reeves. This changes the timeline."

"Agreed. I'll call her tomorrow morning from the burner."

Ruby turned from the window. "Jack, if this audit goes bad - if they manufacture cause to fire you - you know they'll try to discredit everything you've found. Make it look like a disgruntled employee making false accusations."

"I know."

"So we need insurance. Something they can't spin, can't discredit, can't make disappear."

Jack understood what she was suggesting. "You want to go public. Leak the information to media."

"Not yet. But we should prepare the option. Get all our evidence compiled in a format that could be sent to investigative journalists if we need to. Give it to someone we trust with instructions to release it if certain conditions are met."

"Like what conditions?"

"Like you getting fired without cause. Like evidence being destroyed. Like the FBI's investigation stalling." Ruby came back to the couch, sat facing him. "I'm not saying we do this lightly. Media exposure has its own risks. But having the option, having it ready, gives us leverage."

Jack thought about his children seeing news stories about their father. About Helen reading newspaper articles questioning his motives. About his professional reputation being debated in public forums.

But he also thought about twelve million dollars in fraud going unpunished. About criminals winning because good people were too afraid of personal cost to fight back.

"Okay," he said. "We prepare the option. But we only use it as a last resort."

"Agreed."

They spent the next two hours compiling a comprehensive evidence package - documents, financial analyses, timeline summaries, corporate structure diagrams. Everything organized for maximum clarity, designed to be understood by journalists without specialized financial knowledge.

Ruby knew someone at the regional investigative journalism nonprofit, a reporter who'd broken several corporate fraud stories. She drafted an email explaining the situation, attached the evidence package, and saved it as a draft.

"If something happens to either of us," Ruby said, "this email gets sent automatically through a delayed delivery service I set up. Forty-eight hours after we miss a check-in, it releases."

Jack looked at the draft email, at the evidence they'd assembled, at the insurance policy they'd just created against their own destruction.

"When did we become the kind of people who need dead man switches?"

"The moment we decided integrity mattered more than safety." Ruby closed the laptop. "Come on. It's late. We both need sleep before tomorrow."

They went to bed but sleep came reluctantly. Jack lay in the dark, listening to Ruby's breathing even out, his own mind refusing to quiet. Tomorrow the audit began. Thursday he'd be interviewed. Somewhere in between, the company would make its move - subtle or aggressive, legal or manufactured.

He thought about his father, facing similar choices with less preparation and fewer allies. He thought about Vietnam, about ambushes you saw coming but couldn't avoid. He thought about Michael's birthday dinner and Emma's dragon books and Sarah's college applications and all the normal future moments that depended on him surviving the next few days intact.

The shrapnel in his ribs ached steadily, a metronome of old pain marking time toward new confrontation.

Some battles you chose. Some chose you. All of them revealed whether you were the person you claimed to be.

Jack had survived firefights and divorce and the slow reconstruction of a life worth living. He'd learned that courage wasn't the absence of fear but the decision to act despite it.

Tomorrow, he'd walk into that office knowing he was being watched, monitored, assessed for weakness. He'd sit through the audit knowing the auditors had been primed to find fault. He'd smile professionally and cooperate fully while documentation and digital surveillance captured everything for later use against him.

And he'd do it anyway.

Because some things mattered more than safety. Some principles were worth defending even when defense was costly. Some fights you couldn't walk away from without losing the only thing that made survival worthwhile.

Ruby shifted in her sleep, moved closer, her warmth grounding him in the present moment. Tomorrow's battles would come. Tonight, he had this: a woman who understood him, trusted him, and chose to stand beside him anyway.

That was worth fighting for.

Everything else was just details.

Jack closed his eyes and slept finally, his dreams a jumble of conference rooms and jungle rivers, audit reports and gunfire, the past and present bleeding together in the way trauma always connected across time.

But when morning came, he'd be ready.

He was always ready.

That was the gift Vietnam had given him - the ability to walk into danger with clear eyes and steady hands.

Tomorrow, he'd need it.

Chapter 9: Recorded

Wednesday morning arrived cold and gray, the kind of weather that matched Jack's mood perfectly. He woke at five-thirty, went through his routine with military precision, and arrived at the office by seven. The audit team was already there.

Cartwright & Associates had set up in a large conference room on the fourth floor, converting it into a temporary command center. Three auditors - two men and a woman, all in their thirties, all wearing the professional uniform of corporate investigators - were arranging laptops, organizing files, and preparing for what Jack assumed would be a methodical dissection of his department's operations.

Martin Cartwright himself was older, mid-fifties, with silver hair and the calm demeanor of someone who'd conducted hundreds of these reviews. He spotted Jack in the hallway and approached with an extended hand.

"Mr. Mercer. Good to meet you in person."

"Likewise." Jack shook his hand, noting the firm grip and direct eye contact. Professional. Assessing.

"We'll be starting with a general overview this morning - department structure, key processes, documentation workflows. Individual interviews begin tomorrow. Your cooperation is appreciated."

"Of course."

Jack went to his desk, logged into his computer - hyper-aware now that every keystroke was being recorded - and began his day with exaggerated normalcy. He reviewed routine reports, responded to standard emails, and avoided accessing anything that could be construed as outside his scope.

At eight-thirty, Frank Delaney sent a department-wide email summoning everyone to the conference room for the audit kickoff meeting. Jack joined his colleagues, noting who seemed nervous, who seemed unconcerned, who was avoiding eye contact.

Monica Chen sat three seats away, her expression professionally neutral. She caught Jack's eye briefly, nodded almost imperceptibly, then looked away.

Cartwright led the meeting with practiced efficiency, explaining the audit scope, timeline, and expectations. Everything by the book. Everything designed to seem routine and non-threatening.

"We'll need access to all departmental files, email archives, and relevant database systems," Cartwright explained. "We'll also be conducting confidential interviews with each team member. These conversations are your opportunity to share any concerns, identify any irregularities you've observed, and help us ensure your department is operating with full compliance."

Jack heard the subtext: they were inviting people to inform on each other, to share suspicions, to point fingers. Standard audit practice, but also an effective way to identify who might be problematic.

After the meeting, Jack returned to his desk and found an email waiting from Katherine Mendoza, his attorney. The representation letter had been sent to the company's legal department and HR at eight AM. By nine-fifteen, he had a response.

The email was from David Brennan, the company lawyer who'd sat in on the HR meeting. It was professionally cordial and subtly threatening in equal measure:

Mr. Mercer, we acknowledge receipt of Ms. Mendoza's letter and respect your decision to retain counsel. Please be assured that the company has no intention of taking any adverse employment action and views the current audit as routine compliance verification. We hope this matter can be resolved cooperatively without escalation. However, we must note that retaining counsel for routine business matters may create unnecessary adversarial dynamics. We encourage direct communication and professional cooperation.

Jack forwarded the email to Mendoza with a single line: *Translation?*

Her response came within minutes: *Translation: "How dare you protect yourself. We're going to make this difficult." Ignore them. All communication through me.*

By mid-morning, the audit team had settled into their work. Jack watched them moving through the department, requesting files, conducting preliminary interviews, taking notes. Everything systematic. Everything documented.

At eleven, his desk phone rang. An internal extension he didn't recognize.

"Jack Mercer."

"Mr. Mercer, this is Derek Vaughn. Do you have a few minutes? I'd like to discuss the audit process."

Jack's pulse quickened. Vaughn rarely contacted him directly. "Of course. Your office?"

"Actually, let's grab coffee. The café downstairs. Say fifteen minutes?"

"I'll be there."

Jack hung up, immediately suspicious. Vaughn wanting to meet off-site, in a public space, away from the audit team's immediate presence. This was either a peace offering or a trap.

He texted Ruby from his personal phone: *Vaughn wants to meet. Coffee shop downstairs. 11:15.*

Ruby: *Don't go alone. Take someone as witness.*

Jack: *Who? Everyone here either works for Vaughn or is scared of him.*

Ruby: *Then record it. Phone in pocket, audio on.*

Jack considered. One-party consent state. Legal to record conversations you were part of. But also potentially inflammatory if discovered.

Jack: *Risky.*

Ruby: *So is meeting him alone. Your call.*

Jack made the decision quickly. He activated his phone's voice recorder, slipped it into his shirt pocket, and headed downstairs.

The café was moderately busy - enough people for privacy through ambient noise, not so crowded that conversation would be overheard. Vaughn was already there, sitting at a corner table with two coffees waiting.

"Jack. Thanks for making time." Vaughn gestured to the seat across from him. "I got you a regular coffee. Hope that's all right."

"Perfect. Thanks." Jack sat, wrapped his hands around the cup, and waited.

Vaughn studied him for a moment with the calculating gaze of someone accustomed to reading people and manipulating situations. "You've been with the company three years now. Solid performer, good reviews, respected by your colleagues. Frank speaks highly of your work."

"I appreciate that."

"Which is why I wanted to talk to you directly, colleague to colleague, about this audit situation." Vaughn leaned forward slightly. "I know it can feel invasive, having external auditors scrutinizing your work. But it's necessary. We operate in a heavily regulated industry. These reviews protect us - protect you - from liability."

"I understand."

"Good. Because I've heard some concerning things. Rumors that you might view this audit as adversarial. That you've retained legal counsel, which suggests you think the company is acting against your interests." Vaughn's tone remained friendly, but his eyes were cold. "I want to assure you, Jack, that's not the case. This is routine. Standard procedure. Nothing personal."

Jack kept his expression neutral. "I appreciate the clarification. Though I'd note that retaining counsel is also standard procedure when navigating complex employment matters. Nothing personal."

Vaughn's smile tightened fractionally. "Of course. Though it does create certain... perceptions. Makes people wonder what you're worried about. What you might be hiding."

"I'm not hiding anything."

"I'm glad to hear that. Because transparency is essential in our line of work. Any irregularities, any concerns about compliance or documentation - those need to be addressed openly, through proper channels." Vaughn paused. "Not through back-channel investigations or unauthorized data access."

There it was. The accusation wrapped in concern. Jack had been accessing data inappropriately, conducting investigations outside his authority, and now the audit would expose his misconduct.

"Everything I've accessed has been within my authorization level and relevant to my job responsibilities," Jack said evenly.

"I'm sure that's your belief. But sometimes enthusiasm can lead to overreach. You're a conscientious employee, Jack. Sometimes conscientious people look for problems that don't exist, see patterns where there's just random noise." Vaughn's tone turned almost paternal. "I'd hate to see you damage your career over misunderstandings."

Jack felt anger building but kept it contained. "What exactly are you suggesting, Derek?"

"I'm suggesting that if you've discovered anything during your routine work that concerns you, the appropriate response is to bring it to management - to me, to Frank - through official channels. Not to conduct independent investigations. Not to involve external parties." Vaughn set down his coffee cup with deliberate precision. "And I'm suggesting that the best outcome for everyone would be for this audit to proceed smoothly, with full cooperation, without any... complications."

"What kind of complications?"

"The kind that come from employees making unfounded accusations. Seeing conspiracies where there's just normal business complexity. Involving lawyers and federal agencies over misunderstandings that could be resolved internally." Vaughn's expression hardened. "That kind of complexity tends to damage careers, Jack. Even when people have good intentions."

Jack understood perfectly. This was a threat dressed as friendly advice. Cooperate, stay quiet, let the audit whitewash whatever they wanted whitewashed, or face professional destruction.

"I appreciate your concern," Jack said carefully. "But I'm confident the audit will find that my work has been professional, thorough, and entirely appropriate."

"I hope you're right." Vaughn stood, signaling the conversation was over. "Just remember - loyalty matters in this company. Team players get rewarded. Troublemakers, even well-intentioned ones, tend to find themselves looking for new opportunities."

He walked away before Jack could respond, leaving Jack alone with his coffee and his racing thoughts.

Jack waited five minutes, then pulled out his phone and stopped the recording. Nearly eight minutes of Vaughn making veiled threats, suggesting Jack had engaged in misconduct, and essentially demanding silence in exchange for career safety.

He texted Ruby: *Got it. All of it.*

Ruby: *Send me the file. Now.*

Jack uploaded the recording to a secure cloud storage, sent Ruby the link, then forwarded it to Katherine Mendoza with a brief explanation. Within ten minutes, both women had responded.

Ruby: *This is retaliation. Clear as day. He's threatening your job for investigating.*

Mendoza: *Perfect. Save this recording in multiple locations. This is exactly what we need if they terminate you - proof that adverse action was tied directly to your investigative work. How did he know about FBI involvement?*

Jack thought about that. He and Ruby had been careful. The only people who knew were Agent Reeves and whoever she'd briefed at the Bureau. Unless...

His stomach dropped. The keystroke logging. If they'd been monitoring his computer activity for longer than Paul had realized, they might have seen his initial research into reporting channels. Or his email communications before he'd gotten more cautious.

Or there was a leak at the FBI.

Jack texted Mendoza: *Need to talk. Concerned about information security.*

Mendoza: *My office, 6 PM. Come alone, watch for surveillance.*

The rest of the day passed in mounting tension. Jack worked with robotic precision, hyperaware that everything he did was being logged, analyzed, prepared for use against him. The audit team moved through the department like professional ghosts, polite and thorough and revealing nothing.

At three PM, Monica Chen stopped by his desk with a routine question about documentation formats. As Jack pulled up the relevant files, she spoke quietly without looking at him directly.

"They're going to interview me tomorrow morning. First one up, nine AM."

"Okay."

"They're going to ask about you. About whether I've observed any unusual behavior, inappropriate data access, unauthorized investigations."

Jack's hands stilled on the keyboard. "What are you going to tell them?"

"The truth. That you're thorough, professional, and the best analyst in the department." Monica's voice dropped even lower. "But Jack, you should know - Vaughn met with Cartwright privately this morning. Before the kickoff meeting. I saw them in Vaughn's office, door closed, very serious conversation."

"Did you hear anything?"

"No. But Cartwright came out looking like someone who'd just received very specific instructions about what to find."

Jack nodded slowly, understanding. The audit wasn't independent. It had been compromised before it even started.

"Thanks for the heads up."

Monica left without acknowledging his gratitude, her warning delivered and her own exposure minimized.

Jack finished his day at exactly five o'clock, gathered his things, and left the building. He took an indirect route to Mendoza's office, watching for tails, seeing nothing obvious but trusting his instincts enough to remain cautious.

Mendoza's receptionist had already left for the day. She met him at the door herself, ushered him into her office, and closed the blinds before speaking.

"Tell me everything about the Vaughn conversation. Don't leave anything out."

Jack recounted the meeting, playing the recording for her, explaining the context and the implied threats. Mendoza listened with the focused intensity of a lawyer building a case.

"This is good for us," she said when he finished. "Textbook retaliation. He's directly threatening adverse employment action based on your investigative activity. If they fire you now, we have clear causation."

"He knew about the FBI," Jack said. "How?"

"Several possibilities. Could be they've been monitoring your communications longer than you realized. Could be someone at the Bureau leaked. Could be they have sources in law enforcement who tipped them off about the preliminary inquiry." Mendoza paused. "Or it could be simpler - they're assuming anyone who found what you found would report it to authorities. They're preparing for that scenario whether it's happened yet or not."

"What do I do?"

"You go to work tomorrow. You cooperate fully with the audit. You answer questions honestly but carefully - stick to facts, don't speculate, don't elaborate beyond what's asked. And you document everything." Mendoza pulled out a legal pad. "I'm preparing a whistleblower retaliation lawsuit. We'll file it the moment they take adverse action - if they fire you, demote you, or even significantly change your job responsibilities. But we need more documentation first."

"How much more?"

"Ideally, evidence that the audit is a pretext. That they're using it to manufacture cause for termination. That their real motivation is silencing your investigation." Mendoza looked at him directly. "Can you get me that evidence?"

Jack thought about Monica's warning, about Vaughn's private meeting with Cartwright, about the entire orchestrated performance of institutional corruption.

"I can try."

"Be careful. Don't do anything that could be construed as interfering with the audit or accessing information you're not authorized to see. We need clean evidence, not more ammunition for them to use against you."

Jack left Mendoza's office as darkness settled over the city. The temperature had dropped, winter announcing itself in the sharp edge of the wind. He drove to Ruby's apartment, checking his mirrors compulsively, taking random turns to verify he wasn't being followed.

Ruby answered the door before he could knock, pulled him inside, and wrapped her arms around him without speaking. They stood in her entryway for a long moment, Jack feeling the accumulated tension of the day beginning to crack.

"Rough day?" Ruby asked finally.

"Vaughn threatened me. The audit's compromised. Monica warned me they're coordinating against me. And somewhere there's either a leak or they've been monitoring me longer than we thought."

Ruby guided him to the couch, poured wine, and settled beside him. "Tell me everything."

Jack went through the day chronologically - the audit kickoff, Vaughn's threatening coffee meeting, Monica's warning, Mendoza's assessment. By the time he finished, Ruby was making notes on her ever-present legal pad.

"We need to assume they know about the FBI," she said. "Which means we need to accelerate our timeline."

"How?"

"I'm calling Sarah Reeves tonight. Telling her the company is conducting a compromised audit designed to discredit you and potentially destroy evidence. That changes the calculus for the Bureau - if they think evidence is being destroyed, they can move faster."

"Can they? I thought federal investigations took months."

"Usually. But if there's an imminent threat to evidence preservation, they can expedite. Get emergency warrants, freeze records, even conduct surprise raids if justified." Ruby set down her notepad. "We're past the point of patient investigation. They're coming for you, Jack. We need the FBI to move before they succeed."

Jack felt the situation spiraling beyond his control. Events accelerating, forces mobilizing, the carefully structured life he'd built becoming collateral damage in a fight he hadn't chosen but couldn't avoid.

"What about my kids? Helen? If this explodes publicly..."

"Jennifer knows the basics. She's being careful with the kids. Helen is in a secure facility with restricted visitor access." Ruby took his hand. "Your family is as protected as we can make them right now. The question is whether you're ready for what comes next."

"Which is what?"

"War. Not metaphorical corporate politics. Actual legal, professional, potentially criminal war. They're going to try to destroy you. We're going to try to destroy them. And somewhere in the middle, the truth either survives or gets buried." Ruby's grip tightened. "You can still walk away. Right now. Tell the FBI you're withdrawing cooperation, tell Mendoza to stand down, cooperate with the audit and hope they're satisfied with silence."

Jack thought about his father, who'd tried to fight and lost everything. He thought about the three sailors who'd died when the

RPG hit their boat in the Mekong Delta. He thought about Michael's history project and the lesson Jack had tried to teach about standing up for what mattered.

"I can't walk away."

"I know. I just needed to hear you say it." Ruby leaned against him. "Okay. Then here's what happens next. I call Reeves tonight, explain the situation, push for expedited action. You go to work tomorrow, survive your interview, document everything. Mendoza prepares the retaliation lawsuit. And we wait to see who moves first - them or the FBI."

"And if they move first?"

"Then we fight. In court, in the media, in every available forum. We make this public, messy, and expensive for them. We make sure even if they destroy you professionally, they don't get to do it quietly."

Jack understood what she was offering - a scorched earth strategy that would hurt him almost as much as it hurt them, but would ensure the fraud got exposed regardless of his personal fate.

"Okay," he said. "Make the call."

Ruby pulled out the burner phone, stepped into her bedroom for privacy, and spent twenty minutes talking to Agent Reeves. Jack sat on the couch, drinking wine, thinking about the chain of decisions that had brought him to this moment.

He could have ignored the irregularities. Could have let the audit request scare him into silence. Could have signed the HR acknowledgment and accepted the implicit warning.

But then he'd be someone else. Someone who looked away from corruption because confronting it was costly. Someone who chose safety over principle.

His father had tried to fight and made mistakes. Jack was trying to fight smarter - with allies, with lawyers, with federal authorities. But the fundamental equation remained the same: some things mattered more than security.

Ruby emerged from the bedroom, her expression grim.

"Reeves is briefing her supervisor tonight. They're considering emergency measures - warrant applications, evidence preservation orders, possibly freezing the audit until they can secure company records." She sat down heavily. "But Jack, she was very clear about something. The moment the FBI shows up with warrants, everyone will know you're the source. Your cover is gone. Retaliation becomes inevitable."

"How soon?"

"If they move, probably Friday or early next week. Which means you have maybe forty-eight hours before everything goes public."

Jack thought about his interview scheduled for tomorrow afternoon. About the keystroke logs documenting his every digital move. About Vaughn's threats and Cartwright's compromised independence and the careful machinery of institutional corruption grinding toward his destruction.

Forty-eight hours.

Two days to maintain the fiction that everything was normal while forces mobilized on all sides.

Two days before his life changed irrevocably.

"Okay," Jack said quietly. "Then let's make sure these forty-eight hours count."

They spent the rest of the evening preparing - reviewing evidence, coordinating with Mendoza, backing up files to multiple secure locations. Ruby called her journalist contact, gave them a heads up that a major corporate fraud story might be breaking soon.

Jack called Jennifer, explained that things were accelerating, asked her to keep the kids close for the next few days.

"How bad is this going to get?" Jennifer asked.

"I don't know. But I need you to be ready for my name to be in the news. For reporters to possibly contact you. For the kids to hear things at school."

Jennifer was quiet for a moment. "What do you want me to tell them?"

"The truth. That I found something wrong at work, reported it to authorities, and now I'm dealing with the consequences of doing the right thing."

"They'll understand that. They're your kids, Jack. They know who you are."

After hanging up, Jack sat in the dark apartment, Ruby moving around in the kitchen making tea, the city lights glowing through the windows. Somewhere out there, Derek Vaughn was sleeping soundly, confident in his criminal enterprise. Somewhere, the audit team was preparing their questions for tomorrow's interviews. Somewhere, Agent Reeves was building her case for emergency FBI intervention.

And here, in Ruby's apartment, Jack was choosing to stand his ground despite knowing exactly what it would cost.

The shrapnel in his ribs ached with particular insistence tonight. Old wounds recognizing new battles. Old lessons about survival and sacrifice and the price of principles.

His phone buzzed. A text from Michael: *Dad, is everything okay? Mom seems worried.*

Jack typed back: *Everything's fine. Just some work stress. See you this weekend.*

Michael: *Okay. Love you.*

Jack: *Love you too, buddy.*

He set down the phone, feeling the weight of that exchange. His son, worried but trusting. His daughter's upcoming birthday. Emma's dragon books and Sarah's college applications and all the normal future moments that depended on him surviving the next forty-eight hours with his integrity and his family intact.

Ruby brought him tea, sat beside him in the dark.

"Whatever happens," she said quietly, "you made the right choice."

"Even if it destroys everything?"

"Especially then. Because that's when the choice actually matters."

They sat together in silence, drinking tea, watching the city exist in blissful ignorance of the small war about to erupt within its corporate towers.

Tomorrow, Jack would walk into that office knowing he was being set up for destruction.

Tomorrow, he'd sit for his interview knowing every word would be analyzed for evidence of misconduct.

Tomorrow, forces beyond his control would move toward collision.

But tonight, he had this: a quiet apartment, a woman who understood him, and the clear knowledge that he'd chosen principle over safety.

Some fights you lost. Some you won. All of them revealed who you actually were when everything else was stripped away.

Jack had learned that lesson in blood and fire on the Mekong Delta.

He was about to learn it again in conference rooms and legal briefs and the cold machinery of institutional combat.

But the fundamental truth remained unchanged: you fought for what mattered, or you surrendered your soul.

Jack wasn't ready to surrender.

Not yet.

Not ever.

Chapter 10: Terminated

Thursday morning felt like walking into an ambush you could see coming but couldn't avoid. Jack dressed with particular care - the armor of a pressed shirt and tie, the uniform of professional competence. He arrived at the office early again, the building already humming with the strange energy of an organization under examination.

The audit team had been busy overnight. Their conference room command center now included whiteboards covered in flowcharts and timelines, file boxes stacked against the walls, and the unmistakable atmosphere of investigators who'd found something interesting.

Jack settled at his desk, logged in carefully, and opened his email. The first message stopped him cold.

From: Martin Cartwright

Subject: Interview Schedule Update

Time: 7:23 AM

Mr. Mercer - Due to new information requiring follow-up, your interview has been moved to 10:00 AM this morning instead of 2:00 PM. Please report to Conference Room 4B at that time. Bring any personal documentation of your work activities for the past 18 months, including calendars, notes, or correspondence you maintain outside official company systems.

Jack read it twice, his mind racing. They'd moved his interview up by four hours. They wanted documentation he maintained personally - which was code for evidence he'd been conducting investigations outside official channels.

This wasn't a routine interview anymore. This was an interrogation.

He forwarded the email to Katherine Mendoza with a single word: *Accelerated.*

Her response came within three minutes: *Don't bring ANY personal documentation without talking to me first. Call me. Now.*

Jack grabbed his coffee, walked outside to the parking lot, and called from his personal phone.

"They moved your interview up," Mendoza said without preamble. "That means they found something they think is damaging and want to confront you with it before you can prepare."

"What do I do?"

"First, do NOT bring any personal documentation. They have no right to it, and handing it over gives them ammunition. Second, answer their questions truthfully but narrowly - don't volunteer information, don't speculate, don't explain more than what's asked. Third, if they ask anything about FBI contact, external communications, or legal counsel, you invoke your right to have your attorney present."

"That'll make me look guilty."

"That'll make you look smart. Jack, this is a setup. They're going to ask questions designed to make you admit to accessing data inappropriately or conducting unauthorized investigations. Every answer you give will be twisted and used against you." Mendoza paused. "Are you ready for this?"

Jack thought about Vietnam, about walking point through hostile territory knowing ambushes could come from any direction. "Yeah. I'm ready."

"Call me the moment you finish. Don't discuss the interview with anyone else."

Jack returned to his desk, the three hours before his interview stretching like a tightrope. He worked mechanically, responded to emails with careful blandness, and watched the audit team moving through the department like sharks circling prey.

At nine-fifteen, Monica Chen emerged from Conference Room 4B, her face pale and expression tight. She walked past Jack's desk without making eye contact, went directly to the bathroom, and didn't return for twenty minutes.

When she did, Jack caught her attention with a subtle gesture. She shook her head fractionally - a warning. Whatever had happened in her interview, it wasn't good.

At nine forty-five, Jack's desk phone rang. Frank Delaney.

"Jack, can you stop by before your interview? Just want to touch base."

Jack recognized a warning when he heard one. "On my way."

Frank's office felt like a confessional - glass walls offering the illusion of transparency while conducting conversations everyone knew were private. Frank closed the door, which he rarely did, and gestured for Jack to sit.

"How are you holding up?" Frank asked.

"Fine. Just ready to get the interview over with."

Frank was quiet for a moment, clearly weighing his words. "Jack, I've been with this company twelve years. I've seen a lot of audits. This one is different."

"How so?"

"They're not auditing the department. They're auditing you specifically. Every question they're asking, every file they're reviewing - it all comes back to your work, your access patterns, your analytical methodology." Frank leaned forward. "Someone has convinced them you've been conducting an unauthorized investigation. That you've been accessing data outside your scope, looking for problems that don't exist."

"That's not true."

"Maybe. But perception matters, Jack. And right now, the perception is that you've been overstepping your authority." Frank's expression was pained. "I'm telling you this as a friend - be very careful in that interview. They're not looking for information. They're looking for confirmation of conclusions they've already reached."

"What conclusions?"

"That you're a well-intentioned but overzealous employee who's been seeing patterns that aren't there, conducting investigations you weren't authorized to conduct, and potentially compromising data security in the process." Frank paused. "They're building a case for termination, Jack. For cause. And the interview is their last chance to get you to confirm their narrative."

Jack felt cold settle in his stomach. "Who told you this?"

"No one directly. But I've been in enough meetings where your name comes up, enough conversations that stop when I enter the room. I can read the writing on the wall." Frank met his eyes. "I'm sorry, Jack. I wish I could do more. But I have a family, a mortgage, and twenty-three people in this department who depend on me keeping my job. I can't go to war with Vaughn over this."

"I'm not asking you to."

"I know. But I'm also not going to lie for them. If anyone asks me about your work, I'm going to tell the truth - that you're thorough, professional, and one of the best analysts I've supervised." Frank's jaw tightened. "For what it's worth, I think they're wrong. I think you did find something real, and now they're trying to discredit you before it comes out. But I can't prove that, and I can't protect you."

Jack stood. "I appreciate the honesty, Frank. Really."

"One more thing." Frank pulled a business card from his desk drawer. "Friend of mine, works in compliance at a competing firm. If this goes bad and you need a reference for a new position, call him. Tell him I sent you. He owes me a favor."

Jack took the card, understanding what Frank was offering - a lifeline for after the inevitable happened. "Thanks."

At nine fifty-five, Jack walked to Conference Room 4B. His hands were steady, his mind clear. He'd been in worse situations. He'd survived actual combat. This was just corporate warfare, and he knew how to navigate hostile territory.

The conference room had been arranged deliberately - Martin Cartwright sat at the head of the table, flanked by his two associates. David Brennan, the company's lawyer, sat off to one side. A recording device sat conspicuously in the center of the table.

"Mr. Mercer, thank you for coming." Cartwright gestured to the chair directly across from him. "This is a formal interview as part of our compliance audit. Everything said here will be recorded and may be used in our final report and any subsequent proceedings. Do you understand?"

"I understand."

"Do you have legal counsel present or on standby?"

"I'm represented by Katherine Mendoza. She's aware of this interview."

Cartwright made a note. "Very well. Let's begin. For the record, this is a recorded interview with Jack Mercer, conducted on Thursday, November 16th, at approximately ten AM." He looked up.

"Mr. Mercer, how long have you been employed in the Risk Compliance department?"

"Three years. Since November 2023."

"And during that time, what have your primary responsibilities included?"

Jack walked through his job description, keeping his answers factual and concise. For the first fifteen minutes, the questions were standard - background, training, typical workflow, documentation procedures.

Then Cartwright shifted gears.

"Mr. Mercer, in the past six months, we've identified several instances of you accessing database systems beyond what would be typical for your assigned compliance reviews. Can you explain why?"

"Risk compliance requires comprehensive analysis. Understanding patterns across routes, time periods, and documentation types is part of identifying potential issues."

"But your assigned reviews don't typically cover all international shipping routes simultaneously, correct?"

"Individual reviews don't. But maintaining overall risk awareness does require broader visibility."

Cartwright pulled out a printed report. "On September 23rd, you ran database queries covering eighteen months of shipping records for Los Angeles to Shanghai, Miami to Rotterdam, and

Houston to Singapore routes. Approximately 4,800 individual transactions. Why?"

Jack kept his voice level. "I was conducting trend analysis to identify patterns that might indicate systemic compliance issues."

"Were you asked to conduct this analysis?"

"It falls within my general responsibilities to identify risk."

"But were you specifically asked to analyze those particular routes?" Cartwright's tone sharpened.

"No."

"So you initiated this analysis on your own authority?"

"Yes, as part of my job responsibilities."

One of Cartwright's associates, a woman named Sarah Mitchell, leaned forward. "Mr. Mercer, did you find any compliance issues in those 4,800 transactions?"

Jack knew the trap. If he said no, they'd argue he'd wasted company resources on baseless investigation. If he said yes, they'd ask why he hadn't reported through proper channels.

"I found irregularities that warranted further examination," Jack said carefully.

"What kind of irregularities?"

"Documentation gaps, routing inconsistencies, payment authorizations that didn't follow standard patterns."

"And what did you do with these findings?"

"I conducted additional analysis to determine whether the irregularities represented genuine compliance issues or were explainable through legitimate business complexity."

"Did you report these irregularities to your supervisor?" Cartwright asked.

"Not formally. I was still conducting preliminary analysis."

"So you found what you considered to be potential compliance issues and didn't report them through proper channels?"

"I was building sufficient evidence before making formal allegations."

Brennan, the company lawyer, spoke for the first time. "Mr. Mercer, company policy requires that all suspected compliance violations be reported immediately to your direct supervisor. Were you aware of this policy?"

"Yes."

"So you knowingly violated company policy by conducting an extended investigation without reporting your findings?"

Jack saw the box they were building. Report immediately, and get accused of making baseless allegations. Don't report, and get accused of policy violations. Either way, he was wrong.

"I was following my professional judgment about when findings were sufficiently developed to warrant formal reporting," Jack said.

Cartwright made notes. "Let's talk about data access. Did you export any company data to personal devices or external storage?"

"I occasionally save work-related documents to personal drives for backup purposes. Many employees do this."

"Did you save data related to your unauthorized investigation to personal devices?"

"It wasn't an unauthorized investigation. And yes, I maintained working files on a personal thumb drive."

"Where is that thumb drive now?"

Jack hesitated. The thumb drive was in his home safe, containing comprehensive evidence of the fraud. Admitting its existence gave them grounds to demand it. Denying it could be proven false if they'd already found evidence of the exports.

"In my home," he said finally.

"We'll need you to turn that over," Brennan said. "It contains company data and may be relevant to this audit."

"I'll need to consult with my attorney about that."

Cartwright's expression hardened. "Mr. Mercer, refusing to provide materials relevant to an official audit could be grounds for immediate termination."

"I'm not refusing. I'm requesting time to ensure I understand my legal obligations regarding personal property and company data."

The interview continued for another hour, each question carefully designed to extract admissions of policy violations, unauthorized access, or failure to follow proper reporting procedures. Jack answered carefully, trying to navigate between honesty and self-incrimination, but he could feel the walls closing in.

Finally, at eleven-thirty, Cartwright set down his pen.

"I think we have what we need for now. Mr. Mercer, you should know that our preliminary findings suggest serious policy violations related to data access, unauthorized investigations, and failure to follow proper reporting procedures. We'll be providing a full report to company leadership by end of business tomorrow."

"I'd like the opportunity to respond to those findings," Jack said.

"You'll have that opportunity through the formal review process, if necessary." Cartwright stood. "That concludes this interview. Thank you for your cooperation."

Jack walked out of the conference room feeling like he'd just been through a professional evisceration. Every answer he'd given would be used against him. Every hesitation noted. Every carefully worded response twisted into evidence of guilt.

He went directly to his desk, grabbed his jacket, and headed for the parking lot. He was halfway to his car when his phone buzzed with a text from Ruby: *How'd it go?*

Jack: *Bad. They're building a termination case. Can you pick me up? I shouldn't drive right now.*

Ruby: *Where are you?*

Jack: *Office parking lot. Southeast corner.*

Ruby: *Be there in 15 minutes.*

Jack sat on the curb near his car, the cold concrete grounding him while his mind spun through everything that had just happened. Fifteen minutes felt like an hour, but finally Ruby's Subaru pulled up. He climbed in, and she took one look at his face before pulling him into a brief, fierce hug.

"Tell me on the way," she said, pulling out of the parking lot.

As they drove, Jack recounted the interview - the questions, the traps, the systematic dismantling of his professional integrity. Ruby listened without interrupting, her jaw tightening with each new detail.

"They're going to fire you," she said finally. "Tomorrow, probably. They've built a complete case around policy violations and unauthorized investigations."

"I know. I called Mendoza from the parking lot. She's filing the whistleblower retaliation lawsuit today, before they terminate me."

Ruby's hands tightened on the steering wheel. "Good. Beat them to the punch." She glanced at him. "Where do you need to go? Home? My place?"

"Jennifer's. I need to see my kids. Tell them what's happening before they hear it from someone else."

"Okay." Ruby changed lanes, heading toward Jennifer's neighborhood. "I'll drop you off, or do you want me there?"

"Stay. Please. You're part of this now. They should meet you properly, not just as 'Dad's girlfriend' but as someone who stood with me through all of this."

Ruby reached over and squeezed his hand. "Okay."

They drove to Jennifer's house in comfortable silence, arriving just as the school day was ending. Ruby pulled into the driveway and turned off the engine, but didn't immediately get out.

"You sure you want me to come in?" she asked. "This is a family moment. I don't want to intrude."

"You're not intruding. You're part of this." Jack squeezed her hand. "Besides, Jennifer knows about you. It's time you two actually met."

They walked to the door together. Jennifer answered Jack's knock, took one look at his face, and her expression shifted from curiosity to concern. Then her eyes moved to Ruby, and Jack saw the quick assessment that passed between the two women - measuring, evaluating, understanding.

""Jennifer, this is Ruby Martinez," Jack said. "Ruby, my ex-wife Jennifer Morrison.".

Ruby extended her hand. "It's good to finally meet you. I've heard a lot about you."

Jennifer shook it, her grip firm. "Likewise. Jack's mentioned you. Thank you for being there for him through... whatever this is." She stepped back, opening the door wider. "Please, both of you, come in."

They entered, and Jennifer gestured toward the kitchen. "The kids will be home in about fifteen minutes. David's picking them up from school." She looked at Jack, her concern deepening. "What happened?"

"They're going to fire me. Tomorrow, probably. My lawyer is filing a whistleblower lawsuit this afternoon to establish the retaliation timeline." Jack sat heavily at the kitchen table. Ruby remained standing near the doorway, giving them space. "It's going to be public. Ugly. The kids will hear about it."

Jennifer sat across from him, then glanced at Ruby. "Please, sit. You're part of this conversation."

Ruby moved to the table, sat beside Jack. Jennifer's eyes tracked the movement - how naturally Ruby positioned herself, how Jack's posture relaxed slightly with her presence.

"Then we tell them first," Jennifer said, refocusing on Jack. "Together. Before they hear it from someone else."

"Tell them what? That their father found something illegal at work and is being destroyed for reporting it?"

"We tell them the truth, in age-appropriate terms." Jennifer reached across the table, squeezed his hand briefly - an old gesture from their marriage, comfort without intimacy. "Jack, you're doing the right thing. They're old enough to understand that doing right sometimes has costs."

She glanced at Ruby again. "And I'm glad he's not doing this alone."

Ruby nodded, a moment of understanding passing between the two women. Whatever evaluation had happened in those first seconds at the door, Jennifer had made her decision.

The front door opened. David and the three kids came in, noisy and normal and completely unaware that their lives were about to change. They saw Jack and brightened - it wasn't his custody day, so his presence was a surprise. Then they noticed Ruby.

"Dad! What are you doing here?" Emma ran to hug him, then looked curiously at Ruby. "Who's that?"

"This is Ruby Martinez. She's... someone very important to me. Can we talk for a few minutes? All together?"

Something in his tone made them sober. Sarah's eyes narrowed with teenage perception. Michael's expression went cautious. Even Emma sensed this wasn't a casual visit.

They gathered in the living room - Jack and Jennifer on the couch, David in the armchair, the three kids arranged on the floor like they were young again. Ruby sat in a chair near Jack, close enough to show solidarity but giving the family their space.

"I need to tell you something about what's happening at my work," Jack began. "It's important, and I want you to hear it from me first."

He explained carefully, choosing words appropriate for an eleven-year-old while not patronizing the teenagers. He'd found something wrong at his company - people stealing money, breaking laws. He'd reported it to authorities like you're supposed to. But the people doing the wrong things were powerful, and now they were trying to make it look like Jack was the problem instead of them.

"Are they going to fire you?" Sarah asked bluntly.

"Probably. Tomorrow or the next day."

"That's not fair!" Emma's voice cracked. "You were trying to stop bad people!"

"I know, sweetheart. But sometimes doing the right thing has consequences. Fair or not."

Michael was quiet, processing. Finally, he asked, "Is this like what happened to Grandpa? When you told me about him standing up to the construction fraud?"

Jack felt pride and pain in equal measure. His son understood, connected past to present, saw the pattern.

"Yes. Very much like that."

"Did Grandpa regret it?" Michael asked.

"He regretted some things that came after. But he never regretted standing up to corruption. He told me once that you can't build a life worth living on compromised ground." Jack looked at each of his children. "I'm not going to lie to you. The next few weeks are going to be hard. There might be news stories about this. People at school might ask questions. It's going to be uncomfortable and confusing."

"What do we tell people?" Sarah asked.

"The truth. That your dad found something illegal, reported it, and is dealing with the consequences of doing the right thing." Jack paused. "And that you're proud of him for having the courage to stand up to powerful people doing wrong things."

"We are proud," Sarah said firmly. Michael nodded. Emma climbed onto the couch and buried her face against Jack's shoulder.

They talked for another hour - questions and fears and reassurances. Jennifer and David were solid, united in supporting Jack even as he disrupted their lives too. Ruby stayed mostly quiet, letting the family navigate this moment, but when Emma asked who she was and why she was there, Jack introduced her properly.

"Ruby's been helping me understand the financial parts of what I found. She's a forensic accountant - someone who investigates fraud. But more than that, she's someone who's stood beside me through all of this when it would have been easier to walk away."

Emma studied Ruby with the frank assessment of an eleven-year-old. "Are you Dad's girlfriend?"

"Yes," Ruby said simply.

"Are you going to marry him?"

Ruby smiled. "We haven't gotten that far yet. Right now, I'm just trying to help him through a difficult situation."

"Okay." Emma seemed satisfied with this answer. Sarah and Michael were harder to read, but neither seemed hostile - just cautiously curious about this woman who'd suddenly become part of their father's crisis.

Finally, as evening approached and homework beckoned, Jack stood to leave. He hugged each child tightly, made promises to see them this weekend, and walked out with Ruby.

In Ruby's car, she took his hand. "You did good in there. They understand."

"Emma's eleven. She shouldn't have to understand that the world punishes people for doing right."

"Maybe. But she's also learning that her father is brave. That he stands up for what matters even when it costs him. That's a good lesson, Jack."

They drove to Ruby's apartment in comfortable silence. Inside, Jack finally let himself feel the full weight of the day - the ambush interview, the lawyer's warnings, the conversation with his children. Everything that had been building for weeks was now cascading toward inevitable confrontation.

His phone buzzed. A text from Katherine Mendoza: *Lawsuit filed. Press release going out at 6 PM. Prepare for media attention.*

Jack: *How bad?*

Mendoza: *Local news will definitely pick it up. Possibly regional. We're alleging corporate fraud and whistleblower retaliation. That's newsworthy.*

Ruby read over his shoulder. "Okay. So tomorrow, your name and face will be in the news. Your company will issue statements calling you a disgruntled employee. The legal war will be public."

"Yeah."

"And you're still okay with this?"

Jack thought about the question seriously. Was he okay with his professional reputation being debated in public forums? With his children seeing news coverage questioning their father's motives? With Helen reading articles about her son's career destruction?

"No," he said honestly. "I'm not okay with it. But I'm going to do it anyway."

Ruby kissed him softly. "Then let's make sure you're ready. Media training. What to say if reporters contact you. How to protect yourself while the case proceeds."

They spent the evening preparing - Ruby coaching him on concise responses that didn't compromise the litigation, Mendoza sending over guidelines for media interaction, Jack drafting brief explanations he could give to extended family and friends.

At six PM, Mendoza sent the press release. It was professional, direct, and devastating:

Local Risk Analyst Files Whistleblower Retaliation Lawsuit Against Major Logistics Firm

Jack Mercer, a three-year employee of Regional Logistics Solutions, filed suit today alleging systematic corporate fraud and illegal retaliation for reporting financial crimes to federal authorities. According to the complaint filed in federal court, Mercer discovered evidence of money laundering and customs fraud totaling at least $12 million conducted through shell companies and falsified documentation...

It went on for three paragraphs, laying out the allegations with enough specificity to be credible but enough vagueness to protect detailed evidence. It named Derek Vaughn as a key figure in the alleged fraud. It described the retaliatory audit and threatened termination.

By seven PM, Jack's phone was ringing with unknown numbers. Reporters, presumably. He didn't answer. Ruby had coached him: let your lawyer handle media for now. Don't give interviews until the strategy is clear.

At eight PM, Regional Logistics Solutions issued their own statement:

We are aware of baseless allegations made by a former employee currently under investigation for serious policy violations. The company takes all compliance matters seriously and has conducted a thorough independent audit revealing that Mr. Mercer repeatedly violated data access policies, conducted unauthorized investigations, and failed to follow proper reporting procedures. His allegations are an attempt to deflect from his own misconduct and will be vigorously defended against in court.

"Former employee," Ruby noted. "They fired you without telling you."

Jack's phone rang. This time, the number was from HR. He let it go to voicemail, then listened to the message on speaker:

"Mr. Mercer, this is Linda from HR. Per the findings of our compliance audit, your employment with Regional Logistics Solutions has been terminated effective immediately. You are not to return to company premises. Your final paycheck and information about benefits continuation will be mailed to your address on file. Please return all company property within five business days."

And just like that, Jack was unemployed.

Three years of work, ended by voicemail.

He looked at Ruby, who was already texting Mendoza. Within minutes, his lawyer had issued a follow-up statement noting that the termination had occurred within hours of the whistleblower lawsuit being filed - clear evidence of retaliation.

Jack sat on Ruby's couch, phone buzzing with messages from former colleagues, news notifications, calls from numbers he didn't recognize. His life had become a public spectacle, his character under debate, his choices dissected by people who didn't know him.

But underneath the chaos, something felt clear. He'd done what needed to be done. Principles over comfort. Truth over security. The right thing, even when the right thing came with a devastating price tag.

"You okay?" Ruby asked quietly.

"Ask me in a year."

She smiled faintly. "Fair enough. For tonight, let's just get through tonight."

They ordered dinner, turned off the phone notifications, and sat together in the gradually quieting apartment. Tomorrow would bring new battles - media scrutiny, legal maneuvering, public opinion. Tomorrow, the FBI would hopefully accelerate their investigation now that everything was public. Tomorrow, Derek Vaughn would wake up to see his name in the news connected to fraud allegations.

But tonight, Jack was just a man who'd been fired for doing right, sitting with a woman who'd stood beside him through all of it, trying to figure out what came next.

The shrapnel in his ribs ached steadily - old wounds, old battles, old lessons about sacrifice and survival.

Some fights you won. Some you lost. This one was still undecided.

But Jack had shown up. Had stood his ground. Had refused to compromise what mattered even when compromise would have been easier.

That had to count for something.

Even if right now, it didn't feel like much.

Chapter 11: Aftermath

Friday morning, Jack woke to the disorienting reality of having nowhere to go. No alarm. No commute. No office waiting with its careful choreography of professional routine. Just the empty expanse of a day that should have been a workday but wasn't.

He was in Ruby's bed, the early light filtering through curtains they'd forgotten to close. Ruby was already awake beside him, propped on one elbow, watching him with quiet concern.

"You okay?" she asked.

"Ask me when I figure out what okay means anymore."

She leaned down and kissed his forehead. "Coffee first. Then we tackle the day."

Jack's phone sat on the nightstand, screen dark. He'd turned off notifications last night after the hundredth message from reporters, former colleagues, and people he barely remembered from high school suddenly interested in his story. The digital pile-up of attention felt suffocating.

"I should check messages," he said without moving.

"You should have coffee first," Ruby repeated, more firmly.

She was right. Jack rolled out of bed, pulled on clothes, and followed her to the kitchen. The apartment felt like a bunker - safe, isolated, removed from the storm raging outside its walls. Ruby made coffee with the practiced efficiency of someone who'd spent too many early mornings preparing for difficult days.

"Katherine emailed," Ruby said, handing him a mug. "Wants to meet at ten. Says the company's response has been 'aggressive' and she needs to strategize."

"What does aggressive mean in lawyer-speak?"

"Probably that they're not backing down. They're going to fight this hard and publicly." Ruby sat across from him at the small kitchen table. "Also, Agent Reeves called my cell at six-thirty this morning. The FBI wants to meet with you today. This afternoon, if possible."

Jack wrapped his hands around the coffee mug, feeling its warmth. "They're moving faster."

"The publicity helps. Once fraud allegations are public, the Bureau has more pressure to act. Nobody wants to look like they ignored warnings about twelve million in money laundering." Ruby paused. "But Jack, you need to be ready. Today's going to be intense. Media will be looking for you. Your face is probably already on the news."

As if on cue, Jack's phone began buzzing on the counter where he'd left it. He ignored it.

"I should call Helen," he said. "Before she sees something on TV or hears from someone else."

"Good idea. And your kids - check in with Jennifer, make sure they're okay."

Jack made the calls from Ruby's balcony, away from her well-meaning attention, needing the illusion of privacy for conversations that would be difficult regardless.

Helen answered on the second ring, her voice stronger than it had been weeks ago but still carrying the slight thickness from the stroke.

"Jack? I saw the news."

"Yeah. I figured you might."

"They're saying terrible things about you. That you stole company data, that you're making false accusations." Helen's voice wavered between anger and fear. "Is any of it true?"

"No. They're lying to protect themselves. I found fraud, Mom. Real fraud. Millions of dollars. And now they're trying to destroy my credibility before the truth comes out."

Helen was quiet for a moment. "Your father would be proud. Scared for you, but proud."

"I'm scared for me too."

"Good. Fear keeps you careful." Helen paused. "Are you safe? Do you need anything?"

"I'm safe. I'm with Ruby. I have a good lawyer. The FBI is involved." Jack looked out at the city, morning traffic beginning its daily crawl. "But Mom, this is going to get worse before it gets better. There will be more news stories, more accusations. People will ask you about me."

"Let them ask. I know my son. I know what kind of man you are." Her voice firmed with the stubbornness that had carried her through stroke recovery and decades of difficulty. "You do what you need to do. Don't worry about me."

After they hung up, Jack called Jennifer. She answered immediately.

"I saw the news," she said without preamble. "They're absolutely destroying you. Channel 5 had a whole segment about 'disgruntled employees making false fraud claims.' They interviewed some corporate fraud expert who said most whistleblower cases are bogus."

"How are the kids?"

"Shaken. Sarah's angry on your behalf. Michael's quiet - you know how he gets when he's processing. Emma asked me three times this morning if you're going to jail."

Jack closed his eyes. "Can I talk to her?"

"She's at school. I didn't keep them home - didn't want them to think this was worse than it is. But Jack, other kids are going to see the news. Other parents are going to talk. It's going to be rough for them."

"I know. I'm sorry."

"Don't apologize for doing the right thing. Just... stay in touch. Let them know you're okay. That helps more than you think." Jennifer paused. "Ruby seems solid. I'm glad you have her."

"Yeah. Me too."

After the calls, Jack finally turned on the television. The local morning news was running a story about him - his employee photo from the company website displayed prominently, next to images of the Regional Logistics Solutions building.

"...former compliance analyst Jack Mercer filed an explosive lawsuit yesterday alleging widespread fraud at his employer. The company denies all allegations and says Mercer was fired for policy violations unrelated to his claims. Legal experts say whistleblower retaliation cases are difficult to prove and often stem from workplace disputes rather than genuine fraud..."

They made him look paranoid. Vindictive. A problem employee lashing out after being caught violating policies.

Ruby came to stand beside him, watching the coverage. "They're good at this."

"At what?"

"Controlling the narrative. They get their version out first, frame you as the bad actor, make people skeptical of your allegations before evidence even emerges." She muted the television. "But this is just the opening round. Once the FBI moves, once actual evidence becomes public, the story changes."

"And if the FBI doesn't move? If this drags out for months?"

"Then we fight in court. And if necessary, in the media." Ruby turned to face him. "But right now, we focus on today. Mendoza at ten. FBI at three. One step at a time."

Katherine Mendoza's office felt like a war room. She'd cleared her conference table and covered it with documents - news clippings, legal filings, transcripts of Jack's interview, the company's public statements. She looked like she'd been up most of the night.

"They're not playing around," she said without preamble as Jack and Ruby entered. "The company hired Blackstone & Reed - that's a top-tier litigation firm, very aggressive. They filed a counter-motion this morning seeking sanctions against me for filing a frivolous lawsuit."

Jack sat heavily. "Can they do that?"

"They can try. It won't succeed - your case has clear merit. But it's a tactic to intimidate, to make this expensive and personal for everyone involved." Mendoza pulled out a thick document. "They're also alleging that you breached confidentiality agreements by sharing company data with Ruby and with me. They want a preliminary injunction preventing you from disclosing any additional information."

Ruby leaned forward. "I'm a forensic accountant. Jack showing me data for professional analysis isn't a breach of confidentiality."

"They're arguing it is because you're not employed by the company and weren't engaged through official channels." Mendoza flipped through pages. "It's a weak argument legally, but it creates complications. And it's part of their larger strategy - paint Jack as someone who violated multiple policies, leaked confidential information, and is now making false allegations to cover his own misconduct."

"So what do we do?" Jack asked.

"We respond aggressively. I'm filing our opposition to their motions today. I'm also preparing to take depositions - I want Derek Vaughn under oath within two weeks. I want Monica Chen. I want Paul Hendricks. I want everyone who witnessed the retaliation." Mendoza's eyes were sharp, focused. "And I'm coordinating with the FBI. Agent Reeves reached out this morning. They want full access to all your evidence, and they want to interview you formally today."

"Ruby said three o'clock."

"Correct. Federal Building, downtown. I'll be there with you." Mendoza paused. "Jack, I need to prepare you for what that interview will be like. The FBI doesn't mess around. They'll ask detailed questions, they'll challenge inconsistencies, they'll push you on every piece of evidence. You need to be precise, factual, and completely honest. Any discrepancies between what you tell them and what they can verify will damage your credibility."

"I understand."

"Also, they'll want the thumb drive. The one you told Cartwright about. All your personal files, all your analysis. Everything." Mendoza looked at him directly. "Are you ready to turn that over?"

Jack thought about the thumb drive sitting in his home safe. Months of careful documentation, evidence of fraud, proof of what he'd found. Once he gave it to the FBI, he lost control of it completely.

"Yes. I'm ready."

They spent the next two hours preparing - reviewing timeline, clarifying evidence, rehearsing answers to anticipated questions. By the time they finished, Jack felt simultaneously more prepared and more anxious about the afternoon meeting.

"One more thing," Mendoza said as they were leaving. "The media will keep calling. Don't answer. Don't give statements. Everything goes through me. The company wants you to make mistakes publicly. Don't give them that opportunity."

Back in Ruby's car, Jack checked the time. Noon. The FBI meeting wasn't until three, which gave them a few hours.

"I need to stop by my apartment," Jack said. "The thumb drive is in my safe. The FBI will want it."

Ruby nodded and pulled out of the parking lot, heading toward Jack's place. The drive took twenty minutes through midday traffic, giving Jack time to mentally prepare for seeing his apartment - the place he'd lived alone for three years, the space that represented his post-divorce independence.

When they arrived, the building looked exactly as it always had - a modest complex, well-maintained, nothing fancy. Jack unlocked his door and stepped inside, Ruby following.

The apartment felt stale from days of absence. Mail had piled up under the slot. The air had that closed-in quality of a space left unoccupied. Jack gathered the mail quickly - mostly bills and junk - and headed to his bedroom.

The safe was in his closet, hidden behind a stack of boxes. A small fireproof model, the kind you could buy at any office supply store. Jack had never needed serious security before. He'd never had evidence of federal crimes to protect.

He spun the combination, opened it, and pulled out the thumb drive. Such a small thing to contain so much damage. Months of investigation, millions in fraud, careers that would be destroyed or saved depending on what the FBI did with this data.

"That's it?" Ruby asked from the doorway.

"That's it." Jack pocketed the drive. "Everything I found. Everything that got me fired."

"Everything that might put corrupt people in prison," Ruby corrected.

Jack looked around his apartment - the life he'd built, the independence he'd fought for after the divorce, the carefully constructed routine that had been blown apart. "I should probably start staying here again soon. Get back to normal life."

"You can. But there's no rush."

Ruby's voice was gentle. "Stay at my place as long as you need. Until things settle down."

Jack looked around his apartment - the life he'd built, the independence he'd fought for after the divorce. It felt empty now, almost hollow.

"Yeah. Maybe a few more days at your place. After the FBI meeting, after this weekend with the kids. Then I'll come back."

"Whatever you need." Ruby gestured toward his bedroom.

"Grab some more clothes while we're here. You're running low."

They gathered a few of Jack's things - fresh clothes, toiletries, his laptop - and locked up the apartment. On the way out, Jack grabbed his mail, sorting through it in the passenger seat as Ruby drove.

One envelope stood out - from Regional Logistics Solutions, official company letterhead. Jack opened it carefully.

Inside was his termination letter, official and final. The language was cold and corporate: *"...pursuant to company policy violations... unauthorized data access... failure to follow reporting procedures... terminated for cause effective immediately..."*

Also included: information about COBRA health insurance continuation, final paycheck details, and a reminder that he was prohibited from accessing company property or contacting current employees.

"They're thorough," Jack said, showing Ruby the letter at a stoplight.

She scanned it quickly. "Forward this to Mendoza. It's more evidence of retaliation timing."

Jack photographed the letter and sent it to his attorney. Within minutes, Mendoza responded: *Perfect. This helps us. See you at Federal Building at 2:45.*

They grabbed lunch at a quiet deli, eating in the car while Jack tried to quiet his mind...

Back in Ruby's car, Jack checked his phone. Seventy-three missed calls. Dozens of voicemails. Text messages from people he hadn't spoken to in years.

One message stood out - from Monica Chen, sent at 8:47 AM: *I'm sorry about everything. You were right. I should have helped sooner. Please be careful.*

Jack showed it to Ruby.

"Interesting," she said. "She's reaching out."

"Should I respond?"

"Not yet. She could be setting you up for the company, trying to get you to say something they can use. Or she could be genuinely conflicted because her husband is involved." Ruby pulled out of the parking lot. "Let's see what the FBI says this afternoon. They might want to talk to her too."

They grabbed lunch at a quiet deli, eating in the car while Jack tried to quiet his mind. Everything was moving so fast - termination, lawsuit, media attention, FBI interview. Just three weeks ago, his life had been normal. Routine. Predictable.

Now he was unemployed, publicly accused of misconduct, and about to sit down with federal investigators to discuss corporate fraud and money laundering.

"You're thinking too much," Ruby observed.

"Hard not to."

"I know. But you can't control what happens next. You can only control how you respond." She reached over and took his hand. "You've done everything right so far. You found fraud, you reported it, you protected the evidence. Now you let the system work."

"What if the system doesn't work? What if they're too powerful, too connected? What if this ends with me blacklisted from the industry while they keep stealing?"

Ruby was quiet for a moment. "Then we go to the media. We make this so public, so documented, so undeniable that they can't hide anymore. And even if you get blacklisted, even if your career in logistics is over, you'll know you didn't look away. You didn't let them win without a fight."

Jack squeezed her hand. "When did you get so good at pep talks?"

"Years of practice on myself. After Hammond & Associates fired me, I spent months wondering if I'd made the wrong choice. If I should have just stayed quiet, kept my job, accepted that corruption was the price of security." Ruby's jaw tightened. "But I couldn't live with that. Neither can you. We're both stubborn idiots who think principles matter more than comfort."

"That's one way to put it."

"It's the true way to put it." She smiled faintly. "Come on. Let's go meet the FBI."

The Federal Building downtown was all concrete and security - metal detectors, badge readers, the architectural language of government authority. Agent Sarah Reeves met them in the lobby, dressed in a dark suit that somehow made her look both professional and vaguely threatening.

"Mr. Mercer. Ms. Martinez. Thank you for coming." She gestured toward the elevators. "Ms. Mendoza is already upstairs in the conference room."

They rode up in silence, the elevator's hum filling the space where conversation might have been. Jack felt like he was being taken somewhere important but possibly dangerous - the same sensation he'd had in Vietnam when helicopters carried them toward hot landing zones.

The conference room on the eighth floor was spare and functional. Katherine Mendoza sat at a long table, another FBI agent beside her - a man in his fifties with gray hair and the patient expression of someone who'd investigated thousands of cases.

"Mr. Mercer, I'm Special Agent Thomas Brennan, white-collar crime division supervisor." Not related to the company's lawyer David Brennan, clearly - just unfortunate name coincidence. "I'll be leading this interview. Ms. Reeves will be assisting."

Everyone sat. A recording device was placed on the table, along with a stack of documents Jack recognized as his own evidence package.

"This interview is being recorded," Brennan said formally. "Everything you say here is subject to verification and may be used in federal proceedings. Do you understand?"

"I understand."

"Good. Let's begin." Brennan opened a folder. "Tell me, in your own words, how you first became aware of potential fraud at Regional Logistics Solutions."

Jack took a breath and began. He walked through the timeline methodically - the initial irregularities he'd noticed, the patterns that emerged, the shell companies he'd identified. Brennan and Reeves listened without interrupting, occasionally making notes.

When Jack mentioned Pacific Meridian Holdings and Hemisphere Trade Solutions, Brennan's expression sharpened with interest.

"You identified these shell companies on your own?" Brennan asked.

"I identified the patterns. Ruby - Ms. Martinez - helped me understand the financial structure and confirmed they were shells."

Brennan looked at Ruby. "Ms. Martinez, you're a forensic accountant?"

"Yes. Previously with Hammond & Associates. I conducted an independent analysis of the data Mr. Mercer provided."

"And your conclusion?"

"Systematic money laundering using logistics operations as cover. Conservative estimate of twelve million dollars over eighteen months. Likely more if we had access to complete records."

Brennan made more notes. "Did you report your findings to company management?"

Jack explained the decision not to report internally - that the fraud extended to senior leadership, that reporting through official channels would just trigger a cover-up. Mendoza jumped in, framing it as appropriate whistleblower behavior under the circumstances.

The interview continued for two hours. Brennan probed every detail - why Jack had accessed certain data, how he'd analyzed it, what made him certain the patterns represented fraud rather than legitimate business complexity. Jack answered as precisely as he could, walking the line between confident and defensive.

Finally, Brennan sat back. "Mr. Mercer, what you've described is serious. Money laundering, customs fraud, possibly organized crime connections. But you're also describing a situation where you accessed company data extensively, conducted an investigation outside normal channels, and shared confidential information with external parties."

"I reported to the FBI," Jack said. "That's what whistleblowers are supposed to do."

"Eventually, yes. But you conducted months of investigation first." Brennan's tone wasn't accusatory, just precise. "The company is arguing you violated policies, exceeded your authority, and now you're making fraud allegations to justify your own misconduct. How do I know they're wrong?"

Jack felt anger building but kept it controlled. "Because I have documentation. Evidence. Financial records showing shell companies and false invoicing. I didn't make this up."

"Evidence you obtained through unauthorized access to company systems."

"Evidence I obtained through my job responsibilities as a compliance analyst."

Mendoza leaned forward. "Agent Brennan, my client discovered fraud and reported it to federal authorities. That's protected whistleblower activity. The company's retaliation doesn't change the underlying facts of what he found."

Brennan nodded slowly. "I'm not saying I don't believe Mr. Mercer. I'm saying that proving this case requires more than his analysis of shipping records. We need direct evidence - communications showing knowledge of fraud, financial records connecting payments to specific individuals, testimony from cooperating witnesses."

"What about the shell companies?" Ruby asked. "Pacific Meridian, Hemisphere Trade Solutions, Nexus Global Ventures. Those exist. Jack didn't invent them."

"No. And we've already started investigating those entities. But shell companies alone don't prove fraud. Lots of legitimate businesses use complex corporate structures for tax or liability reasons." Brennan pulled out another document. "What we need is evidence connecting specific people at Regional Logistics Solutions to the creation and operation of these shells for criminal purposes."

Jack remembered the early LLC - Pacific Trade Partners, founded by Derek Vaughn and Marcus Chen. "I found evidence that Vaughn and someone named Marcus Chen co-owned the original company that got restructured into the shell network."

"Marcus Chen," Brennan repeated, writing it down. "Who is he?"

"I don't know much about him. But I think he's married to one of my colleagues, Monica Chen. She's been... conflicted. Giving me warnings, but not directly helping."

"If her husband is involved in fraud, that would explain her behavior." Reeves looked at Brennan. "We should interview her."

"Agreed." Brennan turned back to Jack. "Do you have the thumb drive? The one you mentioned to the auditors?"

Jack pulled it from his pocket, slid it across the table. "Everything's on there. All my analysis, all the evidence I compiled, copies of the company documents I accessed."

Brennan took it carefully, as if it were evidence in a criminal trial - which, Jack realized, it probably would be. "We'll need some time to analyze this. Cross-reference it with our own databases, verify the connections you've identified." He paused. "Mr. Mercer, I want to be clear about what happens next. The Bureau is opening a full investigation based on what you've provided. But investigations take time - weeks, possibly months. We'll need to issue subpoenas, conduct interviews, build an airtight case before we make arrests."

"The company is destroying my reputation right now," Jack said. "Every day they're out there calling me a liar and a thief."

"I understand. But rushing an investigation leads to weak cases and acquittals. We do this right, or we don't do it at all." Brennan's expression softened slightly. "That said, the publicity helps us. Once fraud allegations are public, it's harder for suspects to destroy evidence without it looking suspicious. And your whistleblower lawsuit gives us additional leverage."

Mendoza spoke up. "Agent Brennan, will the Bureau be issuing any statements? My client needs some public validation that his allegations are being taken seriously."

"We can confirm that the FBI is conducting an investigation into financial irregularities at Regional Logistics Solutions based on information provided by a concerned employee. We won't name Mr. Mercer, but people will connect the dots." Brennan stood. "We'll be in touch as the investigation progresses. In the meantime, if you remember anything else, if anyone from the company contacts you, if anything happens that seems threatening or retaliatory - you call Ms. Reeves immediately."

Reeves handed Jack her card. "My direct line. Day or night."

They wrapped up the formalities, signed paperwork, and headed back down to the lobby. Outside, the afternoon had turned gray and cold, matching Jack's mood.

"That went well," Mendoza said as they reached the parking garage.

"Did it? Felt like they were skeptical."

"They're FBI. Skeptical is their default setting. But they're opening a full investigation. That's huge." Mendoza checked her watch. "I need to get back to the office and file our response to the company's motions. Jack, go home. Rest. Try to decompress. This weekend, you focus on your kids and your mother. Monday, we go back to war."

After Mendoza left, Jack and Ruby sat in her car for a long moment without speaking.

"You did good in there," Ruby said finally.

"I gave them everything. Now it's out of my hands."

"That's not a bad thing. You can't carry this alone. The FBI has resources, authority, power you don't have." She started the car. "Come on. Let's get you home."

They drove back to Ruby's apartment, the termination letter sitting on the dashboard like a tombstone for Jack's career.

Inside, Ruby's place felt more like home than his own apartment had - maybe because this was where he'd been living through the crisis, or maybe because Ruby's presence made anywhere feel more grounded.

His phone rang. Unknown number. He let it go to voicemail, then listened to the message on speaker:

"Mr. Mercer, this is Todd Hansen from Channel 7 News. I'd like to give you an opportunity to tell your side of the story. We've heard from Regional Logistics Solutions, but I think our viewers would benefit from hearing directly from you. Please call me back at..."

Jack deleted it.

Another voicemail, this one from a former colleague: *"Jack, it's Dave from accounting. Look, I don't know what to believe right now, but I*

Jack saved that one.

Ruby ordered dinner - Thai food from a place they both liked - and they ate mostly in silence, both exhausted by the day's emotional weight. After dinner, Jack called his kids, letting them hear his voice, reassuring them he was okay. Emma cried a little. Michael asked technical questions about how FBI investigations worked. Sarah wanted to know if there was anything she could do to help.

"Just be yourselves," Jack told her. "And don't let other people's opinions change what you know about me."

After the calls, Jack and Ruby watched mindless television until they were both too tired to think. They went to bed early, Jack grateful for the oblivion of sleep, knowing tomorrow would bring its own challenges.

As he drifted off, Ruby's warmth beside him, Jack thought about what Agent Brennan had said: *Investigations take time. Weeks, possibly months.*

He could survive weeks. He could even survive months.

What he couldn't survive was losing himself in the process - becoming bitter, vengeful, consumed by the fight. His father had done that, let the battle become his entire identity. Jack wouldn't make the same mistake.

He'd fight. But he'd also live. He'd be a father, a son, a partner. He'd find ways to be useful even without a job. He'd protect what mattered while the legal machinery ground slowly toward whatever conclusion it would reach.

The shrapnel in his ribs ached faintly - old wounds, old reminders. Some battles you won quickly. Others took time.

Vietnam had taught him patience. Had taught him that survival sometimes meant enduring rather than attacking.

This was an endurance fight now. Jack could do endurance.

He closed his eyes and slept.

Tomorrow would come soon enough.

Chapter 12: Vindication Delayed

Saturday morning arrived with the peculiar silence of a life disrupted. Jack woke in Ruby's bed, disoriented for a moment before remembering: unemployed, publicly accused, under FBI investigation - though this time as the witness rather than the suspect.

His phone showed dozens of notifications, but one stood out. A text from Jennifer, sent at 6:47 AM: *Kids are asking if they can still come to your place this weekend. I told them yes unless you need space. Your call.*

Jack typed back: *Please bring them. Normal is good right now.*

Jennifer: *They'll be ready at 10. Jack - there are reporters outside your apartment building. Saw it on the news this morning. You might want to meet somewhere else.*

Jack swore quietly. Of course there were reporters. His address was probably public record, easy enough to find once his name hit the news.

Ruby stirred beside him. "What's wrong?"

"Media camped outside my apartment. Can't take the kids there."

Ruby sat up, thinking. "Bring them here. I've got space. Or we could go somewhere public - museum, park, somewhere the reporters won't follow."

"Your place," Jack decided. "I want them to meet you properly anyway. Not just in crisis mode at Jennifer's."

They spent the next hour preparing - Ruby tidying her apartment, Jack mentally rehearsing how to introduce his children to his girlfriend under the extraordinary circumstances of unemployment and public scandal. Not exactly the casual "meet my new partner" scenario he'd imagined.

At ten, Jack drove to Jennifer's house. He'd borrowed Ruby's car, figuring his own vehicle might be recognizable to reporters. The precaution felt paranoid and necessary in equal measure.

Jennifer met him at the door, David standing behind her with the three kids already bundled in coats.

"Morning," Jennifer said, her tone carefully neutral. "They're excited to see you. Sarah's been reading news coverage online - I couldn't stop her. Michael's been quiet. Emma just wants everything to be normal."

"Normal. Right." Jack looked at his children, saw Sarah's defiant expression, Michael's worried eyes, Emma's forced cheerfulness. "We're going to Ruby's apartment. Figured reporters wouldn't know that address."

"Good thinking." Jennifer lowered her voice. "Jack, I know this is a terrible time, but... are you okay? Financially, I mean. If you need help with child support until you find work-"

"I'm okay for now. Savings. Severance pay, ironically." He managed a smile. "But thanks."

The kids piled into Ruby's Subaru, Emma immediately claiming the front seat, Sarah and Michael settling in back. As they drove, Emma peppered Jack with questions - was he in trouble with the police, would he go to jail, when would he get a new job, did this mean they couldn't go to Disney World next summer?

"Not in trouble with the police," Jack answered patiently. "The FBI is investigating my old company, not me. I won't go to jail. I'll find a new job eventually. And yes, we can still go to Disney World."

"Promise?" Emma's voice was small.

"Promise."

At Ruby's apartment, she greeted them at the door with the kind of warm professionalism that came from years of navigating awkward business meetings. She'd set out snacks, queued up a movie on her streaming service, and generally created the atmosphere of a normal weekend visit rather than a crisis gathering.

"Thanks for letting us invade your space," Sarah said with teenage directness. "I know this is probably weird for you."

Ruby smiled. "Your dad's been staying here all week. You're not invading anything."

"So you guys are like, living together now?" Michael asked.

Jack and Ruby exchanged a glance. "More like I'm crashing at her place during a difficult time," Jack clarified. "But yes, we're serious about each other."

Emma studied Ruby with the frank assessment of an eleven-year-old determining whether this new person was worthy of her father. "Do you like dragons?"

Ruby blinked. "I... haven't thought about it much. But sure, dragons are cool."

"Emma's reading a series about dragon riders," Jack explained.

"Which I could tell you about if you want to know," Emma offered hopefully.

"I'd love that," Ruby said, and the genuine warmth in her voice seemed to satisfy Emma's evaluation.

They settled into an easy rhythm - Sarah asking Ruby about her work ("Forensic accounting sounds really cool, actually"), Michael showing Ruby a video game he'd been playing, Emma launching into an enthusiastic synopsis of her dragon book series that somehow lasted forty-five minutes.

Jack watched from the kitchen, making sandwiches, feeling something loosen in his chest. His children were okay. They were adapting. They were meeting Ruby not as a threat to their family structure but as someone who made their father less alone during a hard time.

After lunch, while Emma was absorbed in her book and Michael was playing games on his phone, Sarah pulled Jack aside to Ruby's small balcony.

"I read the news articles," she said without preamble. "They're calling you a liar. Saying you stole company data and made up fraud allegations because you got caught."

"I know."

"But it's not true, right? You actually found real fraud?"

Jack looked at his sixteen-year-old daughter, seeing the intelligence and skepticism that would serve her well in college and beyond. She deserved honesty.

"Yes. I found real fraud. Millions of dollars. And when I reported it, they tried to destroy my credibility so people wouldn't believe me."

"That's really messed up."

"Yes, it is."

Sarah was quiet for a moment, watching the city below. "Some kids at school have been saying stuff. That you're a criminal. That you got fired for stealing. I've been defending you, but..." She trailed off.

"But it's hard when the news keeps repeating their version," Jack finished.

"Yeah."

Jack put his arm around his daughter's shoulders. "I'm sorry you're dealing with this. It's not fair that my choices affect your life at school."

"I'm not sorry you made those choices," Sarah said firmly. "I'm proud you stood up to them. I'm just mad that they're winning right now."

"They're not winning. They're just louder." Jack squeezed her shoulder. "The FBI is investigating. The truth will come out. It'll take time, but it'll come out."

"And if it doesn't?"

Jack thought about that - the real possibility that the powerful would stay powerful, that corruption would be proven but unpunished, that his sacrifice would amount to nothing.

"Then at least I'll know I tried. And you'll know your father wasn't someone who looked away from wrong because confronting it was hard."

Sarah nodded slowly. "That matters."

"It's the only thing that matters in the end."

They went back inside to find Ruby and Emma deep in conversation about dragon mythology, Michael listening with half his attention while still playing his game. Normal. Imperfect. Real.

Jack's phone buzzed. A text from Katherine Mendoza: *FBI issued statement. Media picking it up. This helps.*

Jack pulled up the news on his phone. Sure enough, several outlets were reporting:

FBI CONFIRMS INVESTIGATION INTO REGIONAL LOGISTICS SOLUTIONS

Jack showed the article to Ruby, who read it and nodded with satisfaction. "That changes the narrative. Now it's not just your word against theirs. It's the FBI taking your allegations seriously."

"Will people believe it?" Sarah asked, reading over Ruby's shoulder.

"Some will. Some won't. But it gives us momentum." Ruby glanced at Jack. "Your lawyer's right. This helps."

They spent the rest of the afternoon in determined normalcy - watching a movie Michael picked, playing a board game Emma insisted on, ordering pizza for dinner. Sarah FaceTimed with friends, her voice dropping when she mentioned her dad's situation, defensive and proud in equal measure.

By evening, when David arrived to pick up the kids, they seemed lighter than they'd been in the morning. Emma hugged Jack extra tight, Michael said "See you next weekend, Dad," with his usual teenage casualness that now felt like a gift, and Sarah whispered "Love you" as she left.

After they were gone, Jack and Ruby cleaned up the apartment in comfortable silence.

"They're good kids," Ruby said finally.

"Yeah. They are." Jack gathered pizza boxes. "Thanks for today. For making this feel normal when nothing about it is normal."

"They needed to see you're okay. That you have support. That your life isn't just falling apart even though it looks like it from the outside." Ruby wiped down the counter. "And honestly? I needed to meet them properly. To understand that part of your life."

"What did you think?"

"I think Sarah's going to be formidable when she grows up. Michael's deeper than he lets on. And Emma's going to break hearts someday with that earnest enthusiasm."

Jack smiled. "That's pretty accurate."

His phone rang. Unknown number, but this time something made him answer.

"Mr. Mercer?" The voice was female, professional, unfamiliar. "This is Monica Chen. Please don't hang up."

Jack's pulse quickened. He gestured to Ruby, mouthed "Monica," and put the phone on speaker.

"I'm listening."

"I know you have no reason to trust me. I know I should have helped you sooner, should have spoken up when I saw what was happening." Monica's voice was strained, like she'd been crying or was close to it. "But I need to talk to you. In person. Away from phones that might be monitored."

"Why should I meet with you?"

"Because I'm married to Marcus Chen. And because I know things that could help your case." She paused. "I want to cooperate with the FBI. But I'm scared. I need... I don't know what I need. Advice. Protection. Someone to tell me I'm not insane for thinking about testifying against my own husband."

Jack looked at Ruby, who nodded slowly.

"Where do you want to meet?" Jack asked.

"There's a coffee shop on Maple Street. The Grind. Tomorrow morning, nine AM. Please come alone - if Marcus sees you with lawyers or FBI, he'll know something's wrong."

"How do I know this isn't a setup?"

Monica laughed, the sound bitter. "If they wanted to set you up, they'd do it more cleverly than having the suspected criminal's wife call you directly. I'm taking a huge risk even making this call. Please, Jack. I need to talk to someone who understands what it's like to choose principle over security."

After a long pause, Jack said, "I'll be there. Nine AM."

"Thank you." Monica hung up before he could say anything else.

Jack looked at Ruby. "This could be legitimate. Or it could be a trap."

"Either way, you're not going alone." Ruby's tone left no room for argument. "I'll be there, at a different table, watching. If anything seems wrong, we leave."

"I should tell Agent Reeves."

"Yes. And your lawyer. But Jack - if Monica's genuine, if she's willing to cooperate, she could be exactly what the FBI needs. Direct testimony from someone inside the conspiracy."

Jack called Katherine Mendoza first, explained the situation. She was immediately cautious.

"It could be legitimate. It could be an attempt to get you on record saying something they can use against you. Or it could be worse - physical confrontation, intimidation." Mendoza paused. "But if she's real, if she's ready to flip, this accelerates everything. Let me call Agent Reeves. We'll coordinate. You don't go alone, and you don't agree to anything without FBI involvement."

Next, Jack called Sarah Reeves directly, using the card she'd given him. She answered on the second ring.

"Agent Reeves."

"This is Jack Mercer. Monica Chen just called me. She wants to meet tomorrow morning. Says she wants to cooperate, testify against her husband."

Reeves was quiet for a moment. "Where and when?"

Jack gave her the details. She asked several questions - what exactly Monica had said, her tone, whether she'd mentioned specific evidence. Finally, she made a decision.

"Okay. You go to the meeting. We'll have agents nearby, watching. You wear a wire - get her talking, get her to specify what she knows. If she's genuine, we bring her in immediately for a formal interview. If it's a setup, we intervene."

"A wire? Isn't that entrapment or something?"

"Only if you're trying to get her to say something she wouldn't otherwise say. You're just documenting a conversation she initiated. Completely legal." Reeves's tone was firm. "Mr. Mercer, if Monica Chen is willing to testify, she could give us everything - direct knowledge of the conspiracy, evidence of her husband's involvement, maybe even communications between Vaughn and Marcus Chen. This could be the break we need."

After the calls, Jack sat heavily on Ruby's couch. Tomorrow morning, he'd be wearing a wire, meeting with a woman whose husband had helped steal millions, trying to determine if she was genuine or dangerous.

"You don't have to do this," Ruby said quietly. "You could tell the FBI to handle it themselves."

"No. Monica reached out to me specifically. She's scared. If I back out now, she might lose her nerve entirely." Jack looked at Ruby. "But I am scared. What if it goes wrong?"

"Then the FBI agents watching will intervene. You're not alone in this."

Jack thought about Vietnam, about the times he'd walked into dangerous situations knowing backup was nearby but not visible. The same combination of trust and terror.

"Okay," he said. "Tomorrow, I find out if Monica Chen is an ally or an enemy."

They spent the evening quietly - Ruby reading, Jack watching news coverage that was gradually shifting tone as the FBI confirmation gave his allegations more credibility. Some outlets were still calling him a disgruntled employee. Others were beginning to ask harder questions about Regional Logistics Solutions' denials.

At ten PM, his phone rang again. This time, the number was familiar. Helen.

"Mom? Everything okay?"

"I'm fine. Just saw the news. The FBI is investigating?" Her voice carried relief and worry in equal measure.

"Yes. They're taking it seriously now. It's going to take time, but they're building a case."

"Good. That's good." Helen paused. "Jack, I've been thinking about your father. About the mistakes he made after he tried to do the right thing. Promise me you won't let this make you bitter. Don't let fighting them turn you into someone you're not."

"I'm trying not to."

"I know. But it's easy to lose yourself in a fight like this. To let the anger consume everything else." Her voice softened. "You have children who need you whole, not just righteous. Remember that."

After they hung up, Jack sat with his mother's words. She was right. The temptation to let this battle become his entire identity was strong. To wake up angry, go to bed bitter, measure every day by victories and defeats in a legal war.

But he was still a father. Still a son. Still a man who'd built a life worth living beyond this fight.

Ruby came to sit beside him. "Your mom?"

"Yeah. Reminding me not to lose myself in this."

"Good advice." Ruby took his hand. "Whatever happens tomorrow with Monica, whatever the FBI finds, whatever the lawsuit does - you're still you. Still the man who reads dragon books to his daughter and teaches his son about standing up for what's right. Don't forget that part."

Jack pulled her close. "I won't. I promise."

They went to bed early, knowing tomorrow would bring its own challenges. As Jack drifted toward sleep, he thought about Monica Chen - trapped between loyalty to her husband and knowledge of his crimes, reaching out to the man her husband had helped destroy.

Maybe she was genuine. Maybe she was a trap.

Either way, tomorrow he'd find out.

The shrapnel in his ribs ached faintly, a reminder that some wounds never fully healed but you learned to live with them anyway.

Old pain. New battles. Same fundamental question: who did you want to be when the cost of principle became real?

Jack had answered that question already.

Tomorrow, he'd find out if Monica Chen had reached the same answer.

Or if she was just another weapon in someone else's war.

He closed his eyes and tried to sleep.

Tomorrow would come soon enough.

Chapter 13: The Wire

Sunday morning arrived cold and gray, the kind of November day that threatened rain but wouldn't commit. Jack woke at six, too anxious to sleep longer, and found Ruby already awake beside him, scrolling through her phone.

"Nervous?" she asked without looking up.

"Terrified."

"Good. Keeps you sharp." She set down her phone. "Agent Reeves texted. She wants you at the Federal Building by seven-thirty to get wired up. I'll drive you."

Jack showered, dressed in layers that would hide the recording equipment, and tried to eat breakfast despite his stomach's protest. The toast sat heavy and unwelcome. Coffee helped, but not much.

By seven-fifteen, they were in Ruby's car heading downtown. The city was quiet on Sunday morning, the usual weekday chaos replaced by the stillness of people sleeping in or attending church services. Jack watched the buildings pass, wondering if Monica Chen was awake, wondering if she was as scared as he was.

The Federal Building's weekend security was minimal but present. Agent Reeves met them in the lobby, dressed casually in jeans and a jacket - her weekend attire, Jack assumed, though the gun holstered at her hip suggested she was very much on duty.

"Morning," she said, leading them to the elevators. "How are you holding up?"

"Ask me after the meeting."

They rode up to the eighth floor, to a different conference room than they'd used Friday. Agent Brennan was there, along with a tech specialist - a young woman named Garcia who had a duffel bag full of surveillance equipment spread across the table.

"Mr. Mercer," Brennan said by way of greeting. "Ms. Martinez. Thanks for coming early."

Garcia gestured Jack over. "I'm going to fit you with a wire. It's small, undetectable unless someone's specifically searching for it. Goes here-" she indicated his chest "-with the microphone clipped inside your shirt. The transmitter will be in your waistband, back of your pants. You'll barely feel it."

She worked efficiently, explaining each piece as she attached it. The microphone was smaller than Jack expected, no bigger than a button. The transmitter felt like a slightly bulky cell phone against his lower back.

"Test," Garcia said, stepping back. She put on headphones, nodded. "Good. Clear signal. Try talking naturally."

Jack said a few sentences - his name, the date, what he'd had for breakfast. Garcia made adjustments, checked levels, then gave a thumbs up.

"You're good to go. Just talk normally, let her do most of the talking if possible. The equipment will pick up everything within fifteen feet."

Brennan pulled out a folder. "Here's what we need. First, confirmation that she knows about the fraud - specific details, not just vague suspicions. Second, information about her husband Marcus's role. Third, any evidence she has access to - documents, communications, financial records. Fourth, whether she's willing to testify formally."

"What if she's setting me up?" Jack asked.

"We'll have four agents positioned around the coffee shop. Two inside dressed as customers, two outside in vehicles. If anything goes wrong - if anyone threatens you, if this feels like a trap - you say the safe word and we move in immediately."

"What's the safe word?"

"'Vietnam.' Work it into conversation naturally if you need extraction."

Jack nodded, the irony not lost on him. His past war becoming the code word for present danger.

Reeves checked her watch. "It's eight-fifteen. The coffee shop is twenty minutes away. We'll position agents first, then you arrive at exactly nine. Ms. Martinez, you'll enter separately at eight fifty-five, take a table with clear sightline to Mr. Mercer. You're backup observation, nothing more. If something happens, you do not intervene. You let our agents handle it."

Ruby agreed, though Jack could see she wasn't happy about being relegated to watching.

They drove in separate vehicles - Jack with Reeves and Brennan, Ruby following in her own car. The coffee shop was in a quiet neighborhood, the kind of place that catered to weekend brunchers and studying college students. Nondescript. Public enough to feel safe, not so crowded that conversations couldn't be private.

Jack watched as two agents entered separately, taking tables at opposite ends of the room. One ordered coffee and pulled out a laptop. The other sat with a newspaper. Both looked like typical Sunday morning customers.

At eight fifty-five, Ruby entered, ordered tea, and settled at a table with a clear view of where Jack would sit. She pulled out a book, the picture of a woman enjoying a quiet morning.

At exactly nine AM, Jack walked in.

The coffee shop smelled like espresso and cinnamon. Acoustic music played softly. A handful of customers sat scattered at tables, absorbed in phones or books or quiet conversations. Monica Chen was already there, sitting at a corner table, hands wrapped around a coffee mug like she was trying to absorb its warmth.

She looked terrible. Dark circles under her eyes, hair pulled back messily, no makeup. The polished professional Jack knew from work had been replaced by someone who'd spent the night crying or not sleeping or both.

Jack ordered coffee, paid, and approached her table. "Monica."

She looked up, managed a weak smile. "Jack. Thank you for coming. I wasn't sure you would."

"I almost didn't." He sat across from her, acutely aware of the microphone recording every word. "Why did you want to meet?"

Monica's hands tightened around her mug. "Because I can't do this anymore. Can't keep pretending I don't know what Marcus is doing. Can't watch them destroy you for trying to stop something I've known about for months."

"What have you known about?"

"The shell companies. The false invoicing. The money laundering." She spoke quietly, quickly, like the words had been building pressure and now they were escaping. "Marcus started it with Vaughn almost two years ago. Small at first - just a few questionable transactions, easy to justify as business complexity. But it grew. The amounts got bigger. The structure got more elaborate."

Jack kept his voice level, letting her talk. "How did you find out?"

"I'm his wife. I see the bank statements, the mysterious deposits that don't match his salary. I hear phone calls he takes late at night, stepping into another room so I won't hear details." Monica's voice cracked slightly. "And six months ago, I found documents. Corporate filings for companies I'd never heard of, with Marcus's name on them. I confronted him."

"What did he say?"

"That it was legitimate business. Tax optimization, nothing illegal. That I was overreacting." She finally looked directly at Jack. "But I'm not stupid. I'm a logistics analyst. I understand how this industry works. What he described wasn't tax optimization. It was fraud."

"Why didn't you report it?"

Monica's laugh was bitter. "To who? My husband is committing crimes with my boss's boss. Who do I tell that won't just get me fired or worse?" She paused. "And he's my husband. We've been married eight years. We have a house together, a life. Reporting him meant destroying everything."

"But you're here now."

"Because they're destroying you. Because I watched what they did during the audit - setting you up, manufacturing evidence of policy violations, coordinating with Cartwright to build a termination case. I saw it happening and I said nothing." Tears started, which Monica wiped away impatiently. "I gave you little warnings, tried to help in tiny ways that wouldn't expose me. But that's cowardice, not courage. And I'm done being a coward."

Jack glanced briefly at Ruby, who was watching with focused attention. The agents looked like they weren't paying attention at all, which probably meant they were paying very close attention.

"What do you want to do?" Jack asked.

"I want to cooperate with the FBI. I want to testify about what I know. I want..." She struggled to continue. "I want to stop being complicit in something I know is wrong. Even if it costs me my marriage."

"It will definitely cost you your marriage."

"I know." Fresh tears. "Marcus will hate me. His family will hate me. I'll probably lose the house in the divorce. But at least I'll be able to look at myself in the mirror."

Jack understood that feeling exactly. "What evidence do you have access to?"

"Marcus keeps documents at home. In his office, in a safe. I don't have the combination, but I know where it is. I've seen him open it." Monica leaned forward. "And I have his laptop password. He doesn't know I know it, but I've seen him type it enough times. If the FBI wanted to get into his files..."

"That's illegal search without a warrant."

"Not if I consent to them searching my own home." Monica had clearly thought this through. "We're married. It's my house too. I can give permission for law enforcement to search it."

Jack felt hope rising. If Monica was genuine, if she really had access to Marcus's documents and files, this could be exactly what the FBI needed.

"Monica, if you do this, there's no going back. Marcus will know you betrayed him. Vaughn will know. The company will retaliate."

"They already fired you for less. I know what I'm risking." She met his eyes. "I'm scared, Jack. Terrified. But I can't keep living like this. Can't keep being married to someone I know is a criminal. Can't keep watching good people get destroyed for trying to stop it."

Jack made a decision. "I'm working with the FBI. Have been since before I got fired. If you're serious about cooperating, I can connect you with the agents investigating this."

Monica's relief was visible. "Yes. Please. I don't even know how to contact the FBI on my own. I was hoping you could help with that."

"When could you give them access to Marcus's documents?"

"Today, if they move fast. Marcus is out of town until tonight - business trip to LA. I'm home alone. If the FBI came now, they could search everything before he gets back."

Jack stood. "Wait here. I need to make a call."

He walked outside, pulling out his phone. Agent Reeves answered immediately - she'd obviously been listening to everything.

"She sounds genuine," Reeves said without preamble. "Brennan agrees. We want to bring her in for formal interview right now, and if she consents to home search, we'll execute it this afternoon."

"She's scared. Be gentle with her."

"We will. Bring her to the Federal Building. We'll take it from there."

Jack went back inside. Monica looked up anxiously.

"The FBI wants to talk to you. Now. At their offices downtown. Are you ready for that?"

Monica took a shaky breath, then nodded. "Yes. Let's do this before I lose my nerve."

They left the coffee shop together, Monica following Jack to where Reeves and Brennan waited in an unmarked sedan. Ruby appeared at Jack's elbow as they reached the parking lot.

"Is she for real?" Ruby asked quietly.

"I think so. Guess we'll find out."

Monica climbed into the FBI vehicle without hesitation. Reeves gave Jack a brief nod - acknowledgment of a job well done - and they drove away, leaving Jack and Ruby standing in the parking lot.

"Well," Ruby said. "That was anticlimactic. I expected more drama."

"Me too." Jack felt the wire equipment against his skin, suddenly aware of how tense he'd been. "Can we go back to the Federal Building? I want to give them this recording equipment and find out what happens next."

They drove back downtown, Jack peeling off the wire with relief once they reached the FBI offices. Garcia took the equipment, downloaded the recording, and confirmed everything had been captured clearly.

"Good work," she said. "Clean recording, got everything we need."

Brennan emerged from a different conference room where Monica was presumably being interviewed. "Mr. Mercer, Ms. Martinez. Monica Chen is cooperating fully. She's giving us a sworn statement about her husband's involvement, about Vaughn's role, about the corporate structure. She's also consenting to a search of her home."

"When?" Jack asked.

"Two hours. We're getting a search warrant as backup - even with spousal consent, we want ironclad legality. A judge is standing by to sign it." Brennan's expression was grimly satisfied. "If Marcus Chen has kept documentation, if his laptop has communications with Vaughn or financial records, we'll have them by tonight."

"What happens to Monica?"

"She'll be placed in witness protection temporarily - not full relocation, but secure housing until we can assess whether she's in danger from her husband or Vaughn's organization. After we search the house, she can't go back there. Marcus will know someone talked."

Jack thought about that - Monica giving up her home, her marriage, her entire life to testify against corruption. The same choice Jack had made, the same price.

"Take care of her," he said. "She's terrified but she's doing the right thing."

"We will." Brennan nodded to them both. "You two should go. This will take all day and into the evening. We'll contact you with updates."

Outside the Federal Building, the morning had turned into afternoon. Jack's phone showed missed calls from Jennifer, from Helen, from Katherine Mendoza. He'd deal with them all eventually. Right now, he just wanted to breathe.

"That went well," Ruby said as they walked to her car.

"Yeah. It did." Jack felt cautiously optimistic for the first time in days. "If Monica's testimony is as good as it sounded, if they find evidence in Marcus's files..."

"Then you were right. The fraud is real, provable, and you'll be vindicated."

They drove to Ruby's apartment, where Jack finally returned the phone calls. Jennifer wanted an update - he gave her the sanitized version, leaving out details about wires and FBI operations. Helen just wanted to hear his voice, to be reassured he was safe. Mendoza was thrilled, already planning how Monica's cooperation would impact the civil lawsuit.

By evening, Agent Reeves called with an update.

"Search warrant executed. We recovered extensive documentation from Marcus Chen's home office and safe. Financial records, communications with Vaughn, offshore account information, the whole structure." Her voice carried barely contained excitement. "We also imaged his laptop. Preliminary review shows email chains discussing the laundering operation, payments to customs officials, everything we need."

"How much evidence are we talking about?"

"Enough to charge both Marcus Chen and Derek Vaughn with multiple counts of money laundering, wire fraud, and conspiracy. We're building cases against several others involved. Conservative estimate? We're looking at eight to ten arrests within the next two weeks."

Jack felt something release in his chest - vindication, relief, the knowledge that his sacrifice hadn't been for nothing. "What about Monica?"

"Safe. Secure location. She's been incredibly cooperative. Her testimony plus the documents we seized will make for a very strong prosecution."

After the call, Jack sat on Ruby's couch, trying to process everything. Just this morning, he'd been wired for a potentially dangerous meeting. Now, hours later, the FBI had enough evidence to bring down the entire conspiracy.

"It's really happening," Ruby said, sitting beside him. "They're going down."

"Yeah." Jack pulled her close. "It's really happening."

His phone buzzed with a text from an unknown number. He opened it cautiously.

You've made a terrible mistake. This isn't over.

No signature. No identifying information. Just a threat, clear and simple.

Jack showed it to Ruby, who immediately grabbed her phone to call Agent Reeves back.

"Someone just threatened Jack," she said when Reeves answered. "Text message, unknown number."

"Forward it to me immediately. We'll trace it." Reeves's tone turned serious. "Mr. Mercer, this confirms what we suspected - the organization knows Monica cooperated. They may not know specifics yet, but they know someone talked. You need to be careful."

"How careful?"

"Vary your routines. Don't go anywhere predictable. If anything seems off, call me immediately." She paused. "We're moving faster now because of this. The more threatened they feel, the more dangerous they become. We want arrests before they can retaliate."

After hanging up, Jack and Ruby sat in the growing darkness of her apartment.

"The outline said there would be violence," Ruby said quietly. "Threats against your family."

"Yeah." Jack thought about his children, about Helen, about everyone he cared about potentially becoming targets because he'd exposed fraud. "I need to call Jennifer. Warn her to be extra careful with the kids."

He made the call, explaining without creating panic. Jennifer understood immediately, promised to be vigilant. David would pick up and drop off the kids at school personally. They'd avoid predictable routines.

"Jack," Jennifer said before hanging up. "Thank you for telling me. And thank you for being careful. The kids need their father."

"I know. I'm being as careful as I can."

After the call, Jack felt the weight of it all settling heavy. The FBI was moving. Monica had cooperated. Evidence was mounting. Arrests were coming.

But cornered criminals were dangerous criminals.

And Jack had just helped corner some very powerful people.

The shrapnel in his ribs ached with familiar insistence - old wounds recognizing new danger, old lessons about the difference between winning and surviving.

In Vietnam, Jack had learned that sometimes victory and survival were different goals, and you had to choose which one mattered more.

Right now, survival mattered most.

For himself, for his children, for everyone caught in the blast radius of this fight.

Ruby's hand found his in the darkness.

"We'll get through this," she said.

"Yeah," Jack replied, hoping it was true. "We will."

Outside, the city moved through its Sunday evening routines, unaware that somewhere within its boundaries, powerful men were realizing their crimes had been exposed, their empire was crumbling, and they had nothing left to lose.

Jack closed his eyes and tried not to think about what desperate men might do.

Tomorrow would bring its own battles.

Tonight, he just needed to make it through.

One day at a time.

One threat at a time.

One step closer to either vindication or destruction.

The line between them had never seemed thinner.

Chapter 14: Arrests

Tuesday morning brought the peculiar tension of waiting for violence you knew was coming but couldn't predict. Jack woke with Ruby's alarm, the threatening text from yesterday still vivid in his mind: *You've made a terrible mistake. This isn't over.*

Agent Reeves had called late last night with an update - the number was a burner phone, untraceable, purchased with cash at a convenience store three days ago. Security footage showed a man in a baseball cap and sunglasses buying it. Could have been anyone.

"The Bureau is accelerating the timeline," Reeves had said. "We're preparing arrest warrants for Vaughn and Marcus Chen. Could be as early as Wednesday."

Wednesday. Two days away. Forty-eight hours during which cornered criminals knew they were exposed but hadn't yet been arrested.

Jack made coffee while Ruby showered, his mind cataloging threats and vulnerabilities. His children were the obvious pressure point - Emma at elementary school, Michael at middle school, Sarah at high school. Jennifer and David knew to be vigilant, but vigilance only went so far against determined attackers.

Helen was in the rehab facility, which had controlled access but wasn't a fortress. Ruby's apartment building had security but nothing sophisticated. Jack's own apartment had reporters camped outside - ironically, their presence might actually deter anything violent.

His phone rang. Katherine Mendoza.

"Morning," she said. "Saw the news. FBI executed a search warrant yesterday on Marcus Chen's residence. Media is connecting it to your whistleblower case."

"Yeah. Monica Chen cooperated. Gave them access to everything."

"That's huge for our civil case. Her testimony that the company knew about fraud, that the audit was retaliatory - that's exactly what we need." Mendoza paused. "But Jack, I'm concerned. If they're desperate enough to threaten you, they might try something more aggressive. Have you considered getting out of town for a few days?"

"And go where? Hiding doesn't stop them from targeting my family."

"True. But being a visible target doesn't help either." Mendoza's tone turned practical. "At minimum, vary your routines. Don't be predictable. And for God's sake, if anything happens - any confrontation, any threat - you call 911 first, then call me."

After they hung up, Ruby emerged from the bedroom dressed for work. She'd been taking time off, but her accounting clients still needed attention.

"I have to go to the office today," she said, reading Jack's expression. "Two client meetings I can't reschedule. But I'll be careful."

"Ruby, maybe you should work from home until this settles."

"I've been working from home. These are in-person meetings - small business owners who need quarterly reviews." She squeezed his hand. "I'll be fine. The office building has security. I'll park in the garage, take the elevator directly up. Nobody even knows I'm connected to this."

"They know. If they traced my phone records, if they've been following me, they know."

Ruby was quiet for a moment. "Okay. I'll tell my clients we're meeting virtually today. Not worth the risk."

Jack felt guilty for disrupting her work, but also relieved. "Thank you."

"Don't thank me for being smart." Ruby grabbed her laptop. "I'll set up in the living room. You should call your kids, check in."

Jack called Jennifer first. She answered on the first ring, voice tight.

"Everything okay?" he asked.

"Define okay. Sarah got harassed at school yesterday - some boys calling you a criminal, saying you belong in jail. She got into a shouting match defending you, almost got detention." Jennifer's frustration was evident. "Michael's being bullied online. Some kids from school created a group chat calling him 'son of a fraud' and posting memes about you."

Jack's hands tightened on his phone. "I'm sorry. This is my fault."

"It's not your fault that teenagers are cruel. But Jack, it's affecting them. Sarah's angry all the time. Michael's withdrawn. Emma keeps asking when things will go back to normal."

"Tell them it won't be much longer. The FBI is making arrests this week. Once Vaughn and the others are charged, the narrative changes."

"And if the arrests don't change the narrative? If people still think you're the villain?"

Jack didn't have a good answer for that. "Can I talk to them?"

"They're at school. I'll have them call you this afternoon." Jennifer softened slightly. "Jack, they love you. They believe in you. But watching their father get destroyed publicly is hard on them. Just... be aware of that."

After the call, Jack sat heavily on Ruby's couch. His children were suffering because he'd exposed fraud. Sarah fighting at school. Michael being cyberbullied. Emma's innocence being eroded by adult corruption.

The cost kept climbing.

His phone buzzed. A text from Paul Hendricks, his former IT colleague: *Heard about Monica. Be careful. They're panicking.*

Jack: *How do you know?*

Paul: *Still work there. Overheard Vaughn on phone this morning. He knows someone talked. Very angry.*

Jack: *Are you safe? If they think you helped me...*

Paul: *Keeping my head down. But Jack - watch yourself. Vaughn's not just angry. He's scared. Scared people do stupid things.*

Jack forwarded the exchange to Agent Reeves, who called within minutes.

"We're moving up the arrests," she said. "Tomorrow morning instead of Wednesday. Tuesday at 6 AM."

Simultaneous raids - Vaughn at his home, Marcus is in LA on business - flies back tomorrow morning

"Tomorrow? That's fast."

"We have enough evidence now. Monica's testimony, the documents from Marcus's safe, electronic communications - it's sufficient for prosecution. And frankly, the longer we wait, the more dangerous this gets." Reeves paused. "Where are you right now?"

"Ruby's apartment."

"Stay there today. Don't go out unless necessary. Tomorrow, after the arrests, you can resume normal activities. But for the next twenty-four hours, stay put."

Jack agreed, though staying put felt like hiding. After the call, he tried to focus on productive tasks - updating his resume, applying for jobs, researching new career possibilities. But concentration was impossible with the threat hanging overhead.

Ruby worked at the dining table, occasionally glancing over with concern. By lunchtime, she'd made sandwiches they ate in silence, both too tense to maintain casual conversation.

At two PM, Jack's phone rang. Helen.

"Are you alright?" she asked immediately. "I saw on the news that FBI raided someone's house. They're saying it's connected to your case."

"I'm fine, Mom. The FBI is making arrests tomorrow. This will be over soon."

"Over soon," Helen repeated skeptically. "Jack, even when arrests happen, there will be trials. Months or years of legal proceedings. Public testimony. Media attention. This isn't going to be over for a long time."

She was right. Jack had been thinking in terms of arrests as the finish line. But arrests were just the beginning of a much longer process.

"I know," he said quietly. "But at least the immediate danger should pass once they're in custody."

"Should." Helen's voice carried worry. "Please be careful. I can't lose you."

"You won't. I promise."

After they hung up, Jack felt the weight of everyone's fear pressing down. His mother worried he'd be killed. His children were suffering at school. Ruby had canceled work to stay safe. Jennifer and David were on high alert.

All because Jack had found evidence of crime and reported it.

The cost of doing right kept compounding.

His phone buzzed with a text from Sarah: *Dad, can I come stay with you this week? I hate school right now. Everyone sucks.*

Jack's heart broke a little. His sixteen-year-old daughter wanted to escape to him, not understanding that he was the least safe person to be near right now.

Jack: *Not this week, sweetheart. Things are complicated right now. But this weekend, definitely. We'll do something fun.*

Sarah: *Is it true what people are saying? That you stole company secrets and lied about fraud?*

Jack: *No. It's not true. The FBI wouldn't be arresting people if I'd lied. Trust that.*

Sarah: *I do trust you. I just wish everyone else did too.*

Jack: *Me too. Love you.*

Sarah: *Love you too.*

The afternoon dragged. Jack tried watching television but couldn't focus. Tried reading but the words blurred. Finally, he gave up and just sat on the balcony, watching the city move through its oblivious routines.

Ruby joined him eventually, bringing coffee.

"Tomorrow this time, Vaughn will be arrested," she said.

"Yeah."

"You'll be vindicated."

"Maybe. Or maybe people will still think I'm a disgruntled employee who got lucky that the FBI found something."

Ruby was quiet for a moment. "Does it matter? What people think?"

"It shouldn't. But when your kids are getting bullied at school because of what people think about you? Yeah, it matters."

"Fair point." Ruby sipped her coffee. "For what it's worth, I'm proud of you. Not just for exposing the fraud, but for holding it together through all of this. A lot of people would have cracked by now."

"I've come close."

"But you haven't. That counts."

They sat in comfortable silence as the afternoon faded toward evening. At six PM, Agent Reeves called with a final update.

"Everything's set for tomorrow. Arrest teams will move at six AM simultaneously. Vaughn, Marcus Chen, and three others. We'll have them in custody before most people are awake." She paused. "After the arrests, we'll issue a press statement. Media will know that federal charges have been filed, that the investigation confirmed substantial fraud. Your name will be cleared publicly."

"Thank you."

"Thank us by staying safe tonight. One more night, then this phase is over."

Jack and Ruby ordered dinner, ate while watching mindless television, and went to bed early. But sleep was elusive. Jack lay awake, mind churning through scenarios, calculating risks, worrying about everyone he couldn't protect.

At eleven PM, his phone buzzed with another text. Unknown number.

Enjoy your victory while it lasts. We know where your kids go to school.

Ice flooded Jack's veins. He sat up immediately, showing Ruby the message.

"Call Reeves," Ruby said, already reaching for her phone.

Jack called. Reeves answered groggily but snapped to alertness when he explained.

"Forward that immediately. We'll trace it, though it's probably another burner." Her voice turned hard. "This confirms they're targeting your family. I'm sending agents to your ex-wife's house right now. Protective detail until the arrests happen."

"Jennifer's going to freak out."

"Better freaked out than vulnerable. I'll call her myself, explain the situation." Reeves paused. "Mr. Mercer, we're less than seven hours from arrests. Can you hold out that long?"

"Do I have a choice?"

"Not really. But I need to know you're not going to do anything rash. No confronting anyone, no trying to handle this yourself."

"I won't."

"Good. Stay inside. Lock the doors. We have an agent watching your girlfriend's building. If anything happens, they'll respond immediately."

After hanging up, Jack went to every window in Ruby's apartment, checking locks, drawing curtains. Ruby watched from the couch, her expression tight.

"They're threatening your children," she said quietly.

"Yeah."

"Jack, if they actually try something—"

"They won't get the chance. Jennifer and David will keep them safe. The FBI is providing protection. And tomorrow morning, the people making threats will be in custody." He said it with more confidence than he felt.

His phone rang. Jennifer.

"FBI just called," she said without preamble. "They're sending agents to watch our house. Jack, what the hell is going on?"

"Someone threatened the kids. FBI is being cautious."

"Cautious?" Jennifer's voice rose. "There are federal agents outside my house because someone threatened my children. This is way beyond cautious!"

"Jen, I'm sorry. Tomorrow morning they're arresting everyone involved. This will be over."

"It better be. Because if anything happens to Sarah or Michael or Emma because of your whistleblowing—" She stopped, unable to finish the threat.

"Nothing will happen to them. I promise."

"You can't promise that." Her voice broke slightly. "Jack, I supported you exposing the fraud. I still do. But our children... they have to be the priority. Above everything else."

"They are. They always have been."

Jennifer was quiet for a long moment. "The FBI agent said we should keep them home from school tomorrow. That after arrests happen, the threat level drops. So they'll miss a day of school."

"Better than the alternative."

"Yeah." She exhaled heavily. "Call me after the arrests. Let me know it's really over."

After they hung up, Jack sat in the dark apartment, Ruby beside him, both of them too wired to sleep. The hours crawled past midnight, into the early morning. One AM. Two AM. Three AM.

At four-thirty, Jack gave up on sleep entirely. He made coffee, watched the predawn darkness gradually lighten, and waited for six AM.

At five forty-five, Agent Reeves texted: *Teams in position. Arrests happening in 15 minutes.*

Jack showed Ruby the message. They sat together on the couch, hands clasped, counting down the minutes.

Six AM came and went. Jack's phone stayed silent. Six-fifteen. Six-thirty.

At six forty-three, Reeves called.

"Vaughn is in custody. Arrested at his home without incident. Marcus Chen was taken at LAX when his flight landed - also cooperative." Her voice carried satisfaction. "Three other suspects arrested simultaneously. All in custody, all being processed. It's done."

Jack felt something release in his chest - relief so profound it was almost painful. "Thank you."

"We'll be issuing a press release within the hour. Multiple arrests, federal charges filed, investigation ongoing. Your name will be mentioned as the individual who brought the fraud to light." Reeves paused. "Mr. Mercer, you did good work. This was a significant criminal enterprise. Without your courage, they'd still be operating."

After the call, Jack pulled Ruby into a fierce hug. She held him tight, both of them shaking slightly with relief and exhaustion.

"It's over," she said.

"This part is." Jack thought about trials, testimony, the long legal road ahead. "But yeah. The immediate danger is over."

He called Jennifer immediately. She answered on the first ring.

"They got them," Jack said. "All arrested. Kids are safe."

Jennifer's exhale was audible. "Thank God. I've been awake all night imagining..." She didn't finish. "Okay. I'm telling the kids they can go to school. And Jack? Thank you. For keeping us informed, for being careful, for ending this."

"I didn't end it alone."

"No. But you started it. That took courage."

His children called throughout the morning - Sarah first, fierce and proud; Michael quiet but clearly relieved; Emma just wanting to know if she could go to school like normal.

By nine AM, the news had broken. Every local station was covering the arrests:

FBI ARRESTS FIVE IN MAJOR LOGISTICS FRAUD CASE

Charges include money laundering, wire fraud, conspiracy. Investigation began after whistleblower Jack Mercer reported irregularities...

The narrative was shifting. Jack wasn't a disgruntled employee anymore. He was the whistleblower who'd exposed a multi-million dollar criminal enterprise.

Katherine Mendoza called, practically euphoric. "This changes everything for our civil case. Federal criminal charges support all our allegations. The company will want to settle quickly before more damage is done."

Paul Hendricks texted: *Vaughn escorted out in handcuffs this morning. Everyone at the office in shock. You were right all along.*

Monica Chen called, her voice shaky. "I saw the news. Marcus has been arrested. I should feel vindicated but mostly I just feel sad. Eight years of marriage, gone."

"You did the right thing," Jack said.

"I know. Doesn't make it easier." She paused. "Thank you. For meeting me that day, for connecting me with the FBI. I couldn't have done this alone."

By afternoon, Jack felt like he could breathe properly for the first time in weeks. The threats had stopped. His children were safe. The arrests had happened cleanly, without violence.

He stood on Ruby's balcony, watching the city, and felt the accumulated tension finally beginning to drain away.

Ruby joined him. "How do you feel?"

"Tired. Relieved. Grateful." Jack pulled her close. "Scared of what comes next."

"Trials?"

"Yeah. Months of testimony, cross-examination, media attention. Having my entire investigation picked apart by defense lawyers."

"You'll handle it." Ruby's confidence was absolute. "You've handled everything else."

Jack's phone rang one more time. Agent Reeves.

"Thought you'd want to know - Derek Vaughn just lawyered up and is refusing to talk. But Marcus Chen is cooperating. Full confession in exchange for reduced sentence. He's giving us everything - the complete structure, everyone involved, all the financial details."

"What about Monica?"

"She'll likely avoid charges entirely in exchange for testimony. Spousal immunity plus her cooperation means prosecution would be difficult and probably pointless." Reeves paused. "Mr. Mercer, this case is going to be significant. Major prosecution, probably takes two years start to finish. You'll be a key witness. Are you prepared for that?"

"Do I have a choice?"

"Not really. But I wanted you to understand what you're committing to."

"I understand." Jack looked out at the city, at the life he'd disrupted in pursuit of principle. "I'm ready."

After they hung up, Jack stood in silence for a long moment. The immediate crisis had passed. His family was safe. The criminals were arrested.

But the real fight - the courtroom battle, the public scrutiny, the long march toward actual justice - was just beginning.

The shrapnel in his ribs ached faintly, a reminder that some wounds never fully healed, you just learned to carry them.

Old battles. New wars. Same fundamental truth: you fought for what mattered, and you paid whatever price that fight demanded.

Jack had paid plenty already.

He'd pay more before this was finished.

But standing on Ruby's balcony with her hand in his, knowing his children were safe and the criminals were in custody, he felt something he hadn't felt in weeks:

Hope.

Fragile, tentative, hard-won hope.

It would have to be enough.

For now, it was.

Chapter 15: Breathing Room

Monday morning brought the peculiar tension of waiting for violence you knew was coming but couldn't predict. Jack woke with Ruby's alarm, the threatening text from yesterday still vivid in his mind: *You've made a terrible mistake. This isn't over.*

Agent Reeves had called late last night on the secure line the FBI had provided - a basic prepaid phone used exclusively for case communication. The regular burner phones, untraceable, purchased with cash at a convenience store three days ago. Security footage showed a man in a baseball cap and sunglasses buying it. Could have been anyone.

"The Bureau is accelerating the timeline," Reeves had said. "We're preparing arrest warrants. Tomorrow morning. I can't say more even on this line, but be ready."

Tomorrow morning. Just hours away. The window during which cornered criminals knew they were exposed but hadn't yet been arrested was closing.

Jack made coffee while Ruby showered, his mind cataloging threats and vulnerabilities. His children were the obvious pressure point - Emma at elementary school, Michael at middle school, Sarah at high school. Jennifer and David knew to be vigilant, but vigilance only went so far against determined attackers.

Helen was in the rehab facility, which had controlled access but wasn't a fortress. Ruby's apartment building had security but nothing sophisticated. Jack's own apartment had reporters camped outside - ironically, their presence might actually deter anything violent.

His phone rang - his regular phone, not the FBI secure line. Katherine Mendoza.

"Morning," she said. "Saw the news. FBI executed a search warrant yesterday on Marcus Chen's residence. Media is connecting it to your whistleblower case."

"Yeah." Jack kept his answer vague, aware his regular phone was almost certainly monitored. "Things are moving forward."

"That's huge for our civil case." Mendoza's voice carried carefully controlled enthusiasm - she knew to be cautious on unsecured lines too. "We should talk later today. In person, at my office."

"I'll call you on a secure line to set that up."

After they hung up, Ruby emerged from the bedroom dressed casually. She'd been working from home all week, and today would be no different.

"Client meetings?" Jack asked.

Ruby pulled out her notepad, wrote: *Was going to go in. Changed my mind. Too risky.*

Jack nodded, relieved. They'd been communicating anything sensitive in writing, when they'd first suspected surveillance. The habit had become second nature.

His regular phone rang again. Jennifer.

"Morning," she said, voice tight. "How are things?"

"Hanging in there. You?"

"The kids are struggling. Sarah had issues at school yesterday - some boys giving her grief. Michael's getting bullied online. Emma just wants things to be normal again."

Jack felt his chest tighten. "I'm sorry. This should be resolved very soon. I can't say details on the phone, but soon."

"How soon is soon?"

"Very soon. Tell them to hang in there just a little longer." He paused. "Can I talk to them later today?"

"They're at school. Have them call you this afternoon." Jennifer softened slightly. "Jack, they love you. They believe in you. This is just hard on them."

"I know. It's hard on everyone."

After the call, Jack sat heavily on Ruby's couch. Ruby came over with her notepad: *Your kids okay?*

Jack took the pen: *Being bullied at school. Because of me.*

Ruby wrote: *Not because of you. Because of corruption you exposed. Big difference.*

Jack wanted to believe that, but the distinction felt academic when his children were suffering.

His regular phone buzzed with a text from Paul Hendricks: *Heard about the search warrant. People at the office are freaking out. Be careful.*

Jack texted back: *Thanks for the warning.*

The FBI secure phone rang. Jack stepped into the bedroom, closed the door.

"Mercer," he answered.

"It's Reeves. Status update - can't give specifics, but everything's on track for tomorrow morning, six AM. After that happens, the immediate threat level drops significantly."

"Understood."

"How are you holding up?"

"Been better. My kids are getting harassed at school because of this."

"I'm sorry. That's collateral damage we can't prevent." Reeves paused. "But after tomorrow, the narrative shifts completely. Your vindication will be public and undeniable."

"If we make it to tomorrow."

"You will. We have surveillance on your ex-wife's house, on this building, on your mother's facility. If anyone makes a move, we'll know."

After she hung up, Jack returned to the living room. Ruby looked up questioningly. He wrote on her notepad: *Tomorrow 6 AM. Then it's over.*

Ruby nodded, wrote back: *One more day. We can do one more day.*

The afternoon crawled. Jack tried to focus on job applications, on updating his resume, on anything productive. But concentration was impossible with the weight of tomorrow pressing down.

At two PM, his regular phone rang. Helen.

"Jack? Are you alright? I saw something on the news about FBI raids."

"I'm fine, Mom. Everything's moving in the right direction. I can't discuss details on the phone, but it should all be resolved very soon."

"How soon?"

"Very soon. Maybe even tomorrow." He caught himself - too specific. "I'll call you when I can explain everything."

"You're being careful?"

"Very careful. I promise."

Helen was quiet for a moment. "Your father used to say that the hardest part of doing the right thing wasn't the doing - it was waiting for people to realize you were right. Be patient, Jack. The truth will win."

"I hope so."

After they hung up, Jack felt the weight of everyone's fear and hope pressing on him. His mother's cautious optimism. His children's suffering. Jennifer's barely contained anxiety. Ruby's steady presence.

All of it depending on tomorrow going as planned.

His regular phone buzzed with a text from Sarah: *Dad, can I come stay with you this week? I hate school right now.*

Jack's heart broke a little. He texted back: *Not this week, sweetheart. But this weekend for sure. Things will be better by then. I promise.*

Sarah: *People are saying terrible things about you. I keep defending you but it's exhausting.*

Jack: *I know. I'm so sorry. Just a little longer and the truth will come out. Can you hang in there for me?*

Sarah: *I guess. Love you Dad.*

Jack: *Love you too. So much.*

Ruby came to sit beside him, saw his expression, and pulled out her notepad: *The kids?*

Jack wrote: *Sarah's exhausted from defending me. Michael's being cyberbullied. This is destroying them.*

Ruby wrote: *Tomorrow changes everything. The arrests will shift the narrative completely. They just need to survive one more day.*

Jack nodded, hoping she was right.

The afternoon faded into evening. Ruby made dinner - simple pasta, comfort food. They ate in near silence, both too tense for conversation. Even casual talk felt dangerous now, with the assumption that every word might be monitored.

At six PM, the FBI secure phone rang. Reeves again.

"Final briefing," she said. "Six AM tomorrow, simultaneous arrests. Five suspects total. After the arrests, we'll issue a public statement confirming charges have been filed. Your name will be mentioned as the whistleblower who brought this to light."

"Thank you."

"One more thing. We've intercepted some chatter suggesting they know something's coming. Stay inside tonight. Lock everything. We have agents watching, but don't take chances."

After the call, Jack went through Ruby's apartment methodically - checking every window lock, every door, drawing all the curtains. Ruby watched from the couch, her expression tight with controlled fear.

When he finished, she held up her notepad: *We're really in danger, aren't we?*

Jack wrote: *For the next 12 hours, yes. After the arrests, no.*

Ruby: *What if something goes wrong?*

Jack: *Then the FBI agents watching intervene. We're not alone.*

They tried to settle in for the evening, but both were too wired. Jack attempted to watch television but couldn't focus. Ruby opened a book, stared at the same page for twenty minutes.

At eleven PM, Jack's regular phone buzzed. Text message, unknown number:

Enjoy your victory while it lasts. We know where your kids go to school.

Jack's blood turned to ice. He showed the message to Ruby, who immediately grabbed the FBI secure phone and handed it to him.

Jack called Reeves. She answered on the second ring, alert despite the late hour.

"Someone just threatened my kids." Jack read the message word for word.

"Forward it immediately." Her voice was hard, controlled fury. "I'm dispatching protective details to your ex-wife's house right now. Full coverage until the arrests are complete."

"Jennifer's going to panic."

"Better panicked and safe than calm and vulnerable. I'll call her myself, explain the situation." Reeves paused. "Mr. Mercer, we're seven hours from arrests. Can you hold position that long?"

"Do I have a choice?"

"No. But I need to know you won't do anything stupid. No confronting anyone, no trying to handle this yourself. You stay inside, you let us do our job."

"I will."

"Good. I'm also increasing surveillance on your building. We'll have eyes on every entrance. If anyone approaches, we'll know."

After hanging up, Jack went to every window again, paranoid now, checking locks that were already checked. Ruby wrote on her notepad: *They threatened the kids.*

Jack wrote back: *FBI is protecting them. Jennifer's house has agents now.*

Ruby: *What if that's not enough?*

Jack didn't have an answer for that.

His regular phone rang. Jennifer, her voice shaking with controlled anger.

"FBI just called. They're sending agents to watch our house because someone threatened the kids?"

"I just got the text. I called it in immediately."

"Jack, this has gone too far. Our children—" Her voice broke. "If anything happens to them because you decided to be a hero—"

"Nothing will happen. The FBI is there. David is there. And very soon, everyone making threats will be dealt with.

"You keep saying 'soon.' What if it doesn't fix this?"

I can't say more on the phone."   "It will." Jack said it with more confidence than he felt. "Jen, I'm sorry. I never wanted this to touch the kids."

"But it has. It is." She took a shaky breath. "The FBI says we should keep them home from school tomorrow. That after arrests happen, the threat drops."

"That's smart."

"So they miss school, sit at home scared, while federal agents watch our house. This is insane, Jack."

"I know. But it's almost over."

After they hung up, Jack sat in the dark living room, Ruby beside him. She didn't try to write anything, didn't try to comfort him. Just sat close, solid, present.

The hours crawled. Midnight passed. One AM. Two AM. Three AM.

At four-thirty, Jack gave up on the pretense of sleep. He made coffee in the dark, watched the predawn gray slowly lighten the sky, and counted down the minutes to six AM.

Ruby joined him at five, wordless, handing him the FBI secure phone when it buzzed with a text at five forty-five: *Teams in position. Executing in 15.*

They sat on the couch together, hands clasped, watching the secure phone's screen. Six AM came and went. Six-fifteen. Six-thirty.

At six forty-three, the phone rang.

"It's done," Reeves said without preamble. "Vaughn arrested at his home without incident. Marcus Chen arrested at his residence -

tried to flee out the back but was apprehended. Three other suspects in custody. All being processed now."

Jack felt something release in his chest - relief so profound it made him dizzy. "Thank you."

"We're issuing the press release in twenty minutes. Multiple arrests, federal charges, ongoing investigation. Your role as whistleblower will be prominently mentioned." Reeves paused. "You did it, Mr. Mercer. You exposed a major criminal operation and survived to see justice done."

After the call, Jack pulled Ruby close. She was shaking - adrenaline, relief, exhaustion all at once. They held each other in silence, too wrung out for words.

Jack's regular phone rang. Jennifer.

"They got them?" Her voice was desperate, hopeful.

"All of them. Arrested this morning. It's over."

Jennifer's exhale was audible, shaky. "Thank God. I've been sitting here with David and a baseball bat, watching the front door, terrified someone would..." She didn't finish. "Okay. I'm telling the kids they're safe. That they can go to school tomorrow. That it's really over."

"It's really over. The immediate danger, anyway."

"And Jack? Thank you. For warning us, for keeping us informed, for... for finishing this."

"I couldn't have done it alone."

"Maybe not. But you started it. That took more courage than I think I understood until now."

His children called throughout the morning - Sarah fierce and vindicated, Michael quietly relieved, Emma just happy she could go back to school. By nine AM, the news had broken everywhere:

FBI ARRESTS FIVE IN MAJOR CORPORATE FRAUD CASE

Federal charges filed against logistics company executives. Investigation began with whistleblower Jack Mercer...

The narrative had shifted completely. Jack wasn't a disgruntled employee anymore. He was the person who'd exposed a multi-million dollar criminal enterprise.

Katherine Mendoza called, barely containing her excitement. "This changes everything for the civil case. The company will want to settle immediately before more damage comes out."

Paul Hendricks texted: News is showing Vaughn being arrested at his home. Everyone at the office watching in shock. You were right all along.

Monica Chen called, her voice thick with tears. "Marcus was arrested. Eight years of marriage, ended because I did the right thing. I know it was right. But it still hurts."

"I know," Jack said. "Doing right doesn't make it painless."

"No. But at least I can live with myself now."

By afternoon, Jack stood on Ruby's balcony, watching the city, feeling the accumulated tension of weeks finally beginning to drain. Ruby joined him, wrote on her notepad even though they were probably safe now: *How do you feel?*

Jack took the pen: *Tired. Relieved. Scared of what comes next.*

Ruby: *Trials?*

Jack: *Years of them. But at least the immediate danger is over.*

The FBI secure phone rang one last time. Reeves.

"Wanted to update you - Vaughn lawyered up immediately, refusing to cooperate. But Marcus Chen is singing like a canary. Full confession, complete cooperation, giving us everything in exchange for reduced sentence."

"And Monica?"

"Will likely face no charges. Her cooperation and spousal immunity make prosecution pointless." Reeves paused. "Mr. Mercer, this case will probably take two years to fully prosecute. You'll be a key witness. Multiple court appearances, depositions, testimony. Are you prepared for that?"

Jack looked out at the city, at the life he'd disrupted for principle. "Yes. I'm ready."

After she hung up, Jack stood in silence. The arrests were done. His family was safe. The criminals were in custody.

But the real fight - courtroom battles, public scrutiny, years of legal proceedings - was just beginning.

The shrapnel in his ribs ached faintly. Old wounds. New wars. Same truth: you fought for what mattered and paid whatever price it demanded.

Jack had paid plenty already.

He'd pay more before this was finished.

But standing on Ruby's balcony, knowing his children were safe and justice was beginning, he felt something he hadn't felt in weeks:

Hope.

Fragile, hard-won, real hope.

It would have to be enough.

For now, it was.

Chapter 16: The Offensive

The week after the arrests felt like living in a different world. Jack woke Tuesday morning in Ruby's apartment, sunlight streaming through windows they no longer kept curtained. No more threats. No more surveillance anxiety. Just the ordinary quiet of a weekday morning.

The news coverage had been relentless but favorable. Every local station led with the story: FBI arrests in major fraud case, whistleblower vindicated, charges filed. Jack's employee photo appeared alongside headlines that called him "courageous" instead of "disgruntled."

His phone - the regular one, not the FBI secure line - had been ringing constantly. Reporters requesting interviews. Former colleagues reaching out to apologize or offer support. Strangers sending encouragement.

Katherine Mendoza had called Monday afternoon with news that Regional Logistics Solutions wanted to settle the whistleblower retaliation lawsuit. "They're offering two years' salary plus legal fees," she'd said. "I think we can get more, but it's a serious opening offer."

Jack had told her to negotiate. He wasn't in a hurry to settle - not when the criminal trial would provide additional evidence to support his civil case.

But this morning, Tuesday, he needed to start thinking about practical matters. Like finding a job. Like resuming some version of normal life.

Ruby was already up, dressed for actual work - her first day back at the office since the arrests. She came out of the bedroom looking both relieved and nervous.

"You sure you're ready to go in?" Jack asked.

"I have to sometime. Clients are piling up. And honestly, I need normalcy." She grabbed her keys. "What are you doing today?"

"Job hunting, I guess. Updating Linkedin. Maybe reaching out to some contacts in the industry."

Ruby kissed him. "You'll find something good. Companies love hiring whistleblowers - shows integrity."

"Or shows I'm a liability who'll report any wrongdoing I find."

"Depends on whether they're doing anything wrong." She smiled. "I'll be home by six. We can actually go out to dinner if you want. Like normal people."

After she left, Jack sat with his coffee and laptop, staring at job search websites. Risk Compliance Analyst positions were plentiful, but applying felt strange. Would companies see him as an asset or a threat? Would his whistleblower status make him unemployable in the industry he knew?

His phone rang. Jennifer.

"Hey," he answered. "Everything okay?"

"Better than okay. Sarah's school called - apparently some of the kids who were giving her grief apologized yesterday. Said they'd seen the news and realized they'd been wrong about you." Jennifer's voice carried surprised pleasure. "And Michael's online bullying stopped completely. Kids who were posting memes are deleting them."

"That's good. Really good."

"Emma wants to know when she can see you. I told her this weekend like normal, but she's impatient."

Jack smiled. "Tell her Saturday. We'll do something fun. Maybe that science museum she's been asking about."

"She'll love that." Jennifer paused. "Jack, I'm sorry I snapped at you during the worst of it. When the FBI showed up at my house and the threats came, I was terrified. I said some things I didn't mean."

"You were protecting our kids. You had every right to be angry."

"Maybe. But you were right to see it through. Some things are worth fighting for, even when the cost is high." Her voice softened. "The kids are proud of you. I'm proud of you. You did something hard and important."

After they hung up, Jack felt something settle in his chest. His children were recovering. The public narrative had shifted. Life was beginning to normalize.

The FBI secure phone rang - he still had it, though Reeves said he could return it eventually.

"Mercer," he answered.

"It's Reeves. Quick update - Marcus Chen's cooperation is yielding significant results. He's giving us details on the entire operation, plus names of people we hadn't identified yet. We're building cases against at least three more suspects."

"How long until trial?"

"For Vaughn and the main defendants? Probably eighteen months. Grand jury indictment should come within two months, then pretrial motions, discovery, the usual process." Reeves paused. "You'll be called to testify multiple times - grand jury, possibly pretrial hearings, definitely at trial. Are you employed right now?"

"No. Looking for work."

"You might want to consider consulting work or contract positions. Something flexible that won't conflict with court appearances."

"Great. So my whistleblowing made me unemployable in regular positions."

"Not unemployable. Just complicated." Reeves's tone carried sympathy. "Look, I know this isn't what you signed up for. But you did the right thing, and eventually the industry will recognize that."

After the call, Jack returned to job searching with new parameters. Contract positions. Consulting roles. Anything that offered flexibility and wouldn't demand full-time commitment during an eighteen-month trial.

At noon, his regular phone rang. Unknown number. Jack hesitated, then answered cautiously.

"Mr. Mercer? This is David Wallace from Pacific Compliance Group."

They talked for twenty minutes. Wallace explained that Pacific Compliance worked with companies

We're a consulting firm specializing in corporate risk management and fraud prevention. I'm calling to see if you might be interested in discussing opportunities with us."

Jack's pulse quickened. "What kind of opportunities?"

"We help companies build ethical compliance programs and investigate potential fraud. Given your recent... visibility in the news, we think you'd be an asset. Your experience finding and reporting corporate fraud is exactly what our clients need."

They talked for twenty minutes. Wallace explained that Pacific Compliance worked with companies that wanted to avoid becoming the next Regional Logistics Solutions - firms that hired consultants to independently review their operations and identify problems before they became criminal investigations.

"We're looking for someone with your expertise and, frankly, your credibility. A consultant who exposed twelve million in fraud and testified against his own employer? That sends a message to our clients that we're serious about finding problems." Wallace paused. "The position would be contract-based, flexible hours, project-to-project work. Pay is competitive - probably better than your previous salary. Interested?"

"Very," Jack said. "When can we meet?"

They scheduled an interview for Thursday. After hanging up, Jack felt cautiously optimistic. A job that valued his whistleblowing rather than viewing it as a liability. Work that would let him testify without conflicts. Income that would ease the financial pressure.

He called Ruby to share the news. She answered on the second ring, her voice bright.

"That's amazing! See? I told you companies would want to hire you."

"It's just an interview. And it's contract work, not permanent."

"Contract work with flexibility and good pay sounds perfect for your situation. Take the interview, see what they offer." She lowered her voice slightly. "I'm proud of you, Jack. You're rebuilding already."

That afternoon, Jack drove to Helen's rehabilitation facility. She'd progressed enough to move to outpatient therapy, living in a senior apartment complex with support services. He found her in her new living room, walking with only a cane now, her speech almost back to normal.

"Look at you," Jack said, hugging her carefully. "Practically ready to run marathons."

"Don't push it." Helen gestured to the couch. "Sit. Tell me everything."

Jack filled her in - the arrests, the job interview, the kids recovering from their ordeal. Helen listened with the focused attention she'd always given, asking sharp questions, offering harder truths.

"What about Ruby?" she asked finally. "You two still together through all this?"

"Yeah. She's been..." Jack struggled for words. "She's been everything. I couldn't have survived this without her."

"Then maybe it's time to make that official."

Jack blinked. "Official how?"

"However you want. Move in together. Get engaged. Stop pretending you're just dating when clearly you've been through the kind of crisis that either destroys relationships or cements them." Helen smiled. "She stood by you through unemployment, death threats, and federal investigations. That woman's not going anywhere."

"We've only been together eight months."

"Your father and I got married after six months. When you know, you know." Helen's expression turned serious. "Jack, you've spent three years since the divorce being cautious. Being careful. Making sure everything was perfect before committing. But life isn't perfect. Relationships aren't perfect. Sometimes you just have to trust that what you have is worth building on."

After leaving Helen's apartment, Jack drove aimlessly for a while, thinking about what she'd said. Ruby had stood by him through everything. Had risked her own safety and career to help him. Had welcomed his children into her home during crisis without hesitation.

Maybe Helen was right. Maybe it was time to stop being cautious and start building something permanent.

He stopped at a jewelry store - not to buy anything, just to look. The rings were beautiful and expensive and terrifying in what they represented. Commitment. Permanence. Choosing to build a life with someone.

"Can I help you?" A saleswoman approached, professional and perceptive.

"Just looking," Jack said. "Maybe. I don't know."

"Thinking about proposing?"

"Thinking about thinking about it."

The woman smiled. "That's usually how it starts. Want to see some options? No pressure, just browsing."

She showed him rings - simple bands, elaborate settings, diamonds and sapphires and everything in between. Jack found himself drawn to a platinum band with a modest diamond, elegant without being ostentatious. Classic. The kind of ring Ruby would actually wear.

"How much?" he asked.

The price made him wince. But he had savings. And if the settlement came through, he'd have more. And the consulting job might pay well.

"I'll think about it," he said.

"Of course. Here's my card. When you're ready, I'm here."

He left the jewelry store feeling unmoored, uncertain, hopeful. Marriage felt like a huge step. But Helen was right - he and Ruby had already been through trials that would test any relationship. If they could survive whistleblowing and death threats, they could probably handle normal married life.

That evening, Ruby came home from work energized and talkative. Her clients had been supportive, her day productive, normalcy restored.

"How was your day?" she asked, kicking off her shoes.

"Good. Got a job interview Thursday. Consulting firm that wants to hire me specifically because I'm a whistleblower."

"That's fantastic!" Ruby hugged him. "See? Everything's coming together."

They went out to dinner - their first restaurant meal in weeks. A quiet Italian place, candlelight and wine and normal conversation about work and family and plans for the weekend. No encrypted communications. No security paranoia. Just two people enjoying each other's company.

As they walked back to Ruby's apartment afterward, Jack's hand in hers, he thought about the ring. About Helen's advice. About whether he was ready to ask the question that would change everything.

Not tonight. But soon.

Maybe after the job interview. After he had income secured. After a few more pieces fell into place.

Or maybe he was just being cautious again, overthinking what should be simple.

Ruby looked at him curiously. "You're quiet. What are you thinking about?"

"The future," Jack said. "What comes next."

"What do you want to come next?"

Jack thought about that - about trials and testimony and rebuilding his career. About his children and his mother and the life he'd fought so hard to protect. About the woman walking beside him who'd chosen to stand with him through it all.

"I want things to keep getting better," he said finally. "I want the trial to go well. I want to find good work. I want my kids to be happy."

"And what do you want for us?" Ruby asked quietly.

Jack stopped walking, turned to face her on the sidewalk. "I want us to build something real. Something lasting. I want..." He struggled to articulate feelings that felt too big for words. "I want what we have to become what we're building toward."

Ruby studied his face, understanding passing between them without need for elaboration. "Me too."

They walked the rest of the way in comfortable silence, hands linked, future possibilities hovering unspoken but present.

Back at the apartment, Jack's FBI secure phone rang. Reeves again.

"Sorry to call late. We've got a situation developing. One of the suspects arrested Monday - not Vaughn or Marcus, one of the others - just made bail. He's out as of two hours ago."

Jack felt his stomach drop. "Who?"

"Thomas Kirkland. He was the customs liaison who facilitated the smuggling. Lower-level player, but he has connections to some dangerous people." Reeves paused. "We don't think he's an immediate threat, but I wanted you to be aware. Stay alert, vary your routines, keep your phone close."

"I thought it was over."

"The immediate crisis is over. But until trial, there are still people who might want to intimidate witnesses or retaliate." Her voice carried professional reassurance. "We're monitoring Kirkland. If he approaches you or your family, we'll know. Just be smart."

After hanging up, Jack told Ruby what Reeves had said. She absorbed it with the same calm pragmatism she'd shown throughout the crisis.

"So we're careful again for a while," she said. "We can do that."

"I'm tired of being careful. I want to just live normally."

"Then we do both. We live normally and we stay alert. It's not forever, Jack. Just until trial."

Eighteen months. Jack thought about eighteen months of looking over his shoulder, varying routines, staying alert for threats. It felt exhausting and necessary in equal measure.

But standing in Ruby's apartment, safe and together, he realized something important: he could do eighteen months of caution if it meant getting to the other side. He'd already survived the worst. Everything from here was just endurance.

And he was good at endurance.

Vietnam had taught him that. Divorce had reinforced it. Whistleblowing had proven it.

He could outlast this too.

Jack pulled Ruby close, feeling her warmth and steadiness, and allowed himself to believe that the hard part was really, finally over.

The shrapnel in his ribs was quiet tonight - old wounds resting, old battles receding into memory.

New challenges would come. Trials. Testimony. Eighteen months of legal proceedings.

But for tonight, in this moment, he was safe. His family was safe. The criminals were caught.

That was enough.

Tomorrow would bring its own complications.

Tonight, he just held the woman he loved and let himself breathe.

Chapter 17: Rebuilding

Thursday morning arrived with the crisp clarity of late November, the kind of day that promised normalcy - job interviews, coffee meetings, ordinary life resuming its ordinary patterns. Jack dressed carefully for his interview with Pacific Compliance Group, choosing a suit that projected competence without arrogance. Professional. Credible. The kind of person companies would trust to find their problems.

Ruby had already left for work, her schedule packed with client meetings she'd postponed during the crisis. The apartment felt empty but peaceful, no longer the bunker it had been just days ago.

Jack's regular phone buzzed with a text from David Wallace: *Looking forward to meeting you at 11. Our office is in the Riverside Building, Suite 420.*

Jack confirmed, then checked the FBI secure phone. No new messages from Reeves. No alerts about Thomas Kirkland's movements. Maybe Kirkland really was just lying low, trying to stay out of trouble until his trial.

Or maybe he was planning something the FBI hadn't detected yet.

Jack pushed the thought away. He couldn't live in constant paranoia. The arrests had happened. The immediate threat was over. Life had to move forward.

He grabbed his car keys - his own car this time, not Ruby's Subaru. The reporters had finally left his apartment building, bored once the arrests became old news. Jack drove through familiar streets, watching the city move through its Thursday routines, feeling almost normal for the first time in weeks.

The Riverside Building was downtown, a modern structure with corporate tenants and the kind of sterile professionalism that suggested success without personality. Jack found parking in the garage, took the elevator to the fourth floor, and entered Suite 420 at exactly eleven AM.

Pacific Compliance Group's office was modest but well-appointed - clean lines, contemporary furniture, walls covered with certifications and industry awards. A receptionist greeted him warmly and directed him to a conference room where David Wallace was already waiting.

Wallace was in his fifties, gray hair and sharp eyes, the kind of presence that suggested competence earned through decades of experience. He stood and extended his hand.

"Mr. Mercer. Thank you for coming."

"Thank you for the opportunity."

They settled into the interview - Wallace asking about Jack's background, his compliance experience, his investigative methodology. The questions were sharp but fair, probing Jack's technical knowledge while carefully acknowledging the whistleblower situation without dwelling on it.

"What interests me most," Wallace said after thirty minutes, "is how you identified patterns that others missed. You weren't investigating fraud specifically when you found it. You were doing routine compliance work and noticed irregularities. That's the skill we need - people who see what shouldn't be there."

Jack walked him through the discovery process - the initial suspicions, the careful data analysis, the decision points about when to investigate deeper versus when to escalate. Wallace listened with the attention of someone who understood exactly what Jack was describing.

"Our clients need someone who can do that same kind of analysis but for them proactively. Find problems before they become criminal investigations. Would that interest you?"

"Very much."

"Good. Let me show you what we do."

Wallace spent the next hour explaining Pacific Compliance's model - contract engagements with companies that wanted independent compliance audits, fraud risk assessments, ethics program development. The work was project-based, flexible hours, well-paid. Exactly what Jack needed.

"I'd like to offer you a position," Wallace said finally. "Contract basis to start, with possibility of partnership if things work out. Starting rate is one-fifty an hour, minimum twenty billable hours per week. Most consultants bill thirty to forty hours depending on projects. Interested?"

Jack did the math quickly. Even at minimum hours, that was better than his previous salary. At full engagement, it was significantly better.

"Very interested."

"Excellent. I'll have our legal team draw up the contract. You could start as early as next week if you're available." Wallace extended his hand again. "Welcome to Pacific Compliance."

They shook, finalizing details about onboarding, first projects, administrative logistics. By the time Jack left the office at twelve-thirty, he had a new career path and renewed optimism about the future.

He texted Ruby immediately: *Got the job. Contract consultant, good pay, flexible hours. Starting next week.*

Ruby: *That's amazing! Celebratory dinner tonight?*

Jack: *Definitely. I'll make reservations.*

He was heading toward the elevator, mind already planning where to take Ruby for dinner, when a man stepped out of the stairwell and blocked his path.

Thomas Kirkland.

Jack recognized him from news coverage of the arrests - mid-forties, average height, the kind of forgettable face that worked well for someone facilitating smuggling operations. But there was nothing forgettable about the rage in his eyes.

"Jack Mercer," Kirkland said quietly. "We need to talk."

Jack's combat training kicked in automatically - assess threat level, identify exits, calculate response options. They were alone in the hallway. The elevator was ten feet behind Kirkland. The stairwell door was closer but led to an enclosed space. The receptionist at Pacific Compliance couldn't see them from this angle.

"I don't think we do," Jack said, keeping his voice level.

"Oh, we definitely do." Kirkland moved closer, not quite threatening but invading Jack's personal space deliberately. "You destroyed my life. Cost me my career, my freedom, my reputation. Because you decided to play hero."

"I reported crimes. That's not playing hero, that's following the law."

"You reported *alleged* crimes. You ruined people's lives over allegations." Kirkland's voice rose slightly. "My trial is eighteen months away. Eighteen months of my life in limbo because you couldn't mind your own business."

Jack kept his hands visible, non-threatening, but shifted his weight to be ready if Kirkland escalated to violence. "You facilitated smuggling and money laundering. That's not my allegation, that's what the evidence shows."

"Evidence you stole. Company data you accessed illegally."

"Evidence I obtained through my job responsibilities and reported to federal authorities. Nothing illegal about that."

Kirkland's jaw tightened. "You think you're safe now? You think because Vaughn and Marcus are locked up, this is over?"

"I think you're out on bail and talking to a prosecution witness, which violates the conditions of your release. The FBI is probably listening to this conversation right now." Jack pulled out his phone slowly, deliberately. "I can call Agent Reeves if you'd like to discuss this with federal supervision."

"Put the phone down."

"No."

Kirkland's hand moved toward his jacket pocket. Jack reacted on instinct - stepped inside Kirkland's reach, trapped the arm before it could draw whatever was in the pocket, and used Kirkland's own momentum to drive him back against the wall. The moves came from muscle memory, combat training drilled into him forty years ago in the Navy.

Kirkland struggled, but Jack had position and leverage. He pinned Kirkland's arm, reached into the jacket pocket, and pulled out not a gun but a folded envelope.

"What's this?" Jack asked, maintaining control.

"Read it," Kirkland spat. "Go ahead. Read what's going to happen to you and your family if you testify."

Jack kept Kirkland pinned with one hand, opened the envelope with the other. Inside was a single page, typed text:

Drop the charges or your children pay the price. Emma Mercer, Riverside Elementary School. Michael Mercer, Hamilton Middle School. Sarah Mercer, Westside High School. We know where they are. We know their schedules. Drop the charges or we make them disappear.

Ice flooded Jack's veins. His grip on Kirkland tightened involuntarily, combat instinct warring with legal restraint. He wanted to break this man's arm. Wanted to put him on the ground permanently. Wanted to eliminate the threat the way he'd been trained to do.

But he wasn't in Vietnam. This wasn't a war zone. And Jack wasn't twenty-two anymore.

"You just threatened to kidnap my children," Jack said, his voice deadly quiet. "That's a federal crime. Witness intimidation, conspiracy, terroristic threats. You're going to prison for a very long time."

"I'm already going to prison because of you!" Kirkland struggled again. "At least this way, you suffer too!"

Jack pulled out his phone - the FBI secure line - and called Reeves, still maintaining control of Kirkland.

She answered immediately. "Mercer, what's wrong?"

"Thomas Kirkland just confronted me at the Riverside Building, fourth floor. He physically threatened me and delivered written threats against my children. I have him detained. I need FBI response now."

"On the way. Stay on the line. Don't let him go."

Jack could hear Reeves coordinating over radio, agents mobilizing, response teams moving. The elevator dinged. Two FBI agents emerged, weapons drawn, moving with practiced efficiency.

"Jack Mercer?" the lead agent confirmed.

"That's me. This is Thomas Kirkland. He just threatened to kidnap my children." Jack handed over the envelope. "Written threat. He admitted to it verbally. I have him detained but haven't harmed him beyond necessary restraint."

The agents took over, cuffing Kirkland professionally while reading his rights. Kirkland was shouting now, claiming Jack had attacked him, that this was entrapment, that his lawyer would destroy everyone.

The lead agent looked at Jack. "You okay? Injured?"

"I'm fine. He didn't get a chance to hurt me."

"Did you hurt him?"

"Restrained only. Standard defensive techniques. Nothing excessive."

They took Kirkland away, still shouting threats. David Wallace had emerged from Pacific Compliance's office, along with his receptionist, both looking shaken.

"Mr. Mercer, are you alright?" Wallace asked. "Should I call security?"

"FBI's here. I'm fine." Jack took a shaky breath. "I'm sorry you had to witness that."

"Don't apologize. You handled it... impressively. Military training?"

"Navy. A long time ago."

Wallace studied him for a moment. "The job offer stands, Mr. Mercer. Obviously this situation complicates things, but if anything, it confirms you can handle pressure. We'll talk next week once things settle."

Agent Reeves arrived twenty minutes later, taking Jack's statement in detail. The building's security cameras had captured everything - Kirkland approaching, the confrontation, Jack's defensive restraint, the threat delivery.

"He violated bail conditions by approaching you," Reeves said. "The written threat against your children is a separate federal charge. His lawyer can scream entrapment all he wants, but this was his choice, his action, captured on video."

"What about my kids? That threat—"

"We're placing protective details at all three schools. Immediate response. And Kirkland's bail is being revoked. He'll be back in custody within the hour, and this time there's no bail. He's done."

Jack felt the adrenaline starting to fade, leaving exhaustion in its wake. "He said this wasn't over. That Vaughn and Marcus being arrested didn't end it."

"He's right that the organization is bigger than we initially realized. We've identified three more suspects based on Marcus Chen's cooperation. But Jack, they're scared now. Desperate. That makes them dangerous but also sloppy. This stunt Kirkland just pulled? That's desperation. And it just bought him five more federal charges."

After giving his statement, Jack sat in his car in the parking garage for a long time, hands shaking with delayed reaction. He'd been in a physical confrontation. Had pinned a suspect. Had received direct threats against his children.

And his first instinct had been violence. Not restraint, not calling for help - pure combat response, honed four decades ago and still living in his muscle memory.

The shrapnel in his ribs ached sharply, reminding him of other times when violence had been the answer, when eliminating threats was the mission.

But he'd controlled it. Had used only necessary force. Had ended the confrontation without serious injury to anyone.

That had to count for something.

He called Jennifer. She answered immediately, hearing something in his voice.

"What happened?"

Jack explained - the confrontation, the threats, the FBI response. Jennifer's breathing turned sharp and panicked.

"They threatened to kidnap our children? Jack, this is—"

"FBI is putting protective details at all three schools right now. The man who made the threats is being taken back into custody. His bail is revoked. He can't get near the kids."

"Can't or shouldn't? Because there's a difference!"

"Jennifer, I'm scared too. But the FBI is taking this seriously. The schools will have agents watching. Kirkland is going back to jail. We're doing everything possible."

"Is it enough?" Her voice broke. "Is it ever enough when people are threatening to kidnap your children?"

Jack didn't have a good answer. "I don't know. But it's all we can do right now."

After they hung up, Jack called each of his children - Sarah first, then Michael, then Emma. He explained without creating panic, told them about the extra security at school, promised them they were safe.

Emma cried. Michael went quiet in the way that meant he was processing. Sarah got angry, wanting to know why bad people got to keep threatening them even after being arrested.

"Because the justice system is slow," Jack told her. "Because bail exists even for people who shouldn't get it. Because the world isn't fair or just, it just is."

"I hate this," Sarah said.

"Me too, sweetheart. Me too."

By the time Jack finished the calls, it was mid-afternoon. He drove to Ruby's office, needing to see her, to ground himself in something solid after the morning's chaos.

She came downstairs immediately when he texted, took one look at his face, and pulled him into a fierce hug in the parking lot.

"Reeves called me," she said. "Told me what happened. Are you okay?"

"Physically, yes. Emotionally..." Jack struggled to articulate the complicated tangle of fear, anger, and residual combat adrenaline. "I almost hurt him badly, Ruby. When he threatened my kids, I wanted to break his arm. Wanted to put him down permanently. The instinct was so strong."

"But you didn't. You controlled it."

"Barely."

Ruby pulled back, looked at him directly. "Jack, you were attacked by a desperate criminal who threatened your children. Having violent instincts in that situation is normal. What matters is that you controlled them. You used only necessary force. You handled it exactly right."

"It didn't feel right. It felt dangerous."

"Dangerous to who? To Kirkland? Good. He should be scared of you." Ruby's voice turned fierce. "You're not a violent man, Jack. But you're a protective father with combat training. Those two things aren't contradictory. They're why your kids are still safe."

Jack wanted to believe that. Wanted to accept that his violence was justified, controlled, appropriate. But the line between controlled violence and excessive force felt thinner than he'd like.

They sat in Ruby's car in the parking garage, Jack gradually coming down from the adrenaline high, Ruby's presence anchoring him back to normalcy.

"I got the job," Jack said eventually. "Before Kirkland showed up, Wallace offered me the position."

"That's good. Really good." Ruby squeezed his hand. "See? Good things are still happening. You're not just surviving anymore, you're rebuilding."

"Feels like I'm still just surviving."

"Then we survive together. That's all we can do."

That evening, after Ruby finished work, they went to Jack's apartment instead of hers. He needed to be in his own space, surrounded by his own things, reclaiming the normalcy that kept getting disrupted.

The apartment felt stale from disuse but comfortingly familiar. Jack opened windows, let in fresh air, and tried to settle back into the life he'd built before whistleblowing had blown it apart.

Agent Reeves called at seven PM with updates.

"Kirkland is back in custody, no bail this time. We've also arrested two associates of his - people who helped draft the threat letter. We're building a conspiracy case that should put all of them away for a long time."

"What about the other suspects Marcus Chen identified?"

"Three more arrests coming next week. We're being methodical, building solid cases before we move. But Jack, I won't lie to you - this is going to drag out. More arrests mean more trials, more testimony from you, more opportunities for desperate people to try desperate things."

"So I'm looking over my shoulder for the next eighteen months?"

"Not constantly. But yes, you need to stay alert. Vary routines. Keep the secure phone close. Report anything suspicious immediately." Reeves paused. "For what it's worth, what you did today was textbook. You controlled a dangerous situation, didn't escalate beyond necessity, and gave us another criminal to prosecute. That's good work."

After she hung up, Jack sat with Ruby on his couch, the city lights visible through the window, life moving forward in its ordinary patterns below.

"Eighteen months," Jack said. "That's how long until trial. Eighteen months of this."

"We can do eighteen months."

"Can we? Really? Because I'm exhausted and it's only been a few weeks since the arrests. How do I do eighteen months of protective details and security paranoia and threats against my family?"

Ruby turned to face him. "The same way you did Vietnam. The same way you survived your divorce. The same way you've survived everything else - one day at a time, with people who love you helping carry the weight."

Jack pulled her close, feeling her warmth and steadiness, and tried to believe it was possible. Eighteen months wasn't forever. It was finite. Survivable.

He'd survived worse.

The shrapnel in his ribs ached steadily - old wounds that never fully healed but taught him he could carry pain and keep moving forward anyway.

Tomorrow he'd call Pacific Compliance and confirm his start date. He'd coordinate with the FBI about security protocols. He'd check in with his children and his mother and everyone affected by his choice to fight corruption.

But tonight, he just sat with Ruby in his reclaimed apartment and breathed.

One day survived.

Eighteen months to go.

He could do this.

He had to.

Because the alternative - surrendering to fear, letting corruption win, teaching his children that threats worked - was unacceptable.

So he'd endure. He'd adapt. He'd survive.

Just like he always had.

Just like he always would.

Chapter 18: The Wait

The weekend arrived with the complicated relief of crisis survived but not resolved. Jack spent Saturday with his children at the science museum Emma had requested, FBI protective detail following at a discrete distance. The agents were good at their jobs - invisible enough that the kids could almost forget they were being watched, present enough that Jack felt marginally safer.

Emma was fascinated by the geology exhibits, Michael gravitated toward the space exploration displays, and Sarah spent most of the time on her phone but claimed she was having fun anyway. Normal teenage behavior that felt like a gift after weeks of crisis.

They had lunch at the museum café, the kids arguing good-naturedly about whether astronauts or deep-sea explorers faced more danger. Jack watched them, memorizing these ordinary moments, knowing they were precious specifically because they'd almost been taken away.

"Dad, you're staring," Sarah said, not looking up from her phone.

"Just enjoying watching you three be yourselves."

"That's weird."

"I'm a dad. Weird is part of the job description."

Michael grinned. Emma launched into an enthusiastic explanation of plate tectonics that demonstrated she'd actually been paying attention to the exhibits. Sarah rolled her eyes but listened, and Jack felt something settle in his chest.

His children were okay. Shaken, but recovering. The bullying at school had stopped once the arrests made news. The cyberbullying had evaporated. People who'd been cruel were now apologetic or silent.

Public vindication had its benefits.

After the museum, Jack drove them back to Jennifer's house. David answered the door, greeted the kids warmly, then gestured for Jack to step inside for a moment.

"Jennifer wanted me to talk to you," David said quietly once the kids had scattered upstairs. "She's worried about you. Says you're holding it together for everyone else but not dealing with your own stress."

Jack felt defensive instinct rise, then forced it down. David was trying to help, not criticize.

"I'm managing," Jack said.

"Are you? Because from an outside perspective, you've been unemployed for two weeks, threatened multiple times, physically confronted by a suspect, and you're facing eighteen months of being a prosecution witness while trying to rebuild your career and maintain custody schedules." David's tone was kind but direct. "That's a lot for anyone to manage."

"What's your point?"

"My point is that Jennifer and I want to help. If you need the kids to stay here more while you get settled in your new job, that's fine. If you need someone to talk to about the stress, I've got a therapist I can recommend. If you need anything - anything - you ask." David met his eyes. "We're not enemies, Jack. We're co-parents. Your wellbeing affects the kids. Let us help."

Jack felt something loosen slightly. "Thank you. Really. I'll... I'll think about the therapist recommendation."

"Good. And Jack? You did the right thing. Exposing the fraud, testifying, all of it. The kids know that. Jennifer knows it. I know it. Don't let the stress make you doubt it."

Driving back to his apartment, Jack thought about David's words. Therapy. The idea felt both necessary and like an admission of weakness. He'd survived Vietnam without therapy - though in fairness, PTSD wasn't even recognized as a diagnosis back then. He'd survived his divorce through sheer forward momentum.

But maybe survival wasn't the same as healing. Maybe getting through something wasn't the same as processing it.

Ruby was at his apartment when he arrived, having spent the day catching up on her own work. She looked up from her laptop when he entered.

"How was the museum?"

"Good. Kids are doing better." Jack sat beside her on the couch. "David suggested I see a therapist. For stress management."

Ruby closed her laptop. "What do you think about that?"

"I think I don't have time for therapy when I'm starting a new job, coordinating with FBI testimony schedules, and trying to maintain some version of normal life."

"So you think you need it but you're resistant."

Jack smiled despite himself. "When did you become a therapist?"

"I'm not. But I did see one after the Hammond & Associates disaster. Helped me process the anger and betrayal without letting it consume me." Ruby took his hand. "There's no shame in getting help, Jack. Especially when you've been through what you've been through."

"I'll think about it."

"Good." She squeezed his hand. "Now, I have a question for you. And I want you to answer honestly, not just tell me what you think I want to hear."

Jack felt his pulse quicken slightly. "Okay."

"Are we living together or are you just crashing at my place during crisis mode?"

The question hung between them, direct and unavoidable. Jack thought about the past few weeks - how he'd spent more nights at Ruby's apartment than his own, how her place felt more like home than his empty apartment, how naturally they'd fallen into domestic routines.

"I don't know," he admitted. "I've been so focused on surviving that I haven't thought about what we're actually doing."

"Well, think about it now. Because I'm fine with you staying indefinitely. I'm fine with this being our place instead of my place. But I need to know if that's what you want or if you're just... existing in the moment until you figure out what comes next."

Jack looked at her - this woman who'd stood beside him through unemployment, death threats, and federal investigations. Who'd risked her own safety to help him expose fraud. Who'd welcomed his children into her home during crisis without hesitation.

"I want to live with you," he said. "Not temporarily, not until crisis ends. Actually live together. Build something permanent."

Ruby's expression softened. "Yeah?"

"Yeah." Jack felt something settle into certainty. "I was looking at engagement rings last week. Before the Kirkland confrontation. Didn't buy anything, just... looking. Thinking about asking you to marry me someday."

"Someday like when?"

"I don't know. After the job starts. After things settle down. After—"

"After you stop being scared of commitment?" Ruby's tone was gentle, not accusing.

Jack nodded. "Yeah. That."

"Jack, I'm not asking you to propose. I'm asking if you want to live together. Those are different questions with different answers." She shifted to face him fully. "I know you're cautious. I know the divorce hurt you. I know you need to be sure before making big commitments. That's fine. But I also need to know if we're building toward something or if I'm just... here until you figure out what you really want."

"You're not just here. You're—" Jack struggled to articulate feelings that felt too big for words. "You're the person I want to build everything with. The person I trust completely. The person who makes me want to stop being cautious and just... commit."

"Then commit. Move in with me properly. Bring your stuff, consolidate households, build something together." Ruby smiled. "We can talk about marriage later. Right now, I just want to know if you're staying or leaving."

"Staying," Jack said without hesitation. "Definitely staying."

They sealed it with a kiss that felt like promise and relief in equal measure. Later, they made plans - which furniture to keep, which to donate, how to combine two separate lives into one shared space. Practical decisions that felt momentous simply because they represented commitment.

Sunday, Jack started the process of packing up his apartment. Ruby helped, sorting through belongings accumulated over three years of divorced bachelor life, deciding what mattered and what could be left behind.

"You have a lot of books," Ruby observed, surveying the overflowing bookshelf.

"Guilty. Reading is how I decompress."

"We'll need more shelves at my place. Our place." She smiled at the correction.

By evening, they'd packed most of his essentials - clothes, books, personal items. The furniture could wait. What mattered was the commitment, the decision to stop hedging and start building.

Jack's phone rang. Helen.

"How are you doing, Mom?"

"Better question is how are you doing. I saw on the news that someone confronted you. Are you hurt?"

"I'm fine. FBI handled it. The guy's back in custody."

"Jack, when does this end? When do you get to stop fighting and just live?"

"Eighteen months until trial. After that, it should really be over."

Helen was quiet for a moment. "That's a long time to live under threat."

"I know. But I can do eighteen months. Especially now that I have help."

"Ruby?"

"Yeah. We're moving in together. Actually, officially together."

Helen's voice brightened. "That's wonderful. Really wonderful. She's good for you, Jack."

"She's better than I deserve."

"Don't sell yourself short. You're a good man who did a hard thing. You deserve someone who sees that." Helen paused. "Have you thought about marrying her?"

"Yes. But I'm not rushing it. Too much happening right now."

"Fair enough. Just don't wait too long. Life is short, and good women don't stay unattached forever."

After they hung up, Jack thought about his mother's words. Ruby had said marriage could wait, but Helen was right - waiting too long meant risking losing something precious.

Maybe after he started the new job. Maybe after the first grand jury testimony. Maybe after something felt settled enough to justify planning a future.

Or maybe he was overthinking again, looking for perfect timing that would never arrive.

Monday morning, Jack drove to Pacific Compliance Group's office for his first official day. David Wallace met him with genuine warmth, clearly unfazed by the Kirkland confrontation that had happened in this very building just days earlier.

"Welcome officially to the team. Let me introduce you around."

The office was small - five consultants including Jack, two administrative staff, Wallace as managing partner. Everyone knew about Jack's whistleblower situation; Wallace had apparently briefed them all. But instead of wariness, Jack encountered respect.

"Glad to have you," said Maria Santos, a senior consultant who specialized in healthcare fraud. "We need someone who's actually been through it, not just studied it academically."

The other consultants echoed the sentiment. They treated Jack like a colleague who'd earned his place through experience, not like a liability who might attract trouble.

Wallace set Jack up with workspace, technology, and his first assignment - reviewing compliance procedures for a mid-sized manufacturing company that wanted independent assessment before going public.

"Nothing dramatic," Wallace explained. "Just solid analytical work. Show them what good compliance looks like, identify gaps, recommend improvements. Build your credibility with straightforward projects before we throw you into complex investigations."

Jack appreciated the measured approach. He'd had enough drama for a lifetime. Straightforward analytical work sounded perfect.

He spent the day reviewing the manufacturing company's documentation, finding the kind of work simultaneously challenging and comfortable. This was what he was good at - identifying patterns, assessing risk, recommending improvements. The difference was that now he was doing it proactively instead of reactively, helping companies avoid problems instead of cleaning up after them.

At lunch, Maria joined him in the break room.

"How's your first day going?"

"Good. Really good, actually. Feels right."

"Wallace told us about the confrontation last week. That guy who threatened you." Maria's expression was serious. "You handled it well. A lot of people would have folded or escalated too far. You did exactly right."

"Didn't feel right at the time. Felt terrifying."

"Welcome to consulting. Sometimes doing the right thing feels terrifying." She smiled. "But you get used to it. And eventually, you realize the fear means you're taking risks that matter."

Jack thought about that throughout the afternoon. The fear meant you're taking risks that matter. His entire whistleblowing experience had been terrifying specifically because it mattered - to his family, his career, his principles, justice itself.

Maybe fear wasn't weakness. Maybe it was just proof you had something worth protecting.

By the time he left the office at five-thirty, Jack felt something he hadn't felt in months: professional contentment. He had meaningful work. Colleagues who respected him. Income to support his family. A future that looked like more than just survival.

Ruby was already at the apartment - their apartment now - when he arrived. She'd started organizing his books, integrating them with hers, creating a shared library.

"How was day one?" she asked.

"Perfect. Really perfect." Jack kissed her. "Thank you."

"For what?"

"For believing I'd land on my feet. For standing by me when I couldn't see past the next crisis. For being the kind of person who makes commitment feel like opportunity instead of obligation."

Ruby pulled him close. "You did the hard part. I just stood beside you."

"That was the hard part. Anyone can fight alone. Finding someone willing to fight with you - that's rare."

They spent the evening continuing the process of combining households, making room for each other's belongings and lives. It felt domestic and profound in equal measure - the small acts of commitment that transformed two separate existences into one shared future.

Jack's FBI secure phone rang at eight PM. Reeves.

"Quick update - we've arrested the three additional suspects Marcus Chen identified. All in custody, all being charged. The criminal network operating within Regional Logistics Solutions has been effectively dismantled. The company itself is still operating under new interim management, but the people running the fraud are all in custody or cooperating." You're still facing testimony obligations, but the immediate threat level has dropped significantly."

"So I can stop looking over my shoulder?"

"You can look over your shoulder less frequently. Stay alert but resume normal life. We'll notify you of any new developments." Reeves paused. "You're doing great, Mr. Mercer. Most whistleblowers crack under this pressure. You're holding together and rebuilding. That's impressive."

After she hung up, Jack sat with the news. "The criminal network was dismantled. The immediate threats were over. Life could actually normalize."

He'd survived.

Not just physically, but professionally, emotionally, relationally. He'd exposed massive fraud, endured retaliation, protected his family, found new work, and committed to building a future with someone he loved.

The cost had been enormous. But he'd survived.

Ruby joined him on the couch, took his hand. "Good news?"

"The best. More arrests. "The criminal network is dismantled. Immediate threat over." "So we can really start living normally?"

"Yeah." Jack pulled her close. "We really can."

That night, lying in bed with Ruby asleep beside him, Jack thought about the past two months. From discovering fraud to being fired to arrests to confrontations to new job to moving in together - a lifetime of change compressed into weeks.

The shrapnel in his ribs was quiet tonight, old wounds resting, old battles receding into memory where they belonged.

New challenges would come. Grand jury testimony. Trial preparation. Eighteen months of legal proceedings. But those were scheduled challenges, predictable and manageable.

The immediate crisis - the death threats, the confrontations, the desperate criminals - that was over.

Jack closed his eyes and slept deeply for the first time in months, no longer listening for threats in the darkness, no longer calculating exit strategies and defensive positions.

Just sleeping. Just resting. Just being a man who'd fought hard and survived intact.

Tomorrow would bring new challenges.

But tonight, he was safe. His family was safe. His future was secure.

That was enough.

More than enough.

It was everything.

Chapter 19: Breaking Point

Winter settled over the city with the slow inevitability of time passing. Jack's first month at Pacific Compliance Group blurred into routine - client meetings, compliance reviews, analytical work that felt both challenging and safely distant from the personal stakes of his whistleblower experience. The work was good. The money was better. Life was normalizing in ways that should have felt satisfying but somehow felt hollow.

The problem was waiting.

The grand jury indictment had come through in mid-December, formally charging Derek Vaughn, Marcus Chen, and six others with multiple counts of money laundering, wire fraud, conspiracy, and customs violations. The indictment was sealed until arraignment, which was scheduled for early January. After that would come pretrial motions, discovery, more motions, and eventually - maybe a year from now - actual trial.

Jack's testimony wouldn't be needed for months. Katherine Mendoza was negotiating his civil settlement, but Regional Logistics Solutions' new management was dragging out the process, clearly hoping Jack would accept less money to avoid prolonged litigation. The FBI had stopped calling with updates; the investigation was complete, the case built, the criminals in custody or cooperating.

Everything was in motion, but none of it required Jack's active participation. He was just... waiting. Existing in the space between crisis and resolution, unable to move fully forward because the past wasn't quite finished with him.

Ruby noticed, of course. She always noticed.

"You're restless," she observed one evening in mid-December as they sat in their shared apartment - still strange to think of it as truly shared, not just Ruby's place where Jack happened to live.

"I'm fine."

"You're not fine. You've been pacing every night for a week. You're sleeping badly. You're distracted during conversations." She set down her book. "Talk to me."

Jack thought about denying it, then didn't. Ruby deserved honesty.

"I don't know what to do with myself. For two months, everything was urgent - find evidence, expose fraud, survive threats, rebuild career. Now everything's just... waiting. The trial won't happen for a year. My testimony won't be needed for months. I'm supposed to just live normally while this thing hangs over everything."

"That's hard for you. The waiting."

"Yeah. I'm not good at waiting." Jack ran his hand through his hair. "In Vietnam, waiting was when bad things happened. Waiting for contact. Waiting for ambush. Waiting to find out if the guy next to you was going to make it or die from his wounds. Action I could handle. Waiting drove me insane."

Ruby was quiet for a moment. "You know what helped me after Hammond & Associates? After I reported the fraud and got fired and spent eighteen months waiting for the SEC investigation to conclude?"

"What?"

"Therapy. And accepting that healing doesn't happen on a schedule." She moved closer to him on the couch. "Jack, you've been through trauma. Multiple traumas, actually. The fraud discovery, the retaliation, the threats, the physical confrontation. You survived all of it, but you haven't processed any of it. You've just been moving from crisis to crisis without stopping to feel what it did to you."

"I don't have time to fall apart."

"I'm not suggesting you fall apart. I'm suggesting you acknowledge that what you went through was traumatic and give yourself permission to feel it." Ruby took his hand. "You told David you'd think about seeing a therapist. Have you?"

"No."

"Why not?"

Jack struggled to articulate resistance that felt both reasonable and irrational. "Because therapy means admitting I can't handle it alone. Because I'm supposed to be strong for my kids, for my mother, for you. Because—"

"Because you've been trained since Vietnam to just power through and not show weakness?" Ruby's tone was gentle but firm. "Jack, going to therapy isn't weakness. Acknowledging trauma isn't failure. You did something incredibly difficult and survived. That's strength. Asking for help to process it is also strength."

Jack thought about that. "Did therapy really help you? After Hammond?"

"Yes. Took six months of weekly sessions before I stopped having panic attacks every time my phone rang. Took another six months before I could trust that doing the right thing hadn't permanently destroyed my life." Ruby's expression turned vulnerable. "I didn't tell you this before, but after I was fired, I spent three weeks barely leaving my apartment. I was terrified. Convinced everyone in the industry knew I'd betrayed Hammond, convinced I'd never work again, convinced I'd made a terrible mistake."

"But you got through it."

"With help. With therapy. With time." She squeezed his hand. "You don't have to do this alone, Jack. You don't have to just endure until trial. You can actually heal."

That night, Jack lay awake long after Ruby had fallen asleep, thinking about healing versus endurance. He'd spent his entire adult life enduring - Vietnam, divorce, whistleblowing. Survival had become his default mode. But Ruby was right; survival wasn't the same as healing.

The nightmares started three days later.

They weren't new nightmares. They were old ones, Vietnam vintage, the kind that had plagued him for years after coming home and then gradually faded to manageable frequency. But the stress of whistleblowing had apparently reawakened them.

The first one jerked Jack awake at two AM - the Mekong Delta, the RPG impact, the screaming, the blood, the desperate scramble to save crew members who were already dead. He woke gasping, disoriented, Ruby's hand on his shoulder anchoring him back to present reality.

"You're okay," she said quietly. "You're safe. You're home."

Jack's heart was racing, sweat soaking his shirt despite the winter cold outside. He sat up, trying to control his breathing, trying to separate past from present.

"Vietnam?" Ruby asked.

"Yeah. Sorry. I didn't mean to wake you."

"Don't apologize." She sat up beside him. "Does this happen often?"

"Used to. Right after I got back. Then occasionally over the years. Thought I was past it." Jack wiped sweat from his face. "Guess the stress brought them back."

"Do you want to talk about it?"

Jack almost said no, almost retreated behind the walls he'd built between his war experience and everyone in his current life. But Ruby had shared her trauma. Maybe he owed her the same honesty.

"It's always the same dream. The morning we got hit. I see the RPG coming but I can't move fast enough to warn everyone. The explosion happens in slow motion. Then I'm trying to help the wounded but my hands won't work right and people are dying and I can't save them."

Ruby pulled him close. "I'm sorry. That sounds terrifying."

"The worst part is that it's mostly accurate. That's really what happened. I did see the RPG coming but too late. People did die while I tried to help them. The dream is just my brain replaying the worst day of my life on repeat." Jack leaned into her warmth. "I thought I'd dealt with it. Forty years later, you'd think it wouldn't still affect me."

"Trauma doesn't expire. It just waits for stress to bring it back." Ruby paused. "Will you at least consider calling a therapist? Not for me, but for yourself?"

"Yeah. I'll call someone. I promise."

The nightmares continued. Not every night, but often enough to disrupt sleep and leave Jack exhausted. Ruby never complained about being woken up. She just held him until he could breathe normally again, grounding him in present safety.

By Christmas, Jack had finally made an appointment with Dr. Rebecca Mitchell - a therapist specializing in PTSD and trauma. The first session was scheduled for early January, after the holidays but before the arraignment.

The holidays themselves were complicated. Jack had custody of the kids for Christmas Eve, Jennifer and David for Christmas Day. Helen joined them for Christmas Eve dinner at Jack and Ruby's apartment - the first time Helen had seen the fully combined household.

"It suits you," Helen said, looking around at the merged furniture and combined libraries and photographs of Jack's children sharing shelf space with Ruby's family photos. "This looks like a real home, not just a place to sleep."

"It feels like a real home," Jack agreed.

The kids seemed comfortable with Ruby now, no longer treating her as "Dad's girlfriend" but as a natural part of his life. Emma showed Ruby her new dragon book series. Michael asked Ruby for help with a math problem, casually accepting her explanation. Sarah engaged Ruby in a surprisingly adult conversation about forensic accounting career paths.

Watching his family interact with the woman he loved, Jack felt something settle into certainty. This was right. This was what building a future looked like.

Helen pulled Jack aside while Ruby and the kids were absorbed in a board game.

"When are you going to ask her?" Helen said quietly.

"Ask her what?"

"Don't play dumb. When are you going to propose?"

Jack glanced at Ruby, laughing at something Emma said. "I don't know. Soon. After the arraignment, maybe. After things settle more."

"Things are never going to settle completely. There's always going to be something - trial preparation, testimony, legal proceedings. If you wait for perfect timing, you'll wait forever." Helen squeezed his arm. "She's good for you. Your kids love her. You're clearly in love with her. What are you waiting for?"

"Permission, maybe. From you, from the kids, from myself."

"Well, you have my permission. I suspect the kids would approve. So the only person stopping you is you." Helen's expression softened. "Don't let fear of commitment cost you something precious. Your father and I weren't perfect, but we built something real. You deserve the same."

After Christmas, Jack found himself returning to the jewelry store he'd visited months ago. The same saleswoman recognized him.

"Back again?" she said warmly. "Still thinking about it?"

"More seriously this time." Jack looked at the platinum band with the modest diamond that had caught his attention before. "This one. Can I see it again?"

She brought it out, let him examine it, explained the specifications and warranty and return policy. The ring was beautiful, understated, exactly the kind of thing Ruby would appreciate.

"I'll take it," Jack said before he could overthink the decision.

The purchase felt momentous and terrifying and absolutely right. He had the ring sized, bought a simple box, and hid it in the back of his sock drawer - the most cliché hiding spot imaginable, but Ruby respected his privacy enough not to snoop.

Now he just needed to figure out when and how to ask.

New Year's Eve arrived with the weight of transition. Jack and Ruby spent it quietly at home, no parties or crowds, just the two of them and a bottle of wine and the TV showing Times Square celebrations they didn't really watch.

"What are you hoping for in the new year?" Ruby asked as midnight approached.

"For the trial to go well. For my kids to be happy. For the nightmares to stop." Jack paused. "For us to keep building what we've started."

"We will. All of it." Ruby raised her glass. "To surviving and healing and building futures worth fighting for."

They toasted, kissed at midnight, and went to bed with the new year stretching ahead full of possibility and obligation in equal measure.

The first week of January brought Jack's first therapy session with Dr. Mitchell. Her office was comfortable but professional, designed to feel safe without being overly decorated. She was in her fifties, calm presence and direct gaze that suggested she'd heard every variation of human trauma and remained unshocked by any of it.

"Tell me why you're here," she said after introductions.

Jack explained - the whistleblowing, the retaliation, the threats, the confrontation with Kirkland. The nightmares returning. The sense of being stuck in limbo waiting for trial. The feeling that he should be fine but wasn't.

Dr. Mitchell listened without interrupting, taking occasional notes. When Jack finished, she asked, "What do you want from therapy?"

"To stop having nightmares. To feel normal again. To not be constantly on edge waiting for the next crisis."

"Those are reasonable goals. But I want to be clear about what therapy can and can't do. I can help you process trauma, develop coping mechanisms, understand your stress responses. I can't make the trial go away or guarantee the nightmares stop immediately. Healing takes time."

"How much time?"

"Depends on the person and the trauma. Some people see improvement in weeks. Others take months. You've experienced multiple traumas - Vietnam, divorce, whistleblowing - that are probably all connected in your stress response. We'll work through them systematically."

They spent the rest of the session establishing baseline - Jack's current symptoms, his support system, his coping mechanisms. Dr. Mitchell gave him homework: keep a journal tracking nightmares and triggers, practice breathing exercises when stress spiked, continue leaning on his support network.

"One more thing," she said as the session ended. "You mentioned feeling like you should be fine because you survived. Let go of that expectation. Survival and wellness are different things. You can survive and still be wounded. Acknowledging wounds isn't weakness."

Jack left the session feeling simultaneously exposed and relieved. He'd admitted to a professional that he was struggling. That felt like progress, even if nothing else had changed yet.

The arraignment happened on a cold Monday in mid-January. Jack attended as an observer, not required to testify but wanting to see the defendants formally charged. Katherine Mendoza accompanied him, along with Agent Reeves.

The courtroom was exactly as Jack had imagined - wood paneling, high ceilings, the machinery of justice operating with formal precision. Derek Vaughn was brought in first, wearing an orange jumpsuit, looking significantly less polished than the executive Jack remembered. Marcus Chen followed, then the other defendants, each entering pleas of not guilty through their attorneys.

The judge set trial for November - ten months away. Pretrial motions and discovery would consume the intervening months.

Outside the courthouse afterward, reporters swarmed. Jack had been briefed by Mendoza on what to say and what to avoid.

"Mr. Mercer, do you feel vindicated seeing the defendants arraigned?"

"I'm relieved that the justice system is working. My role was to report what I found. The FBI and prosecutors are doing the rest."

"Do you regret becoming a whistleblower?"

"No. I did what was necessary. Would I prefer my life hadn't been disrupted? Of course. But I don't regret exposing crime."

"What message do you have for other potential whistleblowers?"

Jack thought about that carefully. "Document everything. Get legal counsel early. Protect your family. And understand that doing the right thing has costs. But those costs are worth it."

The news coverage that evening was favorable - Jack portrayed as principled whistleblower, defendants as criminals facing justice. The narrative had fully shifted from where it started months ago.

That night, Jack and Ruby sat in their apartment, the arraignment behind them, the trial ten months ahead.

"How do you feel?" Ruby asked.

"Tired. Relieved it's started. Dreading ten more months of this hanging over everything."

"We'll get through it. Same way we got through everything else."

Jack pulled the ring box from his sock drawer where he'd hidden it. His hands were shaking slightly as he opened it, showing Ruby the platinum band with its modest diamond.

Her eyes widened. "Jack..."

"I'm not great at romantic speeches. And this timing is probably terrible with the trial ahead and everything still complicated. But Helen was right - there's never going to be perfect timing. There's just now." Jack took a breath. "I love you. You stood by me through the worst crisis of my life. You welcomed my children without hesitation. You make me want to stop being cautious and just commit to building something real. Ruby Martinez, will you marry me?"

Ruby was crying, which Jack hoped was good. "Yes. Absolutely yes."

He slid the ring onto her finger - it fit perfectly. She pulled him into a kiss that felt like promise and relief and future all at once.

"I was starting to think you'd never ask," Ruby said when they finally broke apart.

"I was starting to think the same thing. Helen told me to stop waiting for perfect timing."

"Your mother is very wise." Ruby looked at the ring, then at Jack. "When do you want to get married?"

"I don't know. After trial, maybe? Or before? I don't want to wait too long, but I also don't want our wedding overshadowed by legal proceedings."

"How about this summer? June or July, before trial preparation gets intense. Small ceremony, immediate family, nothing elaborate."

"That sounds perfect."

They spent the evening making plans - potential venues, who to invite, how to tell their families. Ordinary wedding planning that felt extraordinary simply because it represented commitment in the face of ongoing uncertainty.

Jack called his children the next morning to tell them. Sarah squealed with excitement. Emma asked a million questions about the wedding. Michael said "Cool, Dad" with teenage casualness that masked genuine happiness.

Jennifer was thrilled. "Ruby's good for you. I'm really happy for you both."

Helen cried happy tears. "Finally. I thought you'd wait forever."

The nightmares didn't stop after the engagement, but they became less frequent. Therapy was helping, slowly. Dr. Mitchell was teaching Jack to recognize triggers, to ground himself in present reality when past trauma intruded.

Work at Pacific Compliance continued steadily. Jack was building a reputation as the consultant companies hired when they wanted brutally honest assessment of their compliance programs. His whistleblower experience gave him credibility; his analytical skills gave him results.

Winter faded toward spring. The trial date loomed but felt manageable with seven months still ahead. Jack and Ruby set a wedding date - July 15th, a Saturday, simple ceremony at a garden venue Jennifer had recommended.

Life was moving forward. Healing was happening. The future was taking shape.

The shrapnel in Jack's ribs ached less frequently now, old wounds finally beginning to rest as new foundations were built.

Some battles you survived. Some you won. And some you learned to carry while still building something worth living for.

Jack had done all three.

And somehow, impossibly, he was happy.

Not completely healed. Not without scars or nightmares or lingering trauma.

But happy.

Building a future with a woman he loved. Maintaining relationships with children who respected him. Working at a job that valued his integrity.

The trial would come. Testimony would be difficult. Legal proceedings would drag on.

But Jack was ready.

He'd survived worse.

And this time, he wasn't surviving alone.

He was building.

And that made all the difference.

Chapter 20: Vows

Spring arrived with the tentative hope of things growing after long dormancy. Jack's therapy sessions with Dr. Rebecca Mitchell had become a weekly routine, slowly untangling decades of survival mechanisms and making space for actual healing. The nightmares hadn't stopped completely, but they'd become less frequent, less vivid, more manageable.

Work at Pacific Compliance Group had settled into a rhythm Jack found deeply satisfying. He'd completed three major consulting projects, earning respect from clients and colleagues alike. David Wallace had hinted at making Jack a partner within the year if things continued going well.

The wedding planning had taken on a life of its own, primarily driven by Ruby and Jennifer working together with surprising compatibility. Jack's role seemed to be mostly nodding agreement and writing checks, which suited him fine. He cared about marrying Ruby, not about the details of flowers and catering.

But underneath the normalcy, the trial loomed. Seven months until November. Seven months of pretrial motions, discovery disputes, and preparation for testimony that would put Jack on a witness stand defending every decision he'd made.

Katherine Mendoza called in early March with news about the civil settlement.

"Regional Logistics Solutions is offering three hundred fifty thousand plus full legal fees," she said. "That's up significantly from their initial offer. I think we can push for four hundred, but it'll mean dragging out negotiations another few months."

Jack did the math quickly. Three fifty after taxes would be roughly two-forty. Enough to rebuild savings depleted during unemployment, fund the wedding, and create a financial cushion.

"Take it," he said. "I don't want to drag this out. I want it done."

"You're sure? We could probably get more."

"I'm sure. The money is good, but closure is better."

Mendoza negotiated final terms, and by mid-March, Jack had a signed settlement agreement. The money would arrive after a thirty-day waiting period, but the legal battle with his former employer was officially over.

He told Ruby that evening over dinner - takeout Thai food eaten at their kitchen table, the kind of mundane domestic moment that felt precious.

"How do you feel?" Ruby asked.

"Relieved. It's one less thing hanging over us. The criminal trial is still there, but at least the civil case is resolved."

"Three hundred fifty thousand is substantial."

"Yeah. Enough to feel vindicated without feeling like I'm profiting from exposing crime." Jack paused. "I want to put most of it in savings. Some toward the wedding. Maybe take the kids on a real vacation this summer before trial preparation gets intense."

"That sounds perfect." Ruby reached across the table, took his hand. "We're really doing this, aren't you? Building a normal life while waiting for trial."

"Trying to. Dr. Mitchell says it's important to keep living, not just existing in limbo."

"Dr. Mitchell is smart."

Jack smiled. "She is. Though she keeps pushing me to talk more about Vietnam, which I'm not great at."

"What does she say about it?"

"That trauma doesn't expire, that my whistleblower experience probably triggered old PTSD from the war, that I can't fully heal from one without addressing the other." Jack shrugged. "She's probably right. I'm just not ready to go that deep yet."

"That's okay. Healing happens at the pace it happens."

April brought Jack's first major trial preparation session with the prosecution. He met with Assistant U.S. Attorney Michael Torres and his team at the federal courthouse, spending four hours going through his testimony in detail.

Torres was in his forties, sharp and methodical, the kind of prosecutor who left nothing to chance.

"Defense is going to attack your credibility hard," Torres explained. "They'll paint you as a disgruntled employee who fabricated evidence to justify illegal data access. We need your testimony to be airtight - no inconsistencies, no uncertainty, no gaps they can exploit."

They walked through Jack's discovery of the fraud, his investigative methodology, his decision to report to the FBI. Torres probed every detail, playing devil's advocate, anticipating defense strategies.

"When you accessed shipping records for those eighteen months, did you have explicit authorization to pull that much data?"

"I had general authorization for compliance analysis. The specific scope was within my judgment as a Risk Analyst."

"But you weren't asked to conduct that specific analysis?"

"Risk analysts are expected to proactively identify potential issues. That's the job."

"Defense will say you exceeded your authority."

"Then defense is wrong. Company policy explicitly authorized Risk Analysts to conduct broad-based assessments."

Torres nodded, satisfied. "Good. That's the energy I need. Confident, factual, unshakable. The jury needs to see you as the professional who found crime, not the troublemaker who went looking for problems."

After the session, Jack felt simultaneously prepared and anxious. The trial was real, approaching, unavoidable. In seven months, he'd be on that witness stand with twelve strangers deciding whether to believe him.

Agent Reeves called that evening with an update.

"Marcus Chen's cooperation continues to be valuable. We've identified two more individuals involved in the money laundering network - both have agreed to plea deals in exchange for testimony. That strengthens our case significantly."

"How's Monica doing?" Jack asked. He'd thought about her occasionally, wondering how she was managing the aftermath of her husband's arrest.

"She's testifying at trial as a government witness. Divorced Marcus last month. Started over with a new job in a different city." Reeves paused. "She asked me to tell you thank you, if I talked to you. Said meeting you that day gave her courage to do the right thing."

Jack felt something complicated - pride and sadness mixed together. "Tell her I hope she's doing okay."

"I will."

The wedding planning accelerated as July approached. Ruby and Jennifer had found a garden venue that could accommodate fifty guests - immediate family, close friends, a few colleagues. Simple, intimate, exactly what Jack and Ruby both wanted.

Sarah was thrilled to be a bridesmaid. Emma was ecstatic about being a junior bridesmaid. Michael accepted his role as groomsman with teenage stoicism that masked genuine happiness.

Helen was recovering well enough to attend, though she'd need assistance. Jennifer and David had offered to help coordinate logistics, treating the wedding as a family event despite the complexities of divorce and remarriage.

One evening in May, Jack and Ruby sat on their apartment balcony watching the sunset, the city stretching out below them.

"Nervous about the wedding?" Ruby asked.

"Nervous about making it real. Nervous about deserving you. Not nervous about wanting to marry you - that part I'm certain about."

Ruby smiled. "You deserve happiness, Jack. You deserve a partner who sees who you really are. Stop questioning whether you've earned it."

"Easier said than done."

"I know. But try anyway." She leaned against him. "What are you most looking forward to about being married?"

Jack thought about that. "Not having to qualify our relationship anymore. Not introducing you as my girlfriend or my fiancée but just as my wife. Having that simple certainty."

"I like that." Ruby was quiet for a moment. "What are you most worried about?"

"That the trial will consume everything. That November will come and suddenly all our attention will be on testimony and verdicts and I'll be too stressed to be a good husband."

"Then we build in protections now. We agree that the trial doesn't take over our entire lives. That we still have date nights and normal conversations and moments that aren't about fraud or testimony." Ruby turned to face him. "The trial is important. But it's not more important than us. We survived whistleblowing and threats and confrontations. We can survive a trial."

Jack pulled her close, believing it because she said it with such certainty.

June arrived with the peculiar acceleration of time before major events. The wedding was six weeks away. Trial was five months away. Jack's testimony preparation intensified - mock cross-examinations with Torres, reviewing documents, ensuring his memory of events matched the evidence exactly.

Dr. Mitchell's therapy sessions focused on managing anticipatory anxiety.

"You're catastrophizing," she observed during one session. "Creating worst-case scenarios about trial and letting them dominate your thoughts."

"What if the jury doesn't believe me? What if Vaughn's lawyers make me look incompetent? What if—"

"Jack, stop. Those are all possibilities, but you're treating them as certainties." Dr. Mitchell leaned forward. "What's the evidence that the jury won't believe you?"

"I don't know. Maybe they'll think I'm lying."

"Based on what? You have FBI confirmation, documentary evidence, cooperating witnesses, and a settlement from your former employer. The evidence supports your testimony. You're not walking into that courtroom alone with just your word."

Jack knew she was right intellectually. Emotionally, the anxiety persisted.

"How do I stop catastrophizing?"

"Practice. When you notice yourself spiraling into worst-case thinking, pause and ask: what's the evidence? What's actually likely? What can I control right now?" Dr. Mitchell smiled. "And remember - you've already survived the worst part. The investigation, the retaliation, the threats - that's over. Trial is just telling the truth under oath. You're good at truth."

Jack thought about that for the rest of the week. He was good at truth. That's what had gotten him into this situation - inability to ignore wrongdoing, compulsion to report what he found, commitment to honesty even when lying would be easier.

The wedding was three weeks away when Jack's children asked to meet with him - all three together, without Jennifer or Ruby present. They gathered at a coffee shop near Jack's apartment on a Saturday afternoon.

"This feels serious," Jack said, looking at their solemn faces.

"It is," Sarah said. "We want to talk about the wedding and the trial and everything."

Jack's stomach tightened. "Okay. Talk."

Sarah glanced at her siblings, clearly designated spokesperson. "We know you're stressed about trial. We know you're worried about testimony and whether the jury will believe you. And we want you to know something important."

"What's that?"

"We already believe you. All of us. Completely." Sarah's voice was fierce. "Even when other kids were saying terrible things about you, even when the news was calling you a liar, we never doubted. Not once."

Michael, 15 years old, nodded. "You're the most honest person I know. If you say there was fraud, there was fraud."

Emma, twelve years old and earnest added, "And we're really happy you're marrying Ruby. She's nice and she makes you smile more."

Jack felt his throat tighten with emotion. "Thank you. All of you. That means more than you know."

"We also want you to stop worrying so much about protecting us from stress," Sarah continued. "We're old enough to handle knowing when things are hard. You don't have to pretend everything's fine."

"I'm not—"

"Dad, you totally do," Michael interrupted gently. "You always act like everything's under control even when it's obviously not. It's okay to admit when you're scared or stressed."

Jack looked at his children - Sarah, seventeen and wise beyond her years; Michael, fifteen and perceptive; Emma, twelve, and still believing the best of everyone. When had they grown up enough to offer him support instead of just receiving it?

"Okay," he said quietly. "I'm scared about trial. Scared the jury won't believe me, scared of being cross-examined, scared of failing after everything we've been through."

"You won't fail," Emma said with absolute certainty. "You're too good at being right."

Jack laughed despite the emotion. "I hope the jury thinks so."

"They will," Sarah said firmly. "Because you'll tell the truth and the truth is obvious. Bad people did bad things. You reported it. Now they're going to prison. That's how this ends."

Jack wanted to believe in his daughter's simple faith in justice. Wanted to trust that truth was enough, that juries were wise, that the right outcome was inevitable.

Dr. Mitchell would probably say he was catastrophizing again, creating anxiety about unlikely negative outcomes instead of trusting the process.

His children were right. The evidence supported him. The truth was clear. He just needed to show up and testify honestly.

Everything else was beyond his control.

The wedding was two weeks away when the settlement money finally arrived - three hundred fifty thousand dollars appearing in Jack's bank account like validation in numerical form. He'd been vindicated legally, financially, publicly.

Now he just needed to be vindicated in criminal court.

But that could wait until November.

First, he had a wedding to attend.

His own wedding.

To a woman who'd stood beside him through the worst crisis of his life and chosen to build a future anyway.

That felt like the best possible outcome of the past year's chaos - not just surviving, but finding someone worth surviving for.

Jack looked at the ring on Ruby's finger, the wedding date circled on their calendar, the life they were building together, and felt something he hadn't felt in a long time:

Uncomplicated happiness.

Not happiness despite stress or happiness while anxious or happiness contingent on trial outcomes.

Just happiness.

Simple, real, earned happiness.

The shrapnel in his ribs was quiet, old wounds resting as new foundations were built.

Two weeks until the wedding.

Five months until trial.

A lifetime of days between crisis and resolution, filled with work and family and love and ordinary moments that mattered more than any courtroom verdict.

Jack was ready.

For all of it.

The wedding, the trial, the future.

He'd survived worse.

And this time, he wouldn't just survive.

He'd thrive.

Because that's what happened when you stopped just enduring and started actually living.

You built something worth protecting.

And then you protected it.

Whatever it took.

For as long as it took.

Starting with a wedding.

And continuing with everything that came after.

Chapter 21: Unraveling

July fifteenth arrived with cloudless blue skies and the kind of perfect summer weather that felt like benediction. Jack woke early at his mother's apartment - he'd spent the night before the wedding separated from Ruby per tradition, while she remained at their place with Sarah and Emma helping her prepare.

His phone showed dozens of messages - his children confirming arrival times, Helen checking that her transportation was arranged, Katherine Mendoza wishing him happiness, Agent Reeves sending congratulations, colleagues from Pacific Compliance offering support.

And one from Ruby, sent at six AM: *Last day of being engaged. Ready to be married instead?*

Jack typed back: *More than ready. See you at the altar.*

The morning passed in a blur of activity. Jack dressed carefully in the suit they'd chosen - charcoal gray, simple, elegant. Michael arrived at ten to help with final preparations, looking surprisingly adult in his own suit.

"You nervous, Dad?" Michael asked as they adjusted ties in the bathroom mirror.

"Terrified. But the good kind of terrified."

"Ruby's great. You're making the right choice."

"I know. Doesn't make it less scary to commit to forever."

Michael smiled. "Forever's not scary when it's with the right person. At least that's what Mom says about David."

Jack appreciated the mature perspective from his fifteen-year-old son. "Your mom's right. As usual."

By noon, they were heading to the venue - a botanical garden on the outskirts of the city, all flowering trees and manicured paths and a small pavilion where the ceremony would take place. Fifty white chairs arranged in neat rows, an archway covered in roses, the kind of simple beauty that needed no embellishment.

Jennifer and David had arrived early to coordinate logistics. Sarah and Emma were with Ruby, helping her prepare in a private room at the venue. Helen was settling into a chair near the front, looking stronger than she had in months.

Jack stood under the rose arbor with the officiant - a judge Katherine Mendoza had recommended, someone who specialized in small, meaningful ceremonies. The chairs began to fill. Jack's colleagues from Pacific Compliance. A few former coworkers from Regional Logistics who'd supported him during the crisis. Ruby's clients and friends. The people who'd stood by them through everything.

The string quartet began playing. Sarah walked down the aisle first, radiant in her bridesmaid dress, followed by Emma, who managed to be both dignified and excited simultaneously. They took their positions. Michael stood beside Jack as best man.

Then Ruby appeared.

She wore a simple cream-colored dress, elegant without being elaborate, her hair down in loose waves. She carried a small bouquet of wildflowers. She was beautiful in the understated way Jack loved most - authentic, unpretentious, entirely herself.

Jennifer walked beside Ruby, giving her away in a gesture that felt profound - Jack's ex-wife supporting his new marriage, treating Ruby like family. They reached the arbor, Jennifer squeezed Ruby's hand, then took her seat beside David.

Ruby stepped up beside Jack, her eyes bright with emotion.

"Hi," she said quietly.

"Hi," Jack replied, feeling everything else fade except this moment, this woman, this commitment.

The ceremony was brief. The judge spoke about partnership, about choosing each other daily, about building something worth protecting. Jack and Ruby had written their own vows.

Ruby went first, her voice steady despite tears threatening. "Jack, you're the bravest person I know. Not because you exposed fraud or testified or survived threats, but because you keep showing up. For your kids, for your mother, for me. You choose to be present even when it's hard. You choose honesty even when lies would be easier. You choose to build even when tearing down would be safer. I'm honored to build a life with you. To be your partner in everything that comes next. I love you completely."

Jack took a breath, steadying himself. "Ruby, you stood beside me through the worst crisis of my life. You risked your own safety and career to help me expose corruption. You welcomed my children and accepted my complicated family without hesitation. You saw me at my absolute worst and chose me anyway. You taught me that healing is possible, that commitment doesn't have to be terrifying, that love can be simple even when life is complicated. I promise to show up for you the way you showed up for me. To choose you daily. To build something real and lasting. I love you more than I can articulate."

They exchanged rings - the platinum band Jack had bought months ago, and a matching band Ruby had chosen for him. The judge pronounced them married. Jack kissed his wife - his wife - and felt something settle into permanent certainty.

The reception was held in the garden, tables arranged under string lights, the kind of intimate celebration that focused on connection rather than spectacle. Jack and Ruby moved through their guests, accepting congratulations, feeling the weight of community support.

Helen pulled Jack aside during dinner, tears in her eyes. "Your father would be so proud. You found someone who matches your integrity and your courage. Don't mess this up."

"I'll do my best."

"You'll do better than that. You learned from your father's mistakes. You'll build something that lasts."

Sarah gave a toast that was surprisingly eloquent for a seventeen-year-old. "Dad taught us that doing the right thing matters more than being comfortable. Ruby taught us that standing beside someone through crisis is what love actually looks like. Together they're teaching us that you can survive hard things and still build something beautiful. We love you both. Welcome to the family, Ruby."

Emma's toast was shorter but equally moving. "I'm really happy my dad found someone who makes him smile this much. Also Ruby likes dragons which is very important."

The laughter that followed felt like release - joy after tension, celebration after survival, hope after crisis.

As evening arrived, Jack and Ruby had their first dance to a song they'd chosen together - something about building homes and choosing each other and weathering storms. They swayed together under string lights while their combined families watched, and Jack felt the accumulated stress of the past year finally begin to lift.

"We did it," Ruby whispered. "We got married."

"Yeah. We really did." Jack pulled her closer. "No regrets?"

"None. You?"

"Just that I didn't ask you sooner."

They danced until other couples joined them - Jennifer and David, Sarah with a friend from school, Helen being carefully guided by Michael. The garden filled with music and laughter and the sound of people choosing joy.

The wedding ended around ten PM. Jack and Ruby said their goodbyes, accepted final hugs and congratulations, and left for the hotel where they'd spend their wedding night. They'd planned a brief honeymoon - just a long weekend at a coastal resort, since Jack's trial preparation couldn't accommodate more time away.

In their hotel room, they collapsed onto the bed, exhausted and happy and married.

"How do you feel?" Jack asked.

"Like we just survived the most public declaration of commitment possible and now we get to actually be married instead of just planning to be married." Ruby kicked off her shoes. "Also like my feet hurt."

Jack laughed. "Mine too. Worth it though."

"Definitely worth it."

They changed out of their wedding clothes, ordered room service, and spent the evening being quietly together without the pressure of guests or family or performance. Just two people who'd chosen each other, committed publicly, and now got to build the private reality of marriage.

Later, lying in bed with Ruby asleep beside him, Jack thought about the past year. From discovering fraud to being fired to arrests to threats to trial preparation to this - married, stable, employed, healing. The journey had been brutal. But it had led here.

To a woman who matched his integrity. To children who respected him. To work that valued his principles. To a life worth protecting.

The trial still loomed - four months away now. But Jack felt ready in ways he hadn't before. He wasn't fighting alone anymore. He was part of something larger than himself - a marriage, a family, a commitment to building futures instead of just surviving presents.

The shrapnel in his ribs was quiet tonight, old wounds finally resting.

New battles would come. November would bring testimony and cross-examination and verdict anxiety.

But tonight, he was just a man who'd gotten married to someone he loved.

That was enough.

More than enough.

It was everything.

The honeymoon was exactly what they needed - three days of ocean air and quiet restaurants and long walks on the beach. They talked about everything except fraud and trials and testimony. They made plans for their future - where to travel next year, whether to buy a house together, how to blend their lives more completely.

Ruby brought up children on their last evening, sitting on the hotel balcony watching the sunset.

"I know you have three kids already," she said carefully. "But have you ever thought about having more? With someone else?"

Jack considered the question honestly. "I'm sixty-two. You're forty-six. Biology is against us, and honestly, I'm exhausted just thinking about babies at this age."

"That's fair." Ruby smiled. "I'm not saying I want kids. I'm just asking if you'd thought about it."

"Have you wanted kids? Before now, I mean."

"I thought I did. When I was younger, married before briefly. But it didn't work out, and eventually I accepted that maybe motherhood wasn't my path." She paused. "Being a stepmother to your kids feels right though. I like being part of their lives without the pressure of being their mom. Jennifer's already doing that job well."

"You're good with them. They love you."

"I love them too." Ruby leaned against him. "So we're agreed? No new babies, just the family we've already built?"

"Agreed. Our family is complete as it is."

They flew back Sunday evening, returning to their apartment and regular life. Jack had taken Monday off, giving them one extra day of married normalcy before work resumed.

Tuesday morning, he returned to Pacific Compliance Group wearing his wedding ring and receiving congratulations from colleagues. David Wallace pulled him aside with genuine warmth.

"Welcome back. How was the wedding?"

"Perfect. Simple, exactly what we wanted."

"Good. You deserve some happiness after the year you've had." Wallace paused. "I wanted to talk to you about something. We're expanding the partnership structure. I'd like to offer you junior partner status starting next quarter. Increased equity, more client management responsibility, higher compensation."

Jack felt surprise and gratitude in equal measure. "That's... thank you. Yes. Absolutely yes."

"You've earned it. Your work has been exceptional, and your reputation is bringing in new clients. Companies specifically request you because they trust someone who's been through real fraud investigation." Wallace smiled. "Being a whistleblower was costly, but it's also made you valuable in ways traditional consultants aren't."

The promotion felt like vindication - professional recognition that his integrity had worth beyond legal victories. He called Ruby during lunch to share the news.

"That's amazing! See? Everything's coming together."

"Yeah. It really is." Jack paused. "I keep waiting for the other shoe to drop. For something to go wrong."

"That's trauma talking. Dr. Mitchell would tell you to stay present, acknowledge the good things happening, stop catastrophizing." Ruby's voice was gentle. "We're allowed to be happy, Jack. We've earned it."

July faded into August. Jack's trial preparation intensified - more sessions with Torres, more document review, more mock cross-examinations. But it felt manageable now, balanced against work and marriage and ordinary life.

Helen's recovery continued steadily. She'd graduated to outpatient therapy, was living independently with minimal support, had regained most of her speech and mobility. Jack visited weekly, sometimes with Ruby, watching his mother rebuild her life the same way he was rebuilding his.

The kids adjusted to the new family structure with surprising ease. Sarah was preparing for college applications. Michael was thriving academically. Emma had started middle school, still reading dragon books, still believing the best of everyone.

September arrived with the crisp promise of autumn. Trial was two months away. Torres sent Jack the final witness list - he'd be testifying second day of trial, after the FBI agents who'd conducted the investigation. Monica Chen would testify third day. Marcus Chen would testify for the prosecution in exchange for his reduced sentence.

"Defense will try to rattle you," Torres explained during their final prep session. "They'll bring up your divorce, your unemployment, anything to suggest you had motivation to fabricate evidence. Stay calm, stick to facts, remember that the evidence supports you."

"What if they ask about the physical confrontation with Kirkland?"

"They probably will. Be honest - he approached you, he threatened your children, you restrained him using appropriate force. That makes you look protective, not aggressive. They want to paint you as violent or unstable. Don't give them ammunition."

Jack practiced his testimony until he could recite facts without hesitation, answer challenges without defensiveness, maintain composure under pressure. He was ready as he'd ever be.

October arrived with falling leaves and cooling temperatures. One month until trial. Jack took his kids on the vacation he'd promised - a week in the mountains, hiking and campfires and quality time before testimony consumed his attention.

Sitting around the campfire their last night, Sarah asked the question her siblings were probably also thinking. "Are you scared about trial?"

"Yeah. Terrified of messing up, of saying something wrong, of the jury not believing me."

"But you're going to do it anyway," Michael observed.

"I don't have a choice. I have to testify."

"You always have a choice," Emma said seriously. "You could run away or lie or give up. But you won't, because you're brave."

Jack looked at his twelve-year-old daughter, stunned by her simple wisdom. "I don't feel brave. I feel scared and stressed and tired."

"That's what brave means," Sarah said. "Doing the hard thing even when you're scared. You taught us that."

Jack thought about that for the rest of the week. His children believed in him. Ruby believed in him. Helen believed in him. The FBI, the prosecutors, his colleagues - they all believed in him.

Maybe it was time he believed in himself.

The last weekend before trial, Jack and Ruby stayed home, avoiding crowds and stress. They cooked dinner together, watched movies, existed in the calm before the storm.

Sunday night, lying in bed, Ruby asked, "What do you need from me this week?"

"Just be there. At trial, at home, in all the moments between. That's enough."

"I will be. Every day. Every moment." She kissed him softly. "You're going to be amazing. The jury is going to believe you. Justice is going to win."

Jack wanted to believe her simple faith. Wanted to trust that truth was enough, that juries were wise, that the system worked.

Dr. Mitchell would tell him to let go of what he couldn't control, focus on what he could - showing up, telling the truth, trusting the process.

Monday morning arrived gray and cold. Trial day. Jack dressed in a suit that projected professional competence. Ruby drove him to the courthouse, squeezed his hand before he entered.

"I love you. You've got this."

"I love you too."

Inside, the courthouse machinery was already in motion. Jurors gathering. Defendants arriving. Prosecutors preparing. The massive apparatus of justice beginning its slow, careful process.

Jack found Torres in a conference room, doing final preparation.

"Ready?" Torres asked.

"As I'll ever be."

"Good. Remember - confidence, facts, truth. The evidence supports you. Trust it."

Jack nodded, feeling the weight of everything that had led to this moment. The fraud he'd discovered. The retaliation he'd survived. The family he'd protected. The life he'd rebuilt.

All of it coming down to testimony, cross-examination, and twelve strangers deciding whether to believe him.

The bailiff called them to order. Trial was beginning.

Jack's moment was coming.

And somehow, impossibly, he was ready.

The shrapnel in his ribs ached faintly - old wounds recognizing new battles, old lessons about courage and truth coming full circle.

Some fights you chose. Some chose you.

This one had chosen him.

But he was going to finish it.

On his terms. With his truth. Regardless of the outcome.

Because that's what integrity demanded.

And integrity was all that mattered in the end.

Chapter 22: Sentencing

The trial began with all the formality Jack had expected and none of the drama television had prepared him for. Monday morning, the courtroom filled slowly - jurors settling into their box, Judge Patricia Reynolds taking her bench, prosecutors and defense attorneys arranging documents with careful precision.

Derek Vaughn sat at the defense table looking significantly older than Jack remembered - hair grayer, face thinner, the polish of corporate success replaced by the wear of months in custody. Marcus Chen sat at a separate table with his own legal team, having negotiated his cooperation deal but still facing charges. The other defendants - Thomas Kirkland, three customs officials, and two shell company facilitators - occupied additional tables, creating a crowded defense presence.

Jack sat in the gallery with Ruby beside him, watching the machinery of justice begin its slow work. Agent Reeves testified first, walking the jury through the FBI's investigation - how Jack's report had triggered scrutiny, what the evidence showed, how the criminal network operated. She was precise, professional, unshakable under cross-examination.

The defense attorneys tried various strategies - suggesting the FBI had relied too heavily on one disgruntled employee's accusations, questioning why it took so long to investigate if the fraud was so obvious, implying that routine business complexity had been misconstrued as crime. Reeves deflected every attack with calm competence.

"Mr. Mercer's initial report was credible, specific, and supported by documentation he'd compiled. Our investigation confirmed every major allegation he made. The evidence speaks for itself."

Day one ended with foundation laid - the FBI believed Jack, had investigated thoroughly, and found substantial criminal activity. Jack went home exhausted despite having done nothing but watch.

"How are you feeling?" Ruby asked that evening.

"Like I'm waiting for my execution but it keeps getting delayed." Jack managed a weak smile. "Tomorrow's my day. Torres said ten AM."

"You're ready. You've practiced this testimony dozens of times."

"Practice is different from twelve strangers judging whether I'm credible."

Ruby pulled him close. "Those twelve strangers are going to see exactly what everyone else sees - a man who found crime and reported it. Truth has a way of being obvious."

Jack wanted to believe her. Spent the night trying to sleep, managing only fitful rest punctuated by anxiety dreams that weren't quite nightmares but weren't peaceful either.

Tuesday morning arrived cold and clear. Jack dressed carefully, ate breakfast he didn't taste, and arrived at the courthouse by eight-thirty. Torres met him in a conference room for final preparation.

"Remember - answer the question asked, don't volunteer extra information, stay calm under cross-examination. They're going to try to rattle you. Don't let them."

"What's the worst they can do?"

"Attack your credibility. Suggest you fabricated evidence because you were unhappy at work. Imply you accessed data illegally. Make you look unstable or vindictive." Torres met his eyes. "But we've prepared for all of it. Stick to facts, stay composed, trust the evidence."

At ten-fifteen, the bailiff called Jack's name. He walked to the witness stand feeling every eye in the courtroom tracking his movement. The Bible was offered for swearing in, Jack's hand steady as he took the oath.

Torres began with softball questions - Jack's background, his employment at Regional Logistics Solutions, his job responsibilities. Establishing credibility, building foundation, making Jack comfortable before harder material arrived.

"Mr. Mercer, can you explain what first made you suspicious about potential fraud at your company?"

Jack had practiced this answer extensively. "I was conducting routine compliance reviews of international shipping documentation. I noticed patterns - certain routes consistently showed gaps in customs paperwork, payments to intermediary companies that didn't match standard procedures, documentation that met minimum legal requirements but seemed designed to obscure rather than clarify."

"What did you do when you noticed these patterns?"

"I pulled more data, analyzed it systematically, tried to determine whether these were legitimate business practices I didn't understand or potential compliance issues that needed escalation."

"And what did your analysis show?"

"That the patterns were systematic, involved multiple shell companies, and appeared designed to launder money through legitimate shipping operations while evading customs duties and financial reporting requirements."

Torres walked Jack through the entire discovery process - the data pulls, the analysis, the identification of Pacific Meridian Holdings and Hemisphere Trade Solutions, the connection to Nexus Global Ventures. Each answer carefully constructed to show methodical investigation, not paranoid conspiracy theorizing.

"At what point did you decide to report your findings?"

"When I confirmed the shell company connections and calculated that at least twelve million dollars had been moved through these structures over eighteen months. That was clearly beyond routine business complexity and needed to be reported to authorities."

"Why didn't you report to your supervisors first?"

"Because my analysis showed that senior management, including Derek Vaughn, had authorized many of these transactions. Reporting internally would likely have triggered a cover-up rather than investigation."

Torres spent two more hours walking Jack through his decision to contact the FBI, the subsequent retaliation, the manufactured audit, the termination for cause. Building a narrative of systematic whistleblower persecution.

"Mr. Mercer, did you ever fabricate or falsify any evidence?"

"No. Everything I reported was based on actual company documentation I accessed through my legitimate job responsibilities."

"Did you have any personal grudge against Derek Vaughn or your employer?"

"No. I liked my job and wanted to keep it. I reported fraud because I couldn't ignore it, not because I wanted to cause problems."

Torres turned him over to defense for cross-examination. Vaughn's attorney, Robert Sanderson, was exactly the type Jack had expected - expensive suit, practiced charm, razor-sharp intelligence.

"Mr. Mercer, you were fired from Regional Logistics Solutions, correct?"

"I was terminated, yes."

"For policy violations related to unauthorized data access?"

"I was terminated in retaliation for reporting fraud. The policy violations were manufactured to justify retaliation."

"But you admit you accessed large volumes of company data without specific authorization?"

"I accessed data within my general authorization as a Risk Compliance Analyst. That was my job."

Sanderson tried various angles - suggesting Jack had been unhappy at work, implying his marriage problems and divorce had made him unstable, questioning his objectivity. Jack deflected each attack calmly, sticking to facts, refusing to be rattled.

"Isn't it true you were passed over for promotion six months before you suddenly 'discovered' this alleged fraud?"

"No. I wasn't passed over for promotion. I was content in my position."

"Isn't it convenient that you became a whistleblower right around the time your performance reviews started declining?"

"My performance reviews were consistently strong until after I reported the fraud. The declining reviews were part of the retaliation."

Sanderson spent three hours trying to shake Jack's testimony, finding no significant inconsistencies, creating no dramatic Perry

Mason moments. Jack answered questions steadily, backed by evidence, supported by documentation.

Finally, Sanderson tried one last angle. "Mr. Mercer, you physically assaulted my client Thomas Kirkland, didn't you?"

"I restrained Thomas Kirkland after he approached me in a public hallway, threatened me verbally, and delivered written threats to kidnap my children. I used appropriate defensive force."

"You attacked him."

"I defended myself and protected my family from a threat he initiated." Jack's voice stayed level. "Mr. Kirkland was subsequently arrested for witness intimidation and bail revocation. The security cameras confirmed my account."

Sanderson had no effective response to that. He yielded the witness.

Torres did brief redirect, clarifying a few points, then Jack was excused. He walked back to the gallery feeling wrung out but intact. Ruby squeezed his hand as he sat.

"You were perfect," she whispered. "Absolutely perfect."

Jack didn't feel perfect. He felt exhausted. But he'd survived cross-examination without significant damage. The jury had heard his story. The evidence supported him.

Now it was out of his hands.

The trial continued through the week. Monica Chen testified Wednesday, her account corroborating Jack's - she'd known about the fraud, struggled with the decision to report, finally chosen integrity over loyalty to her criminal husband. She was compelling, sympathetic, clearly torn by the choices she'd made.

Marcus Chen testified Thursday as a cooperating witness, detailing the entire criminal operation - how it started, how it evolved, who was involved, how money moved through the shell companies. His testimony was damning for the other defendants, trading his own reduced sentence for comprehensive exposure of the conspiracy.

Defense attorneys tried to suggest Marcus was lying to save himself, but the documentary evidence supported every major claim he made. Bank records, emails, corporate filings - all of it confirmed the money laundering network's existence and operation.

Friday brought forensic accountants who explained the financial mechanics to the jury in terms designed for laypeople. Ruby had helped Torres prepare this testimony, ensuring complex financial crime was explained simply without being condescending.

The first week of trial ended with the prosecution's case nearly complete. Jack and Ruby went home Friday evening feeling cautiously optimistic.

"The evidence is overwhelming," Ruby said. "Even the defense attorneys seem to know they're fighting a losing battle."

"Juries are unpredictable. We can't assume anything."

"That's your anxiety talking. Dr. Mitchell would tell you to stay present, acknowledge what you can observe, stop catastrophizing about unknowable outcomes."

Jack smiled despite his stress. "You've been paying attention to my therapy."

"Of course. Your healing affects both of us." Ruby kissed him. "Let's not think about trial this weekend. Let's just be married people doing married things."

They spent Saturday with Jack's kids - a normal custody weekend, no trial discussion allowed. Sarah talked about college applications. Michael showed off a video game he'd been playing. Emma read aloud from her newest dragon book, still as enthusiastic about fictional worlds as ever.

Sunday, they visited Helen, who was doing remarkably well - walking without assistance, speech nearly back to normal, independence restored.

"How's trial going?" Helen asked.

"Well, I think. The evidence is strong. My testimony went okay. We'll know more next week when defense presents their case."

"You're handling this better than I expected," Helen observed. "You seem... calm. More centered than during the investigation."

"Therapy helps. Being married helps. Having already survived the worst helps." Jack paused. "And knowing I told the truth helps most of all."

Monday brought the defense case - witnesses claiming the shell companies served legitimate business purposes, experts suggesting the financial structures were complex but legal, character witnesses attesting to Vaughn's integrity.

The prosecution shredded most of it on cross-examination. Torres was methodical, exposing holes in the defense narrative, highlighting contradictions between testimony and documentary evidence.

Tuesday, the defense rested. Closing arguments were scheduled for Wednesday.

Jack attended every day, watching justice unfold in its slow, careful way. The trial had none of the drama television promised - no shocking revelations, no surprise witnesses, no dramatic confessions. Just systematic presentation of evidence, careful questioning, and the gradual accumulation of proof that crime had occurred and these defendants were responsible.

Wednesday morning, Torres delivered his closing argument. An hour of carefully constructed narrative, connecting evidence to testimony to charges. Showing the jury that money laundering had happened, that customs fraud had occurred, that conspiracy existed.

"Jack Mercer found crime and reported it. That's not opinion. That's documented fact. The defendants want you to believe this is all misunderstanding, business complexity misconstrued. But the evidence tells a different story. Shell companies designed to hide money. Falsified customs documents. Systematic evasion of financial reporting requirements. That's not business complexity. That's crime."

Torres hammered the evidence methodically, giving the jury framework for deliberation, making the guilty verdict seem inevitable.

Then Sanderson delivered the defense closing. An hour of suggesting reasonable doubt, questioning motives, implying that prosecutors had overreached.

"Jack Mercer was a disgruntled employee looking for problems. He exceeded his authority, accessed data inappropriately, then fabricated a conspiracy theory to justify his misconduct. Yes, there were shell companies. Yes, financial structures were complex. But complexity isn't crime. Different business practices aren't fraud. The prosecution wants you to convict because transactions look suspicious to government lawyers who don't understand international commerce."

It was the best argument Sanderson could make with the evidence available, but it felt weak against the weight of documentation and testimony.

The judge instructed the jury Wednesday afternoon. Deliberations would begin Thursday morning.

Jack and Ruby went home to wait.

"How long do you think they'll deliberate?" Ruby asked.

"No idea. Could be hours, could be days." Jack felt the familiar anxiety returning. "Everything comes down to twelve people we don't know making a decision we can't control."

"The evidence is overwhelming. They'll convict."

"Probably. But not certainly." Jack ran his hand through his hair. "What if they don't? What if we went through everything - investigation, retaliation, threats, trial - and the jury decides there's reasonable doubt?"

"Then we'll handle it. Together." Ruby took his hand. "But that's not going to happen. Trust the evidence. Trust the jury. Trust that truth matters."

Thursday morning arrived with no verdict. Friday morning, still nothing. The weekend passed in anxious limbo. Jack tried to work, tried to focus on anything besides the jury room where twelve strangers were debating his credibility.

Monday afternoon, the call came. Verdict reached. Court would reconvene at three PM.

Jack and Ruby rushed to the courthouse. The gallery filled quickly - media, interested observers, Jack's supporters. The defendants were brought in, looking tense. The jury filed in, their expressions carefully neutral.

Judge Reynolds took the bench. "Has the jury reached a verdict?"

The foreman stood. "We have, Your Honor."

"On the charge of conspiracy to commit money laundering, how do you find the defendant Derek Vaughn?"

"Guilty."

"On the charge of wire fraud?"

"Guilty."

"On the charge of customs violations?"

"Guilty."

The verdicts continued - guilty, guilty, guilty. All charges, all defendants. Complete conviction across the board.

Jack felt Ruby's hand tighten on his. Felt something release in his chest that had been clenched since the day he'd first noticed suspicious shipping patterns more than a year ago.

Vindication.

Complete, total, undeniable vindication.

The judge thanked the jury, scheduled sentencing for six weeks out, and adjourned. The courtroom erupted in controlled chaos - reporters rushing for statements, defendants being led away in custody, prosecutors accepting congratulations.

Torres found Jack in the hallway outside. "You did it. Your testimony was crucial. The jury believed you completely."

"Thank you. For everything."

"Thank me by living a good life and not reporting any more fraud." Torres smiled. "Though I suspect you'd report it anyway. That seems to be who you are."

Agent Reeves approached next, her expression satisfied. "Congratulations, Mr. Mercer. Justice was served."

"Couldn't have happened without your investigation."

"Couldn't have happened without your courage to report it." Reeves shook his hand firmly. "You're one of the good ones. We need more people willing to stand up like you did."

Katherine Mendoza called that evening. "I'm watching the news coverage. They're calling you a hero."

"I'm not a hero. I just reported a crime."

"That's exactly what makes you a hero. Most people look the other way. You didn't." Mendoza paused. "Your settlement is finalized, the criminal convictions support everything we alleged. You can close this chapter completely."

Jack hung up and turned to Ruby. "It's really over. The trial, the waiting, all of it. They were convicted on all charges."

"I know. I was there." Ruby smiled. "How do you feel?"

"Relieved. Exhausted. Vindicated." Jack pulled her close. "Ready to move forward with our lives without this hanging over everything."

"What do you want to do first?"

"Nothing dramatic. Just... exist normally. Work, family, marriage. The ordinary things that matter more than any courtroom verdict."

That evening, Jack called his children with the news. Sarah was thrilled. Michael said "That's awesome, Dad" with genuine pride. Emma asked if this meant the bad people would go to jail forever.

"Not forever," Jack said. "But for a long time. Long enough that they can't hurt anyone else."

He called Helen, who cried happy tears. Called Jennifer, who congratulated him warmly. Sent messages to colleagues and friends who'd supported him through the ordeal.

The news coverage that night was extensive - local stations leading with the verdict, national news picking up the story. Jack Mercer, the whistleblower who'd exposed millions in corporate fraud, vindicated by jury conviction. His photo appeared alongside headlines about courage and integrity and doing the right thing.

Jack watched the coverage with mixed feelings. The public vindication felt good. The attention felt uncomfortable. He'd never wanted to be a public figure. He'd just wanted to report crime and move on with his life.

But maybe that was the point. Ordinary people doing extraordinary things not for recognition but because the alternative was unacceptable.

Dr. Mitchell called the next morning. "I saw the verdict. How are you processing?"

"Still processing, honestly. It feels surreal that it's actually over."

"It's not quite over. Sentencing still ahead, probably more media attention, continued adjustment to post-trial life. But the major uncertainty is resolved. You were believed. Justice happened." Dr. Mitchell paused. "We should talk in session about what comes next. How you move forward now that the crisis that's defined your life for a year is finished."

"What if I don't know how to not be in crisis mode?"

"Then we work on that. Learning to exist in normalcy after extended trauma is its own challenge. But it's a good challenge to have."

Jack went to work that week feeling lighter than he had in months. His colleagues congratulated him, clients sent supportive messages, David Wallace officially promoted him to partner at the firm's next board meeting.

"Your reputation is bringing in significant business," Wallace explained. "Companies trust you precisely because you've been through this. They know you won't compromise."

Life was normalizing in ways Jack had thought impossible during the darkest days of investigation and retaliation.

But some nights, lying in bed beside Ruby, Jack still felt the weight of what he'd been through. The cost of doing right - unemployment, threats, stress, trauma that still required weekly therapy to process.

"Do you regret it?" Ruby asked one evening when Jack was particularly quiet.

"Reporting the fraud? No. I'd do it again." Jack paused. "But I'm tired in ways I didn't know were possible. Tired of being brave, tired of being the person who stands up, tired of being the example."

"Then don't be. You've done your part. The fraud is exposed, the criminals are convicted, justice happened. Now you get to just be Jack. Husband, father, son, consultant. Not whistleblower, not hero, just... yourself."

Jack wanted to believe that was possible. That he could close this chapter and move forward without the weight of what he'd survived following him everywhere.

Time would tell if Ruby was right.

But for tonight, lying beside his wife in their shared apartment, the trial verdict final and justice served, Jack allowed himself to believe in the possibility of normalcy.

The shrapnel in his ribs was quiet tonight.

Old wounds resting.

Old battles won.

New life beginning.

Finally, impossibly, really beginning.

The fight was over.

He'd survived.

More than survived.

He'd won.

And that had to be enough.

Because it was all there was.

Victory, vindication, and the rest of his life waiting to be lived.

Starting now.

Chapter 23: Decisions

Sentencing was scheduled for six weeks after the verdict, giving defendants time to prepare statements and the court time to review pre-sentencing reports. Jack didn't have to attend, but he wanted to see it through - the final chapter of a story that had consumed eighteen months of his life.

The December morning was cold and overcast, the kind of gray day that matched the gravity of what was about to happen. Jack and Ruby arrived at the courthouse early, found seats in the gallery that was less crowded than during trial. Some media remained, but the frenzy had died down. This was bureaucratic conclusion, not dramatic revelation.

Derek Vaughn was brought in first, looking diminished in his orange jumpsuit. The confident executive Jack had once worked for was gone, replaced by someone who'd spent months in custody awaiting this moment.

Judge Reynolds reviewed the pre-sentencing report, the prosecution's recommendations, the defense's pleas for leniency. Then she addressed Vaughn directly.

"Mr. Vaughn, you were in a position of trust and authority. You chose to abuse that position for personal gain, orchestrating a sophisticated money laundering operation that moved millions through shell companies. Your actions weren't mistakes or lapses in judgment. They were calculated, systematic, and sustained over years.

The harm you caused extends beyond financial damage to the erosion of trust in legitimate business operations."

She sentenced him to fifteen years in federal prison, followed by three years supervised release, and restitution of twelve million dollars to be split among the defendants.

Marcus Chen received eight years in exchange for his cooperation, acknowledging that his testimony had been crucial to prosecution success.

Thomas Kirkland, who'd threatened Jack and violated bail conditions, received twelve years plus additional charges for witness intimidation.

The other defendants received sentences ranging from five to ten years, each proportional to their role in the conspiracy.

Jack watched each sentencing with mixed emotions. Relief that justice was complete. Sadness at lives destroyed by greed and poor choices. Gratitude that it was finally, definitively over.

Outside the courthouse afterward, reporters approached for statements. Jack had prepared something brief with Katherine Mendoza's help.

"Justice was served today. I'm grateful to the FBI, the prosecutors, and the jury for their diligent work. I'm especially grateful to my family, who supported me through this difficult process. I hope this case sends a message that fraud will be exposed and prosecuted, regardless of who commits it."

Simple, gracious, final. He had nothing more to say publicly.

The news coverage that evening focused on the sentences - some commentators arguing they were too harsh, others suggesting they were too lenient. Jack ignored most of it. The sentences were what they were. The criminals would serve time. His role was finished.

That weekend, Jack and Ruby hosted a quiet celebration dinner with his children and Helen. Not celebrating others' imprisonment, but acknowledging survival, vindication, closure.

"So it's really over?" Emma asked, now twelve and still seeking clarity about complex adult situations.

"Really over," Jack confirmed. "The bad people are in prison. The fraud was stopped. Everything's settled."

"What happens now?" Sarah wanted to know.

"Now we live normally. I work at my job. Ruby and I are married. You three keep growing up too fast. Grandma Helen continues recovering. We just... live."

"That sounds boring," Michael observed with teenage bluntness.

Jack laughed. "Boring sounds absolutely perfect after the past year and a half."

Helen raised her glass. "To boring. To normal. To building lives worth living instead of just surviving crises."

They toasted, and Jack felt the weight of the past finally beginning to lift. The investigation was complete. The trial was finished. The sentences were handed down. Every legal obligation was satisfied.

He was free.

Not just legally free, but emotionally free to move forward without the constant weight of pending justice.

The week before Christmas, Pacific Compliance Group held its annual holiday party. Jack attended as a full partner now, his reputation helping bring in substantial new business. Clients specifically requested him, trusting someone who'd been through actual fraud investigation rather than just studying it academically.

David Wallace pulled him aside during the party. "You've exceeded every expectation. Your work is exceptional, your integrity is unquestionable, and you're making this firm significantly more profitable. I wanted to make sure you know how valuable you are."

"Thank you. This place saved me when I needed work. I'm grateful."

"We're grateful to have you." Wallace smiled. "I know the past year was brutal. But you came through it with character intact. That's rare."

Christmas arrived with the gentle normalcy Jack had been craving. He had custody of the kids Christmas Eve, spending it at his and Ruby's apartment with Helen joining them. They cooked dinner together, played board games, watched movies, existed in the ordinary joy of family time.

Emma was fascinated by the concept of married life, asking Ruby questions about what it was like to be married to her dad.

"It's nice," Ruby said diplomatically. "He's a good partner. We balance each other well."

"Do you ever fight?"

"Sometimes. About normal things like whose turn it is to do dishes or where to go for dinner. But we talk through disagreements instead of letting them build up."

"That's boring," Emma declared. "I thought married people had dramatic fights."

"Dramatic fights are overrated," Jack said. "Boring stability is much better."

Sarah, now seventeen and preparing college applications, had become more thoughtful about her father's experience. "Dad, when you were deciding whether to report the fraud, did you think about how it would affect us?"

"Every day. It's part of why the decision was so hard."

"But you did it anyway."

"Because the alternative was teaching you that integrity is optional when it's inconvenient. I couldn't do that."

Sarah nodded slowly. "I'm glad you made that choice. Even though it was hard on us for a while."

Later, after the kids had been picked up by Jennifer and David for Christmas Day, Ruby and Jack sat alone in their quiet apartment.

"First Christmas as a married couple," Ruby observed.

"First of many, hopefully."

"Definitely many." She moved closer to him on the couch. "How are you feeling? Really feeling?"

Jack thought about that honestly. "Lighter than I have in a year and a half. Still processing everything, still in therapy working through trauma. But lighter. Like I can actually plan for a future instead of just surviving the present."

"What do you want that future to look like?"

"This. Us. Work I find meaningful. Family I can support. Time with my kids. Growing old with you. Normal, boring, stable life." Jack paused. "Maybe travel more. Take that trip to Vietnam you've been suggesting."

Ruby had been encouraging Jack to return to Vietnam, suggesting it might help him process old trauma by seeing the country as it was now rather than as it existed in his war memories.

"You're ready for that?" she asked carefully.

"Maybe. Someday. Not this year, but eventually." Jack pulled her close. "One healing journey at a time."

The new year arrived quietly. Jack and Ruby spent New Year's Eve at home, toasting at midnight to futures built on foundations hard-won.

January brought renewed focus on work, continued therapy sessions, and the gradual fading of public attention. Jack's story became old news as new scandals captured media interest. He was grateful for the anonymity returning.

Dr. Rebecca Mitchell continued working with Jack on processing trauma, moving from crisis management to deeper healing.

"You've been in survival mode for so long," she observed during one session. "First Vietnam, then your divorce, then whistleblowing. You're extremely good at surviving. But you're less practiced at simply living without crisis."

"How do I learn that?"

"Practice. Allowing yourself to experience joy without waiting for catastrophe. Building routines that aren't about threat assessment. Trusting that normalcy can be sustained." Dr. Mitchell smiled. "You're doing well, Jack. The nightmares are less frequent, your anxiety is manageable, you're building a stable life. That's progress."

Progress felt slow but real. Jack was sleeping better, worrying less, existing more comfortably in the present rather than constantly calculating future threats.

February brought an unexpected call from Monica Chen. They hadn't spoken since the trial, but she'd kept Jack's number.

"I wanted to thank you," she said without preamble. "I saw the sentencing news. It's really over."

"How are you doing?" Jack asked.

"Better than I expected. Worse than I hoped." Monica's voice carried complicated emotions. "I'm divorced, living in a new city, starting over completely. But I can look at myself in the mirror. That's worth more than I realized."

"It is. That's exactly what it's worth."

"I heard you got married. Congratulations."

"Thank you. Her name is Ruby. She's... she's everything."

"Good. You deserve happiness after what you went through." Monica paused. "We both do, I guess. We made hard choices. Paid steep prices. But we can live with ourselves."

After they hung up, Jack thought about Monica's words. They'd both chosen integrity over comfort, paid enormous costs, and survived with character intact. That had to count for something.

March arrived with early spring warmth. A year since the civil settlement. Eighteen months since the initial arrests. Two years since Jack had first noticed suspicious shipping patterns.

The time felt simultaneously endless and compressed - so much had happened, so much had changed, yet it felt like just yesterday he'd been a regular compliance analyst with an ordinary life.

His children were thriving. Sarah had been accepted to three excellent colleges and was deciding between them. Michael was excelling academically and socially. Emma was still reading dragon books and believing the best of everyone.

Helen had recovered almost completely from her stroke, living independently, attending physical therapy twice weekly out of caution rather than necessity.

Jack's partnership at Pacific Compliance Group was thriving. He'd brought in five major new clients, mentored two junior consultants, and established himself as a respected voice in corporate ethics and fraud prevention.

His marriage to Ruby was everything he'd hoped - partnership built on mutual respect, shared values, and genuine affection. They'd learned each other's rhythms, created shared routines, built a life that felt sustainable and precious.

One evening in late March, Jack and Ruby were cooking dinner together when she asked a question that had clearly been building for a while.

"Do you ever think about what would have happened if you hadn't reported the fraud?"

Jack considered carefully. "Sometimes. I'd probably still be employed at Regional Logistics. Making decent money, maintaining routine, avoiding drama."

"Would you be happy?"

"No. I'd know I'd looked away from crime. That I'd chosen comfort over integrity. That I'd taught my kids that principles are optional when they're inconvenient." Jack set down the knife he was using to chop vegetables. "I'd have kept my job and lost myself."

"No regrets then?"

"Plenty of regrets about how hard it was. About what it cost you and my kids and everyone I love. But no regrets about the choice itself." He pulled Ruby close. "Some things you have to do because they're right, regardless of cost."

"That's what I love about you. That integrity isn't negotiable."

"Sometimes I wish it were. Life would be easier if I could just ignore problems that aren't mine to solve."

"But then you wouldn't be you. And I fell in love with you, not some easier version who looks away from wrong."

April brought the anniversary of Jack's job interview at Pacific Compliance Group. A year building a new career from the wreckage of whistleblowing - starting as a consultant, now a full partner. David Wallace marked the occasion by increasing Jack's partnership stake and compensation.

"You've transformed this firm," Wallace said. "Our reputation has never been stronger. Clients trust us because they know we employ someone who actually stood up to fraud rather than just talking about ethics."

Jack appreciated the recognition but felt uncomfortable with the hero narrative. He'd just done what seemed necessary at the time. The outcomes - good and bad - had followed from that choice.

May arrived with Sarah's high school graduation approaching. She'd chosen Northwestern University, planning to study economics with an eye toward financial regulation. Jack couldn't help but wonder if his whistleblowing had influenced her career path.

"Did my fraud investigation make you want to study financial regulation?" he asked during one of their coffee shop conversations.

"Maybe indirectly. But mostly I'm interested in how systems work and how to make them work better." Sarah smiled. "You showed me that one person can make a difference if they're willing to pay the price. I want to make differences too. Just maybe through policy rather than whistleblowing."

"Whistleblowing is overrated. Policy change sounds much safer."

"Says the man who exposed twelve million in fraud and survived to tell about it."

Jack laughed. "Survived, yes. Thrived, eventually. But I wouldn't recommend the experience."

Sarah's graduation in June was joyful and bittersweet - pride at her accomplishments, melancholy at her childhood ending, excitement for her future. Jack watched his daughter receive her diploma and felt the weight of time passing, of children growing up, of life moving forward whether you were ready or not.

The summer passed in comfortable routine. Jack worked steady hours at Pacific Compliance. Ruby's forensic accounting practice continued growing. They took a week's vacation to Maine, just the two of them, rediscovering the pleasure of time together without crisis or obligation.

Helen celebrated her ninetieth birthday with full recovery from her stroke, joking that she'd survived longer than many of her generation and wasn't planning to slow down anytime soon.

August brought Sarah's departure for college. Jack helped her move into her dorm, met her roommate, tried not to be overly emotional about his oldest child starting adult life.

"I'm proud of you," he told her before leaving. "Not just for getting into Northwestern, but for who you are. You're principled, intelligent, kind. You're going to do great things."

"I learned from the best," Sarah said, hugging him fiercely. "You showed me what integrity looks like even when it costs everything. I'll remember that."

Driving home from Northwestern, Jack felt the peculiar mix of pride and loss that came with parenting - knowing you'd done your job raising them, missing them desperately as soon as they left.

Fall arrived with cooling temperatures and the two-year anniversary of Jack's termination from Regional Logistics Solutions approaching. Two years since his life had been blown apart by the consequences of reporting fraud.

He'd survived. More than survived - he'd rebuilt, remarried, found new work, healed enough to function without constant crisis mode.

The shrapnel in his ribs still ached occasionally, especially before weather changes, but it was old pain now - familiar, manageable, part of who he was rather than something that defined him.

One evening in late September, Jack and Ruby sat on their apartment balcony watching the sunset, the city stretching out below them in all its complicated beauty.

"Happy?" Ruby asked.

"Yeah. Really, genuinely happy." Jack took her hand. "Not perfect, not without stress or struggle. But happy. That's more than I expected two years ago."

"What did you expect two years ago?"

"Honestly? I thought my life was over. That I'd never work again, that my reputation was destroyed, that I'd spent everything for nothing." Jack smiled. "Turns out I was wrong. Life wasn't over. It was just beginning differently than I'd planned."

"Sometimes different is better."

"Sometimes different is exactly what you needed without knowing it."

They sat in comfortable silence as the sun set, painting the sky in shades of orange and pink, the day ending as all days did - making room for whatever came next.

Jack had learned that survival wasn't the same as victory, that victory wasn't the same as happiness, that happiness was something you built daily through small choices and sustained effort.

He'd survived Vietnam. Survived divorce. Survived whistleblowing.

Now he was learning to do more than survive.

He was learning to live.

Really, fully, gratefully live.

With a woman he loved, children he was proud of, work that mattered, principles intact.

That was enough.

More than enough.

It was everything.

The fight was over. The healing continued. The life he'd fought to protect was being lived.

Starting now.

Every day.

For as long as he had.

That was the victory that mattered most.

Not courtroom verdicts or public vindication or financial settlements.

But the quiet, ordinary victory of waking up each morning and choosing to build something worth protecting.

Again and again.

For the rest of his life.

Starting with today.

And continuing with every tomorrow that followed.

Chapter 24: New Foundations

October arrived with the crisp certainty of autumn fully established. Jack sat in Dr. Rebecca Mitchell's office for what had become a biweekly appointment rather than weekly - progress measured in the stretching intervals between sessions.

"You seem different today," Dr. Mitchell observed. "Lighter, maybe."

"I feel different. Like I've finally stopped waiting for the next crisis." Jack settled into the familiar chair. "For two years, I've been in survival mode - anticipating threats, calculating risks, preparing for worst-case scenarios. But lately, I've just been... living. Without the constant underlying anxiety."

"That's significant progress. What changed?"

Jack thought about that. "Nothing dramatic. Just accumulation of ordinary days. Work that's satisfying. Marriage that's stable. Kids who are thriving. Enough time passing that the trauma feels like something that happened rather than something that's still happening."

"The nightmares?"

"Rare now. Maybe once a month instead of weekly. And when they come, I can ground myself faster, return to sleep easier." Jack paused. "I think I'm actually healing instead of just managing."

"You are. Healing isn't linear, and you'll have setbacks. But you've done remarkable work processing multiple traumas - Vietnam, divorce, whistleblowing. That takes courage."

"Or stubbornness."

Dr. Mitchell smiled. "Sometimes those are the same thing. The question is: what comes next? You've survived, healed, rebuilt. Now what do you want?"

It was a question Jack had been contemplating for weeks. What did he want beyond survival and stability? What did a future built on choice rather than reaction look like?

"I want to matter," he said slowly. "Not be famous or recognized, but make a difference. Use what I learned - about fraud, about integrity, about the cost of doing right - to help others navigate similar situations."

"What would that look like practically?"

"I don't know yet. Maybe teaching, maybe writing, maybe consulting work that focuses on helping whistleblowers rather than just preventing fraud." Jack ran his hand through his hair. "I spent two years being the person who reported crime. Maybe I could help others do the same without paying the price I paid."

"That's a meaningful direction. Have you discussed it with Ruby?"

"Not yet. Still forming the idea."

"Talk to her. She's been through parallel experiences - whistleblowing at her previous firm, rebuilding after retaliation. She might have insights about channeling your experience into meaningful work."

That evening, Jack raised the question with Ruby over dinner.

"I've been thinking about what comes next. Beyond partnership at Pacific Compliance, beyond just doing good work. I want to do something that helps other whistleblowers."

Ruby set down her fork, giving him full attention. "What are you thinking specifically?"

"Maybe a foundation. Or a consulting practice focused on whistleblower support. Something that provides resources, guidance, protection for people considering reporting fraud." Jack felt the idea solidifying as he spoke. "I had Katherine Mendoza as legal counsel, you as financial support, the FBI taking me seriously. Most whistleblowers don't have those advantages. They report crime and get destroyed because they're isolated and unprepared."

"You want to be the support system you needed?"

"Yeah. Exactly that."

Ruby considered thoughtfully. "It's a good idea. Important work. But it would be resource-intensive - time, money, emotional energy. And it might mean stepping away from partnership at Pacific Compliance, or at least reducing your role there."

"I know. That's why I wanted to discuss it with you first. It would affect both of us."

"How would it work financially?"

Jack had been thinking about this. "The settlement money is mostly saved. We're financially stable. I could reduce my partner responsibilities, focus on building a whistleblower support organization. Maybe start as a nonprofit, seek foundation grants, build gradually rather than trying to do everything immediately."

"You'd be good at it. You understand the process, the costs, the emotional toll. You have credibility - a whistleblower who was vindicated, who survived, who rebuilt successfully." Ruby reached across the table, took his hand. "But I want you to think carefully about whether you're ready. Two years isn't very long. You're still healing. Taking on other people's trauma while processing your own could be overwhelming."

"That's fair. Dr. Mitchell said something similar."

"What if you start smaller? Write about your experience. Develop a guide for potential whistleblowers. Build resources before committing to full-time advocacy work." Ruby squeezed his hand. "Test whether this is sustainable before making it your entire focus."

Jack appreciated her practical wisdom. Ruby had been through this - the impulse to help others avoid what she'd suffered, the realization that advocacy required boundaries and self-protection.

"You're right. Start small, build gradually, make sure I can sustain it without re-traumatizing myself."

"And Jack? Whatever you decide, I'm with you. If you want to reduce consulting work to focus on whistleblower support, we'll make it work financially. If you want to write a book about your experience, I'll support that. If you decide you need more healing time first, that's okay too."

Over the next few weeks, Jack began researching existing whistleblower support organizations, reading accounts from other whistleblowers, understanding the landscape of advocacy and protection. He discovered that while some resources existed, many were inadequate - focused on legal technicalities without addressing the emotional and financial devastation of retaliation.

He started writing. Not a polished book, just organized thoughts about what he'd learned. What he wished he'd known before reporting fraud. The mistakes he'd made. The things that saved him. The costs he hadn't anticipated.

The writing was therapeutic, forcing him to articulate lessons learned through painful experience. He shared drafts with Ruby, who offered feedback from her own whistleblower perspective.

"This section about protecting your family - that's crucial. Most guides tell you to report fraud but don't prepare you for death threats against your children."

"Should I include specific security measures we took?"

"Yes. Practical details matter. People need to know about protective details, varying routines, the FBI secure phone. Make it concrete."

By November, Jack had compiled forty pages of guidance - a comprehensive primer for potential whistleblowers covering legal preparation, evidence documentation, family protection, financial planning, emotional costs, and long-term consequences.

He sent it to Katherine Mendoza for legal review. She read it overnight and called him the next morning.

"This is excellent, Jack. Really comprehensive and practical. You should publish this."

"Publish how? As a book?"

"Start smaller. Law review article. Ethics journal. Get it in front of compliance professionals and potential whistleblowers. Build credibility as an expert voice, then expand to a book later."

"Would journals publish something written by a non-academic?"

"They'd publish something written by someone who actually lived the experience and has credentials to analyze it. Your Pacific Compliance partnership gives you professional credibility. Your successful whistleblower case gives you experiential authority. That's a rare combination."

Jack spent December refining the document into an article suitable for publication. He focused on practical guidance rather than theoretical analysis, writing for people considering reporting fraud rather than academics studying whistleblower behavior.

He titled it: "The Hidden Costs of Corporate Whistleblowing: A Practitioner's Guide to Surviving Retaliation While Pursuing Justice."

Ruby read the final draft and pronounced it "exactly what potential whistleblowers need - honest, practical, not sugar-coating the costs but showing survival is possible."

Jack submitted it to three compliance and ethics journals in early January. Two responded within weeks expressing strong interest. One published it in their March issue, giving Jack's work immediate visibility within the corporate compliance community.

The response was overwhelming. Jack received dozens of emails from compliance professionals, corporate attorneys, and potential whistleblowers thanking him for articulating what they'd experienced or feared experiencing. Several asked if he offered consulting services for people considering reporting fraud.

David Wallace called him into his office after the article's publication.

"I read your journal piece. Powerful work. It's generating significant attention - three potential clients have mentioned it when requesting your services specifically."

"I didn't write it for marketing purposes."

"I know. That's what makes it effective. You wrote it to help people, and it's helping our firm's reputation as a place with genuine integrity." Wallace paused. "I also notice you're positioning yourself as a whistleblower advocate, not just a compliance consultant. Is that a direction you're considering long-term?"

Jack appreciated Wallace's directness. "Possibly. I want to help other whistleblowers survive what I survived. But I'm not sure how to structure that work yet."

"What if Pacific Compliance created a whistleblower support division? You'd lead it, focusing on consulting with potential whistleblowers, helping them prepare, providing the guidance you wished you'd had. We'd handle the infrastructure and overhead, you'd provide the expertise and credibility."

Jack felt surprise and excitement. "That could work. You'd really support that?"

"It's good business and good ethics. Companies increasingly want independent compliance review that includes whistleblower protection protocols. Having someone who actually lived it gives us unique credibility." Wallace smiled. "Plus, it's the right thing to do. I'd rather help whistleblowers survive than watch them get destroyed by systems designed to silence them."

They spent the next two months developing the structure. Jack would reduce his client hours, focusing instead on whistleblower support and preparation. Pacific Compliance would market this as a specialized service, positioning the firm as supporting corporate integrity through both fraud prevention and whistleblower protection.

By March, they launched the Whistleblower Advisory Services division with Jack as director. The response exceeded expectations - companies wanting to implement better whistleblower protections, individuals needing guidance before reporting fraud, law firms seeking expert consultation on retaliation cases.

Jack found the work deeply meaningful. He was using his hardest experiences to help others navigate similar situations, providing the support system he'd built for himself to people who desperately needed it.

One consultation in particular stood out. A woman named Lisa Rodriguez contacted him about potential accounting fraud at her employer. She was terrified, unsure whether to report, worried about retaliation.

Jack spent two hours walking her through considerations - document preservation, legal representation, FBI reporting procedures, family protection, financial preparation. He was honest about costs and risks while also showing that survival and vindication were possible.

"You survived this," Lisa said at the end. "You reported fraud, got fired, faced threats, and you're okay now. That gives me hope that I could survive it too."

"You can survive it. But make sure you're prepared. Get a lawyer first. Protect your evidence. Talk to your family about potential consequences. Don't do this impulsively - do it strategically."

A month later, Lisa contacted him again. She'd followed his guidance, secured legal counsel, documented evidence comprehensively, and reported the fraud to the SEC. Her employer had retaliated by placing her on administrative leave, but her lawyer was already filing whistleblower protection complaints.

"I'm terrified," she admitted. "But I'd be more terrified if I'd reported without preparation. Your guidance made me ready for this."

Jack realized this was the impact he'd been seeking - not fame or recognition, but tangible help for people facing impossible choices.

By spring, Whistleblower Advisory Services had handled twelve consultations, prevented three people from reporting prematurely without adequate preparation, and helped two successfully report fraud with legal protections in place.

Jack's reputation grew within compliance and legal communities. He was invited to speak at conferences, contribute to ethics discussions, serve on advisory boards for whistleblower protection organizations.

Ruby watched his transformation with approval. "You're thriving. This work suits you."

"It feels right. Like I'm using the worst experience of my life to prevent others from suffering unnecessarily."

"That's meaningful purpose. Not everyone finds that."

Michael graduated high school in May, choosing to attend the state university with plans to study computer science. Emma was finishing seventh grade, still reading voraciously, developing her own sense of justice and fairness that reminded Jack of himself at that age.

Sarah returned from her freshman year at Northwestern full of enthusiasm for economics and financial regulation. She'd interned with a congressional office working on securities fraud legislation, clearly influenced by her father's experience.

"I want to fix the systems that make whistleblowing necessary," she told Jack over coffee during summer break. "Make it so people don't have to risk everything just to report crime."

"That's a bigger goal than what I'm doing."

"Your goal is helping individuals survive. Mine is changing structures so fewer people face that choice. We're working the same problem from different angles."

Jack felt immense pride in his daughter's clarity of purpose and ambition to create systemic change.

Helen, now ninety-one, continued her remarkable recovery and independence. She'd become active in her senior community, volunteering to help other stroke survivors through rehabilitation, turning her own struggle into support for others.

"We Mercers apparently can't help ourselves," she told Jack during one visit. "We survive hard things, then immediately try to help others survive similar hard things. It's genetic stubbornness combined with terminal integrity."

"Is that a compliment?"

"It's an observation. Whether it's a compliment depends on whether you value peace or purpose more."

Summer passed in comfortable routine. Jack's Whistleblower Advisory Services work continued growing. Ruby's forensic accounting practice remained steady. Their marriage deepened through shared commitment to meaningful work and mutual support.

One evening in August, sitting on their balcony watching the sunset, Ruby asked a question that had clearly been building.

"Do you ever think about retiring? You're seventy-two. You've built a successful second career. You could step back, enjoy life, travel, spend time with grandchildren when they eventually arrive."

Jack thought about that. "Sometimes. But I'm not ready yet. This work - helping whistleblowers - it feels too important to stop while I'm still capable of doing it."

"What would make you ready to retire?"

"I don't know. Maybe when I feel like I've done enough. Or when younger people can do this work better than I can. Or when

I'm too tired to keep fighting." Jack took her hand. "What about you? Do you want me to retire?"

"I want you to be happy and healthy. If this work makes you happy without destroying your health, keep doing it. If it starts costing more than it gives, step back." Ruby smiled. "We have enough money. You don't have to work for financial reasons. Only do it if it fulfills you."

"It does fulfill me. Maybe that's what I've learned through all of this - that meaning matters more than comfort, that using your hardest experiences to help others is its own reward."

"Very philosophical."

"I'm old. I'm allowed to be philosophical."

They sat in comfortable silence as the sun set, two people who'd survived crises and built something worth protecting together.

Jack thought about the journey from discovery to vindication to purpose. Two and a half years since he'd first noticed suspicious shipping patterns. Nearly three years since he'd first noticed suspicious shipping patterns. Two and a half years since his termination. Almost two and a half years since the arrests. A year and a half since sentencing. Time enough to survive, heal, and rebuild into something stronger than before.

He'd started as a man trying to do his job with integrity. Became a whistleblower by necessity. Survived retaliation through stubbornness and support. Found vindication through justice. And now was building purpose from pain.

The shrapnel in his ribs was barely noticeable anymore - old wounds fully integrated into who he was rather than defining him.

Some people retired at his age, seeking comfort and ease. Jack had chosen differently - using his remaining years to make his suffering count for something, to help others avoid unnecessary pain while still doing necessary right.

It wasn't the retirement he'd imagined decades ago. But it was better - meaningful, purposeful, aligned with who he'd become through struggle.

"I love you," Jack said to Ruby, the words carrying weight of gratitude and commitment.

"I love you too," Ruby replied. "And I'm proud of you. For surviving, for healing, for building something meaningful from trauma."

"Couldn't have done it without you."

"You could have. But I'm glad you didn't have to."

They sat together as darkness arrived, the city lights emerging below, life continuing in its complex, beautiful, difficult ways.

Jack was at peace.

Not because everything was perfect, but because he'd found purpose in imperfection.

Not because the journey was easy, but because the destination was worth the cost.

Not because he'd escaped suffering, but because he'd transformed suffering into meaning.

That was enough.

More than enough.

It was everything that mattered.

And he'd spend whatever time he had left building on that foundation.

One whistleblower helped.

One person guided through impossible choices.

One life preserved from unnecessary destruction.

That was the legacy worth leaving.

That was the purpose worth pursuing.

That was the decision that defined his remaining years.

And Jack was at peace with it.

Finally, completely, genuinely at peace.

Chapter 25: The End and the Beginning

The call came on a Tuesday morning in late September, two years and ten months after Jack had first noticed suspicious shipping patterns in routine compliance data. Agent Sarah Reeves, whose voice had become familiar through investigation, trial, and aftermath, was calling with news Jack hadn't expected.

"Derek Vaughn died last night. Heart attack in federal prison. He was sixty-eight."

Jack sat down heavily at his desk, processing the information. "Was it... suspicious?"

"Natural causes, confirmed by medical examiner. His health had been declining - stress, poor prison diet, age. It happens." Reeves paused. "I wanted you to hear it from me before it hits the news."

"Thank you."

"How do you feel about it?"

Jack thought about that honestly. "I don't know. Sad that a life ended that way. Relieved that the person who orchestrated my retaliation is gone. Conflicted because I never wanted anyone to die - I just wanted fraud to stop."

"That's a healthy response. Complicated feelings about complicated situations." Reeves's tone softened. "You did good work, Mr. Mercer. Vaughn's death doesn't change that. The fraud was real, the convictions were just, and you helped stop something that would have continued indefinitely without intervention."

After hanging up, Jack sat quietly in his office at Pacific Compliance Group, looking out at the city that had been the backdrop for his transformation from ordinary compliance analyst to whistleblower to advocate.

Derek Vaughn was dead. The primary architect of the fraud that had consumed three years of Jack's life had died in prison, less than two years into his fifteen-year sentence.

Jack felt no triumph. Just the melancholy recognition that corruption had costs for everyone involved - victims, perpetrators, families caught in the blast radius. Vaughn had chosen crime and paid with his freedom and ultimately his life. Jack had chosen integrity and paid with employment, safety, peace of mind. Neither choice had been without profound cost.

Ruby found him still sitting there twenty minutes later, staring out the window.

"Reeves called you too?" she asked.

"Yeah. Vaughn died."

Ruby sat beside him. "How are you processing?"

"I'm not sure. It feels like it should mean something - the man who tried to destroy my life is dead. But mostly I just feel... tired. Tired of this story, tired of being defined by what happened, tired of carrying it around."

"Then maybe it's time to let it go. Not forget it, not pretend it didn't matter. Just let it be something that happened rather than something that's still happening." Ruby took his hand. "You've built a whole new life from the wreckage. You help other whistleblowers survive what you survived. You've turned trauma into purpose. That's the story that matters now, not what Vaughn did or didn't do."

Jack knew she was right. The fraud investigation and trial had been the center of his life for years. But it didn't have to be forever. He could acknowledge its impact while also moving beyond it.

That evening, he told his children about Vaughn's death during a video call - Sarah at Northwestern, Michael at state university, Emma at home with Jennifer and David.

"Does this mean it's really over?" Emma asked, now fourteen and still seeking concrete closure.

"It means the person who started everything is gone. But yes, it's over. The fraud was stopped, the criminals were punished, and now we just live our lives."

"Are you okay, Dad?" Sarah wanted to know. "This must be weird to process."

"It is weird. But I'm okay. Better than okay, actually. I have work I love, a marriage that makes me happy, kids I'm proud of. Vaughn's death doesn't change any of that."

After the call, Jack and Ruby made dinner together, moving through their kitchen with the comfortable coordination of people who'd built routines over years of shared life.

"I've been thinking," Jack said as they sat down to eat. "Maybe it's time to write the book. Not just articles and guidance documents, but a complete account of what happened and what I learned. Get it all out, organized, preserved. Then close that chapter and focus on helping other people without constantly reliving my own experience."

"You'd be good at that. And it would help a lot of people." Ruby paused. "But are you ready? Writing a book means immersing yourself in the memories, the trauma, everything you've worked to process."

"I think that's why I need to do it. One final, comprehensive examination. Then I can move forward without unfinished business."

Over the next six months, Jack wrote his book. He worked early mornings before his Whistleblower Advisory Services consultations, evenings after Ruby went to bed, weekends when the house was quiet. He wrote about discovering fraud, the decision to report, the retaliation, the threats, the trial, the aftermath. He wrote about his children's suffering, his mother's stroke, Ruby's support, the FBI's investigation.

He wrote honestly about costs - unemployment, anxiety, nightmares, the toll on everyone he loved. But he also wrote about survival, healing, vindication, purpose found through pain.

Ruby read drafts, offering feedback from her own whistleblower experience. Katherine Mendoza reviewed for legal accuracy. Dr. Rebecca Mitchell provided perspective on trauma and healing. Agent Reeves confirmed factual details about the investigation.

By March, Jack had a complete manuscript: "The Customs Conspiracy: A Whistleblower's Journey from Discovery to Vindication."

He sent it to literary agents Katherine Mendoza recommended. Three responded with interest. One offered representation, seeing commercial potential in a firsthand whistleblower account that balanced thriller elements with practical guidance.

The agent sold it to a mid-sized publisher specializing in business ethics and true crime. Publication was scheduled for the following year, giving Jack time for edits, revisions, and promotion preparation.

"How do you feel?" Ruby asked when the publishing contract was signed.

"Like I've finally told the complete story. Like I can move forward without it consuming me." Jack pulled her close. "Thank you for supporting this. I know reliving everything wasn't easy for you either."

"Your story needed telling. Not just for you, but for everyone who'll read it and realize they could survive whistleblowing too."

Spring arrived with the annual celebration of survival - three years since Helen's stroke, three years since the investigation began, three years since Jack's life had been irrevocably changed.

Helen, now ninety-two, remained remarkably vital. She'd become a mentor to other stroke survivors in her senior community, turning her own recovery into inspiration for others facing similar challenges.

"We're a stubborn family," she told Jack during one visit. "We survive hard things, then immediately help others survive hard things. It's genetic."

"Is that a compliment or a diagnosis?"

"It's an observation. Whether it's good or bad depends on whether you value peace or purpose."

"I think I've found both. Finally."

"Then you're lucky. Most people only get one."

Sarah graduated from Northwestern in May with a degree in economics and immediate acceptance to law school. She'd decided to specialize in securities regulation, explicitly wanting to create systemic change that would protect whistleblowers through policy rather than just helping individuals survive retaliation.

"You showed me what individuals can do," she told Jack at her graduation. "Now I want to build systems that make it easier for people to do the right thing without sacrificing everything."

Michael was thriving in computer science, talking about using technology to detect fraud patterns more efficiently. Emma had developed into a thoughtful fourteen-year-old, still reading voraciously, now interested in environmental advocacy.

All three had been shaped by their father's choice to report fraud - seeing both costs and rewards of integrity, learning that doing right sometimes meant suffering, understanding that character was built through difficult choices.

Jack's Whistleblower Advisory Services had helped forty-three people over two years. Some decided to report fraud and were facing retaliation with better preparation than Jack had. Others decided not to report after understanding true costs, making informed choices rather than impulsive ones. A few had successfully reported, been vindicated, and rebuilt their lives.

Lisa Rodriguez, the first person Jack had consulted, had won her SEC whistleblower case and received a substantial award. She'd called Jack to thank him.

"I would have reported the fraud anyway because I couldn't live with staying silent. But your guidance made me prepared. I had legal representation, protected evidence, financial cushion. When retaliation came, I was ready. That made all the difference."

"That's the goal - not to stop people from whistleblowing if they're committed, but to help them survive it."

"You saved my career and probably my sanity. Thank you."

Summer brought Jack's seventy-fourth birthday. He and Ruby celebrated quietly with family, no dramatic parties or elaborate plans. Just dinner with his children, Helen, Jennifer and David, the people who mattered most.

"Seventy-four years old," Michael observed. "You're ancient, Dad."

"I prefer 'experienced.'"

"How does it feel?" Sarah asked seriously. "Being this age, having lived through everything you've lived through?"

Jack thought about that. "It feels like I've lived several different lives. Navy in Vietnam, corporate analyst, divorced father, whistleblower, advocate. Each version of myself informed by the previous one, building on lessons learned through experience."

"Which version is the real you?" Emma wanted to know.

"All of them. We're not just one thing. We're accumulations of everything we've survived and chosen and learned." Jack looked around the table at his family. "Right now, I'm a father and husband and grandfather-in-waiting and advocate. That feels like the truest version - built from everything that came before."

Fall arrived with the publication date for Jack's book approaching. His publisher scheduled interviews, speaking engagements, book tour stops. Jack approached the attention with reluctance but recognition that publicity served a purpose - more people reading his story meant more potential whistleblowers prepared for what they'd face.

The book released in October to strong reviews. Business ethics journals praised its practical guidance. Legal publications noted its detailed analysis of whistleblower protections. True crime readers appreciated its thriller elements balanced with honest reflection.

Sales were modest but steady. The book found its audience - compliance professionals, potential whistleblowers, people interested in corporate ethics, readers who appreciated stories of ordinary people facing extraordinary choices.

Jack did a dozen interviews, appeared on several podcasts, spoke at three conferences. He was consistently asked the same question: "Do you regret becoming a whistleblower?"

His answer was always honest: "I regret what it cost my family. I regret the trauma and stress and threat. But I don't regret exposing crime. Some things you have to do because they're right, regardless of personal cost. I'd make the same choice again, but I'd prepare better."

By November, the book tour was complete. Jack returned to his normal routine - Whistleblower Advisory Services consultations, partnership duties at Pacific Compliance, therapy sessions with Dr. Rebecca Mitchell that had become monthly rather than weekly, time with Ruby and his children.

One evening in late November, exactly four years after he'd first noticed suspicious shipping patterns in routine compliance data, Jack and Ruby sat on their apartment balcony watching the sunset.

"Four years," Ruby said. "Seems impossible it's been that long."

"Feels like forever and yesterday simultaneously." Jack pulled her close. "Thank you for surviving it with me. I couldn't have done any of this alone."

"You could have. But I'm glad you didn't have to."

They sat in comfortable silence as darkness arrived, the city lights emerging below, life continuing in its endless complexity.

Jack thought about the journey - discovery to retaliation to vindication to purpose. The costs had been enormous. The rewards had been meaningful. The transformation had been complete.

He was no longer the man who'd timidly reported fraud and hoped everything would work out. He was someone who'd been tested thoroughly and emerged with character intact, someone who'd found purpose in pain, someone who'd learned that survival was just the beginning.

The shrapnel in his ribs was completely integrated now - old wounds that ached occasionally but mostly just existed as part of who he was. Reminders of other battles, other survival, other versions of himself that informed this final iteration.

Some people spent their entire lives avoiding hard choices. Jack had faced multiple crucibles - Vietnam, divorce, whistleblowing - and been forged by each into someone stronger, wiser, more resilient.

He'd learned that integrity wasn't optional, that family was everything, that healing was possible, that purpose could be built from trauma, that ordinary people could survive extraordinary circumstances through stubbornness and support.

Most importantly, he'd learned that doing the right thing had costs but also created meaning that comfort could never provide.

"I love you," Jack said to Ruby, the words carrying weight of gratitude, commitment, and recognition that she'd been essential to his survival and transformation.

"I love you too," Ruby replied. "And I'm proud of you. For everything you've done, everything you've survived, everything you've built from the wreckage."

"Couldn't have done it without you."

"But you did do it. That's what matters. You chose integrity when compromise would have been easier. You survived retaliation when surrendering would have been simpler. You built purpose from trauma when giving up would have been understandable." Ruby squeezed his hand. "You're exactly the person you set out to be - someone who stands up for what's right regardless of personal cost."

Jack felt something settle into permanent peace. Not because everything was perfect, but because he'd lived according to his principles, survived the consequences, and found meaning in the struggle.

The fight was over. The healing was ongoing. The purpose was clear.

He'd exposed fraud, survived retaliation, helped others navigate similar choices, and built a life worth living from the ruins of the life he'd lost.

That was victory.

Not the dramatic courtroom kind, but the quiet, daily kind that came from waking up each morning and choosing to build rather than destroy, to help rather than harm, to stand up rather than look away.

"Ready to go inside?" Ruby asked as the temperature dropped with full darkness.

"Yeah. Let's go home."

Home. Their apartment, their shared life, their chosen family, their built-from-scratch future.

Jack stood, Ruby's hand in his, and walked inside to warmth and safety and the ordinary miracle of having survived extraordinary circumstances.

The story was complete.

The journey was finished.

The man he'd become through struggle was the man he'd remain through peace.

And that was enough.

More than enough.

It was everything.

The shrapnel in his ribs was silent tonight.

Old wounds at rest.

Old battles won.

New life secured.

Forever and always.

Starting now.

Continuing tomorrow.

For as long as he had.

Living not in crisis but in purpose.

Not surviving but thriving.

Not fighting but building.

This was his final foundation.

Built on principles that wouldn't compromise.

Strengthened by struggle that wouldn't break him.

Sustained by love that wouldn't abandon him.

This was enough.

This was everything.

This was home.

And Jack Mercer, whistleblower, survivor, advocate, father, husband, was finally, completely, genuinely at peace.

The end.

And the beginning.

Always both.

Forever.

THE END

AUTHOR'S NOTE

This novel is a work of fiction, but it draws from real patterns observed in corporate whistleblower cases across multiple industries. While Jack Mercer and the characters in this story are fictional, the challenges they face—retaliation, isolation, financial devastation, and threats to family—reflect the documented experiences of actual whistleblowers.

According to the National Whistleblower Center, more than 90% of whistleblowers face some form of retaliation after reporting fraud or misconduct. This can include termination, blacklisting, harassment, and in extreme cases, physical threats. The emotional and financial toll on whistleblowers and their families is often severe and long-lasting.

I wrote *The Customs Conspiracy* to honor those who've chosen integrity over comfort, who've reported wrongdoing despite knowing the personal cost. Their courage makes our institutions more honest and our society more just, even when the price they pay is devastating.

If you're considering reporting fraud or misconduct:

Get legal counsel immediately. Whistleblower retaliation is illegal, but protection requires proper documentation and legal strategy. Don't report without a lawyer.

Document everything. Save emails, memos, financial records, and any evidence of wrongdoing. Keep copies in multiple secure locations outside your workplace.

Protect your family. Discuss potential consequences with your spouse and children. Plan for financial hardship. Consider security measures if threats seem possible.

Know the costs. Whistleblowing may cost you your job, your career, your reputation, and years of your life in legal proceedings. Make this choice with open eyes.

Resources exist. Organizations like the National Whistleblower Center, the Government Accountability Project, and various legal clinics provide support, guidance, and sometimes representation for whistleblowers.

This novel doesn't romanticize whistleblowing. It shows both the necessity of exposing wrongdoing and the profound personal costs of doing so. If you choose this path, do it strategically, with support, and with realistic expectations about what lies ahead.

To every real whistleblower who's paid the price of integrity: your courage matters more than you'll ever know.

ACKNOWLEDGMENTS

This book would not exist without the support of many people who believed in this story and in the importance of telling it honestly.

To my family, who gave me the time and space to write Jack's journey and who listened patiently to countless revisions and doubts—thank you for your unwavering support.

To the beta readers who provided invaluable feedback on early drafts, helping me balance thriller pacing with authentic emotional depth—your insights made this a better book.

To the real whistleblowers whose stories informed this narrative, though your names must remain private—your courage inspired every page. You chose principle over comfort, and our society is better for it.

To the lawyers, compliance professionals, and former FBI agents who answered my questions about fraud investigation, whistleblower protections, and legal proceedings—your expertise ensured authenticity in the details that matter.

To the writing community that supported this project from conception through publication—your encouragement sustained me through the difficult middle chapters of both the book and the writing process.

And finally, to readers who believe that stories about integrity, courage, and the cost of doing right still matter in our complex world—thank you for choosing this book. I hope Jack's journey resonates with you.

ABOUT THE AUTHOR

Jackie L. Smith wrote *The Customs Conspiracy* after extensive research into corporate fraud cases and whistleblower experiences across multiple industries, including many state governments. A lot of fraud disclosures are happening right now. This novel represents years of studying real cases, interviewing compliance professionals, and understanding the personal toll that exposing wrongdoing takes on ordinary people who make extraordinary choices.

He believes that whistleblowers are essential to maintaining integrity in our institutions and governments, and that their stories deserve to be told with both honesty about costs and respect for courage. *The Customs Conspiracy* aims to show both the necessity of reporting fraud and the profound personal consequences of doing so.

When not writing, Jackie L. Smith works on old clocks, plays freecell solitaire (never loses), and loves repairing computers. He lives in Kentucky with his family.

READER'S DISCUSSION GUIDE

Questions for Book Clubs and Individual Reflection:

1. Jack faces an impossible choice early in the novel—report fraud and risk everything, or stay silent and keep his job. What would you have done in his position? Why?

2. The novel shows retaliation in many forms: termination, threats, isolation, and attacks on Jack's credibility. Which form of retaliation do you think was most devastating to Jack and his family?

3. Ruby's support is crucial to Jack's survival. How does their relationship evolve through the crisis? What does the novel suggest about partnership during extreme stress?

4. Jack's children suffer consequences for their father's choice— bullying at school, anxiety, disrupted stability. Is it fair for Jack's decision to affect them? How do you weigh individual integrity against family wellbeing?

5. Helen's stroke happens during the investigation. How does this parallel crisis affect Jack's ability to pursue justice? Do you think the stress contributed to her medical emergency?

6. The novel draws parallels between Jack's Vietnam experience and his whistleblower journey. How are these experiences similar? How do Jack's military survival skills help or hinder him in corporate retaliation?

7. Monica Chen initially stays silent despite knowing about her husband's crimes. Is her eventual cooperation redemptive? How do you judge her earlier silence?

8. The FBI investigation moves slowly while Jack faces immediate retaliation. How does the novel portray the tension between institutional justice and personal survival?

9. Jack loses his job, his income, and nearly loses his family's safety—but he's ultimately vindicated. Do you consider his whistleblowing a success? What would success even mean in this context?

10. The novel shows both the necessity of exposing fraud and the devastating personal cost. Should society do more to protect whistleblowers? What specific protections would help?

11. Jack's therapy with Dr. Mitchell is portrayed as essential to his healing. How does the novel treat mental health and trauma? Is therapy portrayed realistically?

12. Derek Vaughn dies in prison before serving most of his sentence. How does this affect your sense of justice? Should Jack feel satisfied with this outcome?

13. By the end, Jack has built a new career helping other whistleblowers. Is this a satisfying resolution? Does it justify what he lost?

14. The novel is told primarily from Jack's perspective. How might the story be different from Ruby's point of view? From his children's? From Monica Chen's?

15. Corporate fraud in this novel involves money laundering and customs violations. Did the specific type of crime matter to you as a reader, or was the human story more important?

16. Jack's marriage to Ruby happens during the crisis rather than after. What does this timing suggest about their relationship and about finding love during chaos?

17. The title *The Customs Conspiracy* has multiple meanings—physical (Jack's war wounds), emotional (stress points), and systemic (vulnerabilities in corporate structures). Which meaning resonates most with you?

18. Jennifer, Jack's ex-wife, remains supportive throughout his ordeal. How does the novel portray divorced co-parenting? Is this realistic?

19. Thomas Kirkland physically threatens Jack and his children. How does this escalation change the nature of the conflict? When does corporate retaliation cross into criminality?

20. If you were considering reporting fraud at your workplace, would this novel make you more or less likely to do so? Why?

Additional Discussion Topics:

THEMES: Explore integrity, family loyalty, institutional corruption, the cost of truth, survival vs. thriving, and redemption through purpose.

REAL-WORLD CONNECTIONS: Research actual whistleblower cases (Edward Snowden, Reality Winner, whistleblowers in corporate fraud cases). How do their experiences compare to Jack's fictional journey?

MORAL COMPLEXITY: Discuss the novel's refusal to make whistleblowing simple or purely heroic. How does acknowledging costs and consequences make the story more powerful?

CONNECT WITH THE AUTHOR

Enjoyed *The Customs Conspiracy?*

Please consider leaving a review on Amazon, Goodreads, or your favorite book platform. Reviews help other readers discover books they might love and support authors in continuing to write stories that matter.

Recommend this book to friends who enjoy:

- Corporate thrillers with moral complexity

- Stories about ordinary people facing extraordinary choices

- Character-driven narratives that balance suspense with emotional depth

- Realistic portrayals of whistleblowing and institutional corruption

Stay Connected:

Twitter/X: **@CheckerBoa81267**

Facebook: **facebook.com/jacksmith1591**

Thank you for reading *The Customs Conspiracy.* **Your support means everything.**